THE THIRD STORM

LIZ HAMBLETON

For the women of this world.
You're stronger than you think.

CONTENTS

Content Warning   XI

1. Chapter One   1

2. Chapter Two   12

3. Chapter Three   24

4. Chapter Four   36

5. Chapter Five   42

6. Chapter Six   56

7. Chapter Seven   67

8. Chapter Eight   79

9. Chapter Nine   87

10. Chapter Ten   101

11. Chapter Eleven   113

12. Chapter Twelve   122

13. Chapter Thirteen   133

14. Chapter Fourteen   146

15. Chapter Fifteen   156

16. Chapter Sixteen   164

17. Chapter Seventeen   173

18. Chapter Eighteen   182

19. Chapter Nineteen   192

20. Chapter Twenty   200

21. Chapter Twenty-one   209

22. Chapter Twenty-two   216

23. Chapter Twenty-three   224

24. Chapter Twenty-four   234

25. Chapter Twenty-five   240

26. Chapter Twenty-six   249

27. Chapter Twenty-seven   264

The Final Storm   269

Acknowledgments   275

About the Author   276

Content Warning

Although not described in great detail, this book contains on-page mentions of self-harm, assault, drug use, cults, and violent events that one might find triggering. The theme of this book contains an intense subject matter and is sexual in nature.

The National Suicide Prevention Lifeline is a United States-based suicide prevention network of over 160 crisis centers that provides 24/7 service via a toll-free hotline number 1-800-273-8255. It is available to anyone in a suicidal crisis or emotional distress.

CHAPTER ONE

SUPERHEROES

T HE AIR MATTRESS BUMPED against the cement wall of
the basement. It swayed all night, lulling the boys
to sleep despite the raging winds outside. The thud...
thud... thud... a constant for hours as the water underneath us made small waves that poured through the
windows and doors. This flood would be worse than the
last.

I prayed this was the halfway mark. My eyelids
couldn't hold themselves open much longer. I had saved
energy drinks and precious coffee that I rummaged from
abandoned houses after the first storm. I had consumed
every drop, and only adrenaline fueled me tonight. Unfortunately, this horror was my new normal, and my
body no longer produced the surge of energy needed to
stay up all night for the tenth time this month.

Beau and Lewis were asleep, nestled underneath my
arms. Their slow breathing harmonized with the steady
thud against the wall. Blonde hair covered their forehead and crept over their eyes. Things like haircuts had
been the last thing on my mind lately. Anything superfi-

cial or fun that once filled up our weekends left us long ago, as if the floods washed it away.

I couldn't tell them apart until two summers ago. Beau was chasing Lewis through the farm, and Lewis kept looking backward to see his brother at his heels. Lewis turned just in time to run face first into a piece of scrap metal poking out from a wheelbarrow. He sliced his head open, staining his almost white hair magenta with blood. I would give anything to go back to that day, not to undo the damage, but to remember what it felt like to play. I chased the boys in those fields and encouraged their races.

Lewis smiled through the blood, but my sister blamed me until her dying day for not paying enough attention. My negligence had scarred her perfect human. She already hated me for calling the twins BeLew after reading The Jungle Book, so it was no surprise when she added another reason to the pile. I loved the nickname, and no matter how much she seethed, it stuck. I made a quip about Lewis getting a scar and not Beau, whose name meant handsome. She did not find it funny.

I was the fun aunt, the playful sister who dropped the boys over the fence with the chickens so they could chase the birds for hours. The one who lifted them onto my horse, riding bareback around our land faster than my sister ever knew, faster than she would ever allow.

"Rowan, what are you doing?" she would yell from acres away while we played something she presumed was too dangerous. We would come in laughing and she would chastise me. "You won't ever understand how hard motherhood is. You can't say no."

She would say it as an insult and as a threat. I would never have children. I could never understand her struggle. She made hard choices and sacrifices. Her voice rang through my ears. *Did I understand her this night?*

Was it fear of motherhood or fear of survival? They may have been the same. The most important rule was to keep the kids alive. I struggled with the thought and ran my hands through the boys' blonde strands, pushing their hair back. Beautiful boys that slept in a horrible place.

My sister died to save her children. There could have been a better way if there had been more time, but the blessing of time was long gone. *Make your decision and move on*, was the mantra after the world changed.

Did I make the right decision?

The thought circled my mind, and I drifted off to the tune of our thudding mattress. I didn't know how long I was asleep, but I awoke to Lewis prodding my arm with his little hand. Beau lay fast asleep on my chest. The water had risen so high I could sit up and touch the ceiling.

The movement had stopped.

The sound of the wind had stopped.

Silence.

"Lewis, can you stand in the water?" I asked, holding the wall so his movement wouldn't topple the air mattress. "Go ahead, I'm right here." My voice scratched from thirst. The familiar rhyme made me smile, "*water, water everywhere but not a drop to drink.*"

Lewis was the braver of the two. He was the bravest six-year-old I had ever come across, not that I had a great deal of experience with children. That much was evident, considering I had asked him to step into murky water unaccompanied. But I needed to determine how much of a pain in the ass it would be to get out of this house.

He wiggled his small body off the mattress while I gave him a reassuring nod. When he slipped off the side, I knew the water was deeper than I had hoped. He gave a slight smile, keeping his head afloat. "I can't touch," he gurgled and brought his hands to the side of the mattress.

I nudged Beau, waking him. Moments later, he left the mattress, clinging to my hip, fearful of the dark liquid that filled the room. I used my free hand to move floating cardboard and plastic hangers that bobbed on the top of our basement which was now a lake, making my way to the exit. The door was already leaning in at the frame from the beating mother nature had given, and it opened easily.

We trudged out of the water to higher ground. When I turned back, the devastation of our farm stole the breath from my body. Not a single tree had survived the destruction. Many lay down flat while others tangled with the wreckage of homes and power lines.

Our house no longer had a second floor. The barn was gone. There was no rubble, no evidence that it had ever held anything in its walls. It was simply missing, swept up in the mouth of the third storm.

There had been tornadoes a few years ago that had ripped off every roof in the county. Waiting on insurance and repairmen frustrated me, so I'd spent hot days laying tarps atop the holes and balancing on the edges of the second story. All that work, and now there was nothing.

What a waste of effort.

"BeLew, you two have to stay here," I ordered. My voice came out harsher than I wanted. I knelt next to them as they sat in the mud with deflated faces. "You were very brave last night. You can't get the supplies down because the water is too deep. When you see me toss the bags on dry land, you can help by bringing them up here. Don't drag them, carry them. Understand?"

They nodded in unison with identical, anxious green eyes. I wished I had packed towels as I watched the water drip from their hair as they shivered. "The first bag I'll bring will have clean clothes. Put them on and throw your wet ones to the side." They nodded again.

We needed to walk toward Dean's house as soon as possible. I didn't know what time it was, but the sun was high in the sky. I wouldn't walk at night. I didn't want to drive at night, but I might not have a choice. Another storm drew near already. They were back to back, lined up in rows of destruction. Time wasn't on our side.

I left the boys doing the math in my head. There were four bags that I had to untie and remove from the ceiling of the basement, then carry back to BeLew. I would have to do them one by one, and that would take about an hour. Then there was the three-mile walk to Dean's property. With the boys, I had to account for an hour or two. I would encourage them to jog while I dragged the buggy to speed up the process.

The drive was four hours at best, six at most if I had to travel off-road. It would be close to nightfall and the ship left tomorrow before daylight. Dean had made it clear he would ensure we were on board, but I hated to put him in a jeopardizing position. It also made me uneasy knowing I owed Dean. He never said what he wanted for payment, but he would demand something. Dean Riggs always had an ulterior motive.

The boys did well loading the buggy, getting into dry clothes, and waiting patiently as I trekked back and forth. When we were ready to start, I asked BeLew to turn around, and then peeled away my wet clothes. I was unsure of the rules with kids and nakedness, but I needed to air dry for a moment.

Still only silence.

No animals, no electricity, no cars, no one.

Most people abandoned this place after the first storm. They feared the ocean and the walls of water that came from it, tearing apart everything in its wake.

I pray the ocean is our salvation.

I put on my dry clothes and got out some power bars and nuts for BeLew. They gulped their food down while I loaded the rifle and set it on the side of the buggy.

"I want you both to have your eyes on me. What I have to say is important, and you need to listen." They chewed and nodded.

"Do not speak on the trail. Do not walk ahead on the trail. You should always be within an arm's reach of me. Do not touch the gun." Their eyes shifted to the rifle and back to me.

I exhaled heavily. "If you're tired, try to keep going. Pretend you're Captain America, strong and tough. No complaining. We'll sleep when we get to the ship."

Lewis finished his food, walked over to me, and grabbed my hand. Beau came to the other side and clutched my leg while I finished eating. I wiped my hands on my jeans, took the handle of the buggy, and started our walk.

They followed at a trot as their little legs tried to keep up with mine.

A little over an hour in, they weren't slowing down. The sky was completely clear, all the clouds and smog sucked away by the looming storms that had already passed or were on their way.

All we could hear was the sound of our feet on the path. No one said a word, and I pretended my muscles didn't ache all over as I dragged the buggy with one arm and held the rifle with the other.

Lewis stopped on the path, and Beau bumped into his back. The buggy lurched behind me and crashed into the back of my ankle. Lewis turned in my direction, eyes like saucers.

I scanned the area around us, dropping the buggy handle and holding the rifle with both hands. Lewis turned back and pointed towards a ditch to our left. I pointed the rifle and waited.

I barely saw it at first, just a shoe, muddy with untied laces. Then it moved.

Shit.

We had to pass it. This heavily wooded path provided protection. It would be dangerous on the open road with our supplies.

I squatted down and motioned the boys to come closer. "I'm going to walk ahead. Don't move from this spot."

Beau looked down at his feet, and Lewis glanced up into my eyes and whispered, "Okay."

The boys clasped hands, and I turned, walking towards the shoe that was now unmoving.

I could be imagining things. It's been weeks since my last full night of sleep.

My breath felt shallow as I approached as if I couldn't get the oxygen into my lungs. Aware of every sound I made, I crept up to the shoe. My back tensed as I moved forward, lifting my rifle and aiming.

The shoe, which was not covered with mud but blood, was connected to a man's leg. A leg with a wound so encased in filth, I couldn't tell if the gash was in his calf or thigh.

I examined the mangled leg for minutes, and not once did it move. His body laid turned away from me, holding himself, and frozen in its place. I questioned what I'd seen earlier.

He was probably dead. If he was out here when the storm hit, he was definitely dead. There were maybe twenty houses between our farm and Dean's, but that included countless acres of land. He could have come from anywhere.

I stood there, my grip tense on the gun, frozen in time. Then I saw it, the shallow movement of his side. He was breathing. Maybe he was alive, but for how long? In another life, maybe I could've played nurse. Six months ago, I would've rushed to help him. That woman was a stranger to me now... like this man.

The sun was against us, and there was no time for this shit. I could see the start of the clearing ahead... Dean's land.

The man twitched again. I raised one hand and signaled for BeLew to come over. Lewis arrived, with Beau trailing behind him. "Grab the buggy," I said. "Start towards the clearing. I'm right behind you."

Lewis stared at the man in front of us. Out of the corner of my eye, I saw him look at me and then the man once more. I kept my eyes on the body in the ditch and watched his breath as his ribs rose and fell.

I heard BeLew sigh as they got the buggy to move, and it rolled to where I was standing. It stopped, and they stood there, waiting. "I'm right behind you, boys. Go on."

They didn't move.

"BeLew, what's the problem?" Lewis came to my side and looked at the man. "Lewis," I scolded. "Why am I repeating myself?"

He turned and walked on with his brother, one pushing and one pulling the supplies. I brought the gun back to my side and walked backward until we reached the clearing.

The shoe didn't move again.

Beau cried soft tears. His sweet hiccups tore at my heart. Seeing the man must have scared him, but there was no time to console him until we were further along.

I jogged the rest of the way to the site. The cement structure that held Dean's apartment and garage remained intact. His military background and paranoid father had resulted in him creating a near-perfect bomb shelter on their land. Their house appeared destroyed in the distance, but Dean's grey apartment building looked unscathed. I had spent so much time in that house growing up. All that was left of our memories was rubble, and a pang echoed in my heart at all we'd lost. I wondered if Dean's apartment would survive the fourth storm, but it wasn't worth the gamble. I had to move on, and forget this part of my life.

The keypad was on battery, and we had coded my handprint into the system. It unlocked as I pressed my palm to the sensor, and I opened the door, turning back to usher the boys toward me. On the inside, the garage-style gate opened with a crank, and I felt my arms and shoulders burn as I turned and turned and turned until it was completely open, giving Dean's Jeep an exit.

BeLew stood in the doorway. Both boys had tears sprinkled on their cheeks. "Get in the Jeep. Find the keys." I swallowed hard, ignoring their emotions for now, and ignoring mine, too. My gut knotted when I thought about the man. Mothers made tough choices. That's what I did back there.

Loading our bags into the back, I heard the vehicle roar to life with Lewis sitting next to the steering wheel. He had turned the key. I yelled over the engine, "Good, it starts. Both of you step out. Get the red cans over there. Load them in."

Ready to leave, my hands shook with nerves. We were another step closer. "Give me hugs, boys," I said, reaching for them. "We'll be on the road for hours. You can relax. We're okay." I was convincing myself as well.

"Will the man be okay?" Lewis asked.

"He was hurt," Beau added. "Lewis said he needs our help."

I stopped and looked at them both. "Is that why you were crying?"

"You said to be like Captain America," Lewis sniffled. "Captain America would help him."

Beau nodded his head in agreement.

"Get in the Jeep," I ordered. "We can't help him. We need to help ourselves right now."

BeLew climbed in with their heads low. I turned back to tell them to buckle in and saw the glare they gave me... the disgust in their eyes. It cut into my gut.

My sister's words echoed in my head. *You won't ever understand how hard motherhood is. You can't say no.*

Maybe she was right, even in death.

Maybe that's why I backed the Jeep into the clearing as far as it could go. Maybe her words were true even now, as I pulled a nearly lifeless man, eighty pounds heavier than myself, down a dirt path.

I *knew* she was right when I reached the back of the vehicle and saw the smiles on BeLew. The pride that passed between us was so thick I could almost taste it.

"Captain Americas," I panted. "Get the rope so I can pull him up."

Chapter Two

Sam

T HE SUN SET THREE hours into the drive. That was when I pulled over to fill the Jeep with gas. It still had enough, but I feared the worst if we found ourselves out of fuel in the pitch-black of night.

BeLew had moved to the front passenger seat, sharing a seat belt. It was fun for them, still getting used to breaking the rules after a lifetime of, "no you can't do that." Their blonde hair wafted in the slight breeze.

Winds were coming back. Another storm loomed on the horizon. We needed to keep moving.

My eyes skimmed the road and tree line. No sight of anyone or much of anything. A few cars had blown off the road, but there were no houses within sight, let alone people.

The shoe moved.

I had laid him in the back seat, wrapping some seat-belts around his body and tucking a blanket on one side so he wouldn't move much. The extent of his injuries was unclear, but the floorboards beneath him were free of blood. That meant the bleeding had stopped, at least.

BeLew turned their bodies around and peeked through the gaps in their seat. I clucked my tongue at them. "Turn back around and get buckled in." I threw the empty gas can behind me. It bounced on the road and rolled to a stop. I never littered before, but what did it matter now?

I lifted myself onto the side step and leaned over him, placing my hands on the seat by his middle. He was still breathing. *Obviously, Rowan, he just moved.* "Hey," I yelled over his limp body. No movement or reaction. I gently nudged his side with my forearm. "If you can hear me, we are almost there. Now might be a good time to wake up."

BeLew giggled. I turned, giving them a smirk. "Okay, on we go," I said, pushing myself back up.

Just when I shifted away, there was the slight touch of fingers around my wrist. The grip was so weak, but there nonetheless.

I put my other hand on top of his and bent down. I touched my cheek to his and spoke into his ear, "Rest now but pull your shit together later. I can't drag you onboard." His eyes fluttered open for a moment and then closed again. His strength failed, and his hand fell back to the seat. Beneath the dirt and matted hair, he was handsome – strong, covered in muscle. Of course, he was in shape to have survived that long. In another life, I might have been nervous around someone that good-looking. My cheeks would have flushed and I would have stared. By that point, I was too numb to care. Handsome meant nothing if you were dead.

"Aunt Row said shit," Beau giggled.

I grimaced. "Yes, I did, but that doesn't mean you can." We settled back into our seats while I cursed silently to myself.

What the fuck are you doing?

The engine roared back to life, and we continued. Obstacles had forced us to turn around and re-route three times so far, but we'd only lost about an hour. In the weeks leading up to this, I had spent countless nights memorizing the path of every road, detour, elevation, and landmark to get there. I had seen these roads in my sleep for a long time and dreamed of driving us like this.

I used to suffer from a terrible sense of direction. No matter how many times I visited the same place, I still used an app on my phone to get there. Necessity changed a person so they could endure. I hadn't touched the maps in the passenger glove box - there was no need.

It was pitch black when my headlights spotted a pile of cars. A labyrinth of pine trees interlaced the wreckage. They must have been driving in the storm. We were so close - maybe twenty minutes. Turning around again was the last thing I wanted to do, but I had to be pragmatic. Emotional decisions would kill us all.

I stopped the Jeep, grabbed my flashlight, and hopped out. The boys stayed buckled in, now used to the routine. The man was still.

My heart sank as my light illuminated the scene. It was a shitshow - the worst I had seen yet. Maybe these people were trying to make it to the ships, but a dozen cars were nothing more than a pile of twisted metal and wood. No sign of a path or something I could drive over with the Jeep's thirty-seven-inch tires.

So close.

The sound of the wind was stronger now. Time was running out. The ticking clock in my head grew louder.

What do I do?

I heard the noise of an engine in the distance; a loud one. I jogged back to the Jeep and saw headlights faintly in the dark. Someone was coming. The closer we came to the shore, I had expected to see people, but the sound startled me. The roaring engine made my stomach drop. People, at times, proved to be more dangerous than the weather.

Not every stranger meant danger. Help was beyond the pile of metal. Dean was one of many that had planned ahead. There were men that had known what was coming and were going to save who they could, who they loved. In Dean's case, who they needed. They were military through and through, but they were still human. No one wanted children drowning on their conscience.

The noise grew louder. I turned the Jeep around, now resigned to the fact that we would have to take another route, and the headlights blinded me as the car came forward. The road was wide enough to pull to one side. But which side?

I kept slightly to the right, hoping the years of habit would keep the other driver on my left. Closer it came, and I realized it wasn't a car. It was an eighteen-wheeler, and it was flying in the center of the road. I didn't know if it saw the wreckage ahead, but if it slammed on its brakes, the load would slide to one side, taking out anything in its way - taking out this Jeep. I drove forward, playing a game of chicken, but I had to get closer before picking how to go around.

It roared on, not slowing down. Maybe a football field's length stretched between us when it sped up. The truck gunned its engine.

Go right, it's muscle memory; he'll do it too.

I swerved, and the Jeep bounced on the rocks under us as we lost the road. The load of the truck blasted by like a train, loud and angry and not slowing down. BeLew held their ears and shut their eyes. We clipped once, just on the bumper's edge, but enough to fly us around facing the other direction. The tires skidded backward as I let the wheel turn itself on the wet roads. We slid, the tires squealing while I pumped the brakes. The Jeep jolted to a stop, and the man groaned.

We were holding our breath as the truck kept on and then crashed into the wreckage ahead, the front of it barreling through cars and trees until the load turned. Lewis looked up, watching the whole thing. I wanted to cover his eyes, but I couldn't move. I remained frozen in shock.

Then the entire truck skidded on its side, moving debris and shooting sparks into the night sky. It rolled three times until coming to its ultimate resting place, like a break in pool striking the first hit on the table, sending the rack flying. Everything in front of us had shifted in the blow. When the noise stopped, I inhaled, my chest burning from the lack of air.

"Shit," Beau said.

Lewis giggled.

"Don't say shit," I mumbled.

The man remained still.

We could get through now.

"Shit, we can get through," I gasped. Beau shot me a look, and I waved my hand at him repeating, "You still can't say it."

I drove forward at a trepidatious crawl.

Could we be that lucky?

It's odd what you consider lucky when the world falls apart. I had cried when I found instant còffee a month ago scavenging. Tears of joy over shitty bean water and all the time feeling so lucky. This was better.

When we reached the rubble, I could see a clear path ahead. "BeLew," I clipped. "Close your eyes, cover your ears, and put your heads in your laps. I'll tell you when you can sit up and look."

They followed orders without hesitation. They had seen worse, but I wanted to protect them from what carnage lie ahead. This was the last push. No one else could make it through this.

I focused on getting to the other side of the pile-up, never looking inside the surrounding cars. I had to shift gears a few times, gun the engine once, but it was mostly clear. The man didn't move – didn't groan again.

I looked up only once. The wheels of the destroyed eighteen-wheeler sprayed water as they continued to spin and I mouthed, "Thank you," then drove onward, eyes forward toward our destination. His fatal decision saved our lives, but I couldn't stop. Mothers make hard decisions, and we were out of time.

Lights appeared in the distance, and then noise. Glorious noise. How I missed the actual sounds of people and electricity. I had memorized Dean's instructions, but my hands still shook on the steering wheel. I had printed his email, read it one hundred times, and let it drown in the flooding after the second storm.

Pull through to any gate that says division 00046. Use Ashley's ID. She's dead. They don't know, and you look like her. Dye your hair black like her. Her file has two sons and a husband. They don't have their names. They aren't coming. The best lies come from the truth. Go by Rowan, say it's a nickname. Use Beau and Lewis's actual names. They honorably discharged you three years ago. You need to speak to Dean Riggs and then board the ship. Do not talk too much. All answers after your name should be that you need them to radio Dean Riggs. Say it on repeat, I need to speak to Dean Riggs. Please radio Dean Riggs. Look them in the eye when you talk. Tell the boys to fake sleeping. Remember the nuances I taught you - how to tell rank - who to salute - naturally carry in your left hand - all those little things. Good luck.

Military personnel stood in the streets, directing traffic. Everything was wet from rushing water that seemed to come from everywhere but the sky. The streets were busy but moving. Plywood boards with spray-painted numbers propped up against chicken wire gates.

00012, 00017, 00025, 00046

"It's time," I said to BeLew. They immediately went limp in each other's arms, heads drooping, eyes closed, well-rehearsed. I pulled into our numbered gate. Two men went to each side of the Jeep. I looked at BeLew and my hands stopped trembling. I could hear my heartbeat in my ears, but I willed myself to relax. Everything went in slow motion.

You can do this.

"Name," one spit out.

"Officer Lawson, Ashley Rowan Lawson," I responded.

"Who is in the vehicle?"

"My husband and children. Please radio Lieutenant Dean Riggs we have arrived." It came out without my thinking. Everything had been so planned out, yet I had forgotten a cover story for the bonus body we had picked up along the way. One of them pulled out a radio and started the channel. It sounded like static from where I sat, but I heard them say my name through the speaker.

Ashley had a husband. You are fine.

"We need everyone's name," one repeated.

"Beau and Lewis. My husband is S-Samuel. Please radio Lieutenant Dean Riggs," I ordered again.

"We are. Once you are endorsed, please pull up to the red lights."

The radio sputtered again, clearer this time, "Approval granted for Ashley, Beau, and Lewis Lawson."

"And Samuel Lawson, Lieutenant?" the other asked.

I held my breath. My heart sped up in my chest. Dean would be confused, maybe even upset, but he would get the message. He would know the man was with me. I used the name Samuel. He had to understand.

"Approval granted for S-Samuel Lawson."

I exhaled, and I thought I saw the boys breathe out as well. They could hear everything around us but remained perfectly still. Kids were resilient, but BeLew were in a league of their own.

The men waved me forward, and one followed along as I parked the Jeep under the red lights. They sputtered and blinked over me like an abandoned motel sign. I got out and stood in front of him, waiting for direction.

"Those RHIB's leave every fifteen minutes until they can't anymore," the one yelled through the wind. It felt stronger now, stinging my face and pushing me to one side. He eyed the man in the back seat and our bags on the floorboards. "I would make sure everything and everyone is with you when you get on and get off the RHIB."

I lifted my chin, pretending I knew what an RHIB was. "That's going to be a problem. My husband is unconscious. Do you have anything that could help us with our bags or, well, him? And where is the ship?"

"The ships are miles out to sea. The water is too shallow. Storms sucked it all in, so the RHIB's will take you." He pointed to the docks where small inflatable looking boats were bobbing in the water. He was impatient with me, but his eyes were kind.

I touched his arm and stepped closer. "Please. I need to get him to the ship."

He eyed me with suspicion, but I refused to back down. I pressed my body against him. Fuck female pride. We needed help.

"I understand," he nodded. "Listen, you take what bags you and those boys can carry. You won't be able to fit more on board, anyway. Come to the station when you are ready, and I'll carry him to the RHIB."

He turned on his heel and left, and I started digging in the bags. "BeLew get up and grab two things you can't live without. We can't take as much as we thought."

They stood, and both grabbed for their stuffed ducks, shoving them into their shirts. I tossed several things in the front seat I knew wouldn't be coming with us and quickly packed three bags of essentials. The wind whipped my ponytail and made my body tense.

We will not be here for storm four.

I thought we had time, but I also didn't know how far out the ship was. Months of trying to beat the clock, and I always ran out of time. Not today.

"Beau and Lewis, make sure you can carry those bags. Practice holding them because you have to carry one each down there." I pointed at the inflatable boats down below.

I left them to jog back to the station. The one man saw me coming, nudged the other, and met me halfway. "Start down with the boys," he said. "I'll meet you there with your husband. It may take you all a while."

"Thanks," I gasped, realizing how tired I had become at the end of our journey. When we finally made it to a bed, I'd likely sleep for a week.

He pointed to BeLew. "The boys look a lot alike. Strong kids to make it out here."

"Twins. They are strong. Almost like Captain America," I chuckled to myself.

"Not a lot of kids have made it all the way," he mumbled as we reached the Jeep. I winced at his statement and said nothing in return.

The boys each had a bag at their feet, ready to go. I lifted the heaviest one and made a hand gesture for them to walk.

Before I could start after them, the man grabbed my elbow and pulled me to his side. "I had a few of these stocked away. You may need it." He handed me a medical kit, military-grade. There would be medicine in this, including antibiotics. It was more precious than gold right now. Fuck, no one cared about gold anymore. But this, this was... everything.

"T-Thank you," I sputtered, my eyes wide. "This is... I don't even know what to say. I'm so grateful."

"My name is Luke," he said, cocking a smile. "Start down. I'll jog with him."

I walked after the boys, catching up as I shoved the medical kit in my bag, covering it with clothing. I turned, seeing Luke in a slow jog with Samuel draped over his shoulders. His chest extended, showing his muscled frame. He carried my fake husband like he was nothing.

We all reached the RHIB and loaded our things. Another man and woman were aboard, eager for us to get settled so we could leave. The boys sat down, and the woman instinctively smiled at them. Lewis reached out his hand for her to hold, and she did. Beau kept to himself and close to his brother, but he gave a weak smile to her.

I helped Luke get Samuel tied onto the bench so he wouldn't fly off as we made our way over the choppy waters to the ship. Luke looked at the couple as he pulled the last rope around Samuel's limp body. "You will help her load him onto the ship." The couple bobbed their heads in agreement.

Luke stood, and I gave him all the smile I could manage. "Thank you for... for everything, really. And good luck. I wish I could do something for you."

With that, Luke wrapped his arms around my waist and crushed his lips to mine. The woman behind me gasped and BeLew giggled. His kiss grew deeper as he pressed his body against mine, and I heard him moan slightly before he freed my lips. The man driving the

RHIB gave a soft laugh and shook his head. I stood there, dumbfounded. My lips tingled from his attack.

"No offense, ma'am, but I don't think your husband's gonna make it. Figured I'd show you my intentions. Men will line up for a woman like you when he's gone."

He had the biggest grin when he stepped off the RHIB and kicked it, pushing us into open water and starting the last leg of our journey. I sat down next to the boys while they waved Luke goodbye, seemingly unaffected by the encounter.

We sped off. Luke's body grew smaller in the distance until his shadow disappeared and darkness surrounded us. The rush of his kiss wore off, and I gripped the metal seats, searching for something I could see in the night.

Only ocean surrounded us. No ship and no shore. All that remained was darkness... darkness and fear.

CHAPTER THREE

HALLWAYS

O NCE UPON A TIME, I was madly in love. On my thirtieth birthday, my fiancé surprised me with a cruise, all expenses paid. We flew down to Florida and stayed a few nights on the beach before setting the seas for the Caribbean. We laughed, drank, and made love. It was one of my favorite memories. If I closed my eyes, I could still feel the scorching sun. For a few blissful days, I had nothing on my agenda except a book and a margarita.

We'd decided on a destination wedding before we started the cruise. Our wedding was for us, and there was no need to make a big show of it. That time in my life was simple and serene. Things had felt like they were coming together and I'd been happy.

When we arrived at the port, the ship's size and beauty shocked me. How could something so massive stay afloat? The seven days that followed were magical, and if I had a single wish in life, it would be to go back to that time, before all that happened recently, and before I knew too much about what the future held and who my fiance truly was. Ignorance had been my bliss, and it had shrouded me every day, blinding my thoughts and feelings.

That cruise ship would have been a snack for the monstrous vessel looming in front of us. The boarding dock was the size of a grocery store parking lot, and it was just where small boats boarded. What looked like a stadium full of people stood stories above us, holding luggage and belongings. The winds were strong then, and the air filled with mist from the waves.

The Titanic came to mind, and I pushed the horrifying image away as quickly as it came. I knew that it sank, but all aboard, anyway.

"What's your number?" the driver of the RHIB shouted. I stared at him puzzled for a moment, and then Lewis chimed in, "Forty-six."

He grabbed a black marker and turned me around. I felt him draw on the back of my shirt. He flipped me forward and did the same to my front. He then branded Beau and Lewis with the same, *00046*.

"And you all?" he asked the other couple. "Nine-hundred sixteen," they responded.

The RHIB pulled to a water-logged dock, and there was nothing but megaphones and yelling and noise. The precious noise I was so grateful for moments ago pounded in my ears, making no sense.

We stepped out holding our bags, and I bent down to BeLew's ears. "Same rules as the trail. No talking and I should be able to touch you at all times. Hold each other's hands." They nodded their heads and linked fingers. We walked forward, but there were no lines and no order to the madness. The couple had unloaded Sam and set him on the dock, then disappeared.

A man grabbed my shoulder and thrust me to the side. He was shoving people left, right, and forward. BeLew rushed behind me and I felt their hands on my belt loops.

"Please, he needs help. He can't walk," I shouted at no one and everyone at the same time.

"Move on," someone screeched back through a megaphone at us.

More pushing, noise, and mist. I found an empty spot in the crowd of people and lunged forward. BeLew were still clinging to my waist. The shoving of the crowd was growing stronger, anger filling the air. The wind stung my face, and the small boats were bobbing violently in the water. We needed to get further into the ship and quickly.

I had no choice but to get BeLew in and go back for Sam. There were several doorways on the wall of the dock, but people were mostly wandering around, confused about what to do. Others were yelling about friends and family on the boats farther out than ours.

I led the boys to a hallway, and we jogged for a few minutes until I found a small enclave in the wall with some pipes. "Here," I gasped. "Stay right here. Hands on the pipe. I'm coming back." I dropped my bag and ran back to the docks.

The chaotic scene had worsened, but I could see Sam. Two teenage boys were standing over him and looked to be sifting through his pockets. I ran up, "What the fuck do you think you will find in there?" They stiffened. "You can keep it, but help me." They looked at each other and left. *Assholes*. Not that I could have blamed anyone for being the worst version of themselves at that moment.

I grabbed Sam by his shirt and dragged him further towards the hallway. The rushing water covering the dock helped at first, acting as a buoy every time I pulled him towards me, but my shoulders burned immediately. I had to stop and shake out my hands with every second or third pull. He remained unconscious, and I cursed at him with each tug.

Someone came up and touched my arm. I turned to see the thieving boys. They had a plastic tarp from God knows where that had covered God knows what, but I didn't care. I could hardly breathe from exertion. They moved him onto the tarp, grabbed hold of each side, and took my lead towards the hall.

Then the noise started, a huge creaking, and we all turned around as we entered the doorway that led to BeLew.

They were lifting the dock.

Screams followed bellowing indignation at the decision. Boats still lined up to board, but their time was up. And ours might be too if we didn't move. The passengers rushed in our direction, an angry mob full of fear.

Shit.

We needed to run. The crowds would be behind us. I could see it on the teenagers' faces - panic. We raced down the hallway, and I could hear people shoving in at our heels like thunderous cattle. "BeLew, grab a bag and start running forward. I'm right behind you," I screamed. I saw one blonde head peek out from the wall, and then both tiny bodies stood out in the walkway, holding their bags, stuffed ducks shoved down their shirts.

The teenagers behind me yelled, "Run!" and BeLew complied, their little legs carrying them farther down the hall, looking back every so often. I grabbed my bag as I ran past where they had been standing, keeping my pace. I tasted blood in my mouth from my bursting lungs. This was the longest hallway I had experienced in my life, and I could feel the people catching up behind us.

Please, Lord, don't let us get trampled.

Finally, we reached the end, where two men stood in front of ominous double doors. I could see their jaws drop in shock. They turned and propped the doors open and we ran through, bursting inside. We sprinted into the giant room of grey floors and walls with no windows. It resembled a prison, but it thrilled me to be out of that damned hallway.

We raced forward until I felt satisfied that the mob behind us had room to spread out. The teenagers dropped Sam at my feet and gave me a slight smile and nod. BeLew laid down on the cold floor, hands on their panting bellies. The room filled with strangers, and I collapsed to the ground next to the boys.

After a few minutes, we caught our breath and settled in. Using our bags as pillows, I stared at the metal ceiling. Sam was breathing, and there was no sign of bleeding. "What now?" I said to myself, and the boys shrugged their shoulders. We lay there and waited, and the room grew crowded.

My eyes felt heavy, and my body was weak. Every muscle shut down, struggling to move. I propped myself up against Sam and nudged the boys to come and lay their heads in my lap. My head kept dropping, startling me awake until finally, I couldn't fight it anymore.

I don't know how long I slept, but I awoke frantically and checked that no person or belonging had disappeared. BeLew—check, a random stranger I named Sam—check, three bags filled with our lives—check.

"Rowan," I heard, as I was feeling around to verify everyone was present and alive. "Rowan!" I turned around and leaped up at the sight of Dean. He looked terrible, but his cocky smile made up for his sunken eyes and three-day stubble.

"Oh my God, Dean," I cried and yanked him into a hug. He pulled me towards him, into his arms, holding me so tight I could barely catch air. Tears threatened to escape as I held him. For that moment, I pushed away all my fears about Dean and fell limp into his body. "Oh, Dean, I'm so glad you are here. Oh my God, I never thought we would make it."

"Is anyone hurt? Are the boys okay? What about you?" he asked.

"We are worse for wear, but we just need food and sleep. This one," I said, gesturing to Sam, "he's not in good shape. He needs medical attention. I'm surprised he made it this far."

"Who is it?"

"Sam Lawson," I shrugged and grinned.

"Honestly, Rowan. You don't need to keep secrets from me. We are past all that. I would have gotten a boyfriend on board. I love you. I wouldn't hurt you like that." His hand touched my cheek as he spoke, and my heart plummeted. He was lying, but it was a kind lie, one you tell someone you loved once.

I covered his hand with mine as it rested on my face. "Dean, I love you, but I have no fucking clue who this man is," I told Dean the story of his rescue and our daring Captain Americas.

He shook his head and chuckled. "Those boys. Not sure where they got their heart. Sure as hell wasn't their parents. I won't waste time telling you how stupid this was." He was hiding his anger well, but I could see his jaw tick as he spoke. Sam was here, despite Dean's disapproval. There was no undoing it now, but I would pay for it later.

"So, what do we do now?" I could see the room held fewer people. Bodies no longer crammed together shoulder to shoulder. People settled into small piles. Some smiled while others cried.

"I'm taking you to your room. You are in the family barracks. I have a rack for your bags, but we will have to load him on it. Can you carry your things just a little further?"

"Of course. Are you staying with us?"

Dean shook his head and looked over at Sam for the best way to lift him. "I have to stay with the crew. Also, I don't have children so I can't stay in the family units." His eyes lowered as he spoke, visibly bothered by the admission.

"This is no place for a baby, Dean. BeLew are the youngest I've seen."

"You're right about that. It wasn't an easy journey getting here. It won't be easy to live here for the year." He lifted Sam in one motion, and I held the rack steady. Sam's legs flopped over the edge, but he was still limp and didn't seem to mind. Dean started walking, and we all grabbed our things and followed him.

Lewis groaned five minutes in. I shot him a stern look. "It's just... do we have to go into another hallway? The last one sucked."

"Shit," Beau said at Lewis's comment.

Dean's eyebrows shot up. "Oh, you are nailing this parenting thing. They curse and are afraid of a fundamental part of every structure on the planet."

"You didn't have to run for your life in the last hallway," I clipped. "And don't say shit, Beau."

"Can I say shit?" Lewis giggled.

"No one says shit or fuck, or damn, understand?" I yelled.

Their eyes got wide, and I received a few sideways glances from passengers as we entered the hall.

"A-plus, Row. Just drive that point home," Dean cackled.

Frustration pumped through my veins, but so did relief after I heard Dean's laughter. Seeing him lifted my spirits and gave me hope. I could be a mother to these boys and survive a year on the ship. We could make it through the storms and maybe come out on the other side, maybe even be happy. Dean, who had once been the reason for so much pain and heartache, was now my ray of hope.

After another long hike taking countless turns and stairs, we stood in front of a silver door labeled 00046–Lawson, scribbled in black marker.

Dean grabbed a ring with four keys and turned the lock, pushing the door open. The room was a shotgun-style studio. It was long, narrow, and maybe forty feet. There was a murphy bed on the left, held to the wall with chains. To the right was a desk or table, depending on the functionality we'd need, with two chairs. Down the right wall stood a trash can, an empty bookshelf, and a locker. Behind the bed were a sink and more shelves. The back wall held bunk-style murphy beds, also secured with chains so they could be lifted and lowered. There were no windows and no sign of where we were located on the ship.

If every bed was down in the room, no one would be able to walk. I could barely walk through then, but I shot to the rear of the room and started lowering the bunk beds. The boys needed food and sleep — in that order. We had collapsible cups I could fill in the sink, and I still had more snacks in one of our bags. Sheets were already on the beds and the boys began an intense discussion about who would be on the top and bottom bunk.

I heard a creak and chains and saw Dean was lowering the other bed towards the front of the room. Then he lifted Sam and set him on the mattress.

"What are you doing?" I asked.

"You can barely walk, and he's out cold, Row. How would you lift him?"

"Why are you putting him on my bed? He needs medical attention."

"Dammit Row, he can't get in the medical bay for days. Have you looked around? Do you know how many hurt and injured people we are dealing with right now? It's women and children first, anyway. Patch him up as best you can."

"Aunt Row says we don't say dammit," Lewis mumbled, already laying on the bottom bunk.

"You made the choice to save him," Dean pointed out. "So, save him, Row."

"What is this, the Titanic? Shouldn't it be the worst injuries first?" I shot back.

"Listen, I've seen a lot of injuries over my lifetime. If he's still breathing, he'll pull through," Dean snipped, and walked to the locker. He opened it and grabbed some duct tape and soap. "You may need to stitch him and clean him up is all. I'm worried about infection, but there isn't much you can do for that but wait. I'll see what supplies I can bring tomorrow."

"You want me to stitch him up with duct tape?" I stammered.

"It should do the job for now. Luckily, you have it. Cabinets and lockers fly open with the ship's movement when the latches break. Sometimes you have to tape shit closed."

Lewis shot his gaze toward Dean and gave him what we lovingly called the "stink eye." I winked at him and turned my attention back to Dean, moving my hands to my hips.

"That's it, then?" I asked. "You don't care if someone dies?" I might as well have said the words to a brick wall. Dean never cared about my fears or opinions.

"This room divides like this," Dean added, pulling open a collapsible accordion wall, ignoring my question. "It looks flimsy, but it seals the room off nicely so the boys have their own space. You can clip it to either side of the sink so you can wash up. Bathrooms are down the hall to your right and here are the keys. I care people are dying, but, yeah, that's it. Take a moment to realize that you did this to yourself. I can't risk this stranger taking medical care from someone else."

He turned and walked through the narrow door of our new home, throwing the keys on Sam's stomach.

I counted three and knew he held the other one. "D-Dean," I stuttered. "Wait just a minute."

The reality was setting in that I would be alone in that room, responsible for three lives. I had accepted the possibility of our death at the hands of mother nature or Murphy's Law until then. But at that moment, we were safe. If I lost someone in our room that night, it was all on me.

He faced me, raising both hands to either side of the doorway, and leaned forward. "I'd tell you to rest, but I know you'll stay up tending to him, so I best let you do it."

His eyes held a mix of sadness and frustration. Sam was another example that I had failed to follow orders, and it pissed Dean off. He'd risked so much getting us here, and we'd almost thrown it away. I'd let him down, and my stomach churned while I considered what that meant for my future.

I wrapped my arms around his middle and pressed my cheek to his chest, holding his body firm against mine. He dropped his hands from the frame and hugged me back with a shaky exhale. We held each other for too long, breathing together in unison. His body was so familiar to me, and if BeLew weren't watching right then, I would've kissed him with all the strength I had left.

When we broke our embrace, he held my face in his hands and touched his forehead to mine. "Row, I think if you wanted him to make it, you would have given him a different name. Seems a bit... unlucky."

I stepped away and grabbed the door, clenching my teeth to hide the pain from my face. His cruel remark snapped me back to reality. "I was lucky to have Samuel when I did. Lucky for it, Dean. You don't feel that way, and it's your loss." I pulled the door closed as Dean left us, and I began the daunting task of removing Sam's bloody clothes.

CHAPTER FOUR

WOUNDS

I TOLD MYSELF I would find the source of his injury, tend to the wound, and then sleep. Four hours later, I realized something about myself and all women.

We seldom slept because there was always another task, something else that needed attention. Not that women *wanted* to stay up washing bottles, switching laundry, and catching up on work, but there was a non-stop voice in our heads saying, *just one more thing*, and at two in the morning, we'd pass out with our hands on our laptop keyboard.

Sam had a laceration on his left thigh. Something had stabbed him through and through but didn't hit any major arteries. He had muscular legs, and the thickness of his quadriceps had taken the brunt of everything. My assumption was that he had ripped whatever pierced his leg because the gash on one side was monstrous and jagged compared to the other.

There was very little blood when I cleaned him up and I was uncertain of what to stitch, or rather duct tape. Instead, I took a clean long sleeve shirt and folded it like gauze. I had antibacterial ointment in the medical kit, and I slathered his then clean wounds, wrapped the homemade gauze snug, and used the duct tape to hold it all taught.

I hesitated to give him the injectable antibiotics until he showed signs of fever or swelling. I didn't know if we might need them later.

Once there was nothing more I could do for his injury, I gave him a much-needed sponge bath, careful to avoid anything too personal. As I wiped away the dirt, a powerful man appeared underneath. Muscle defined every inch of him. Even lifeless, the strength was apparent.

I would have to wash myself in the sink when it was all done. Sweat dripped from my forehead as I kneeled over him. I had made countless trips to the faucet with our lone towel, rinsing, washing, scrubbing, and sweating.

He never woke up, never even roused.

The boys slept with open mouths and heavy breaths through it all. Satisfied I had done all I could, I resigned to crawling into the bed with Sam. There was a small gap between him and the wall, and I crept over his body, trying to squeeze in without spooning the man.

Impossible.

The bed was slightly bigger than a twin, and Sam was broad and over six feet tall. He was also warm, and no longer smelled like a sewer. Sleep came quickly.

My dreams that night were vivid and burned into my memory. I was at the top of the hill on our farm, looking down at our sunken basement. It seemed so far down as if I was staring out from the cliff of a mountain. Then I fell through the air and plummeted into the water. I tried to swim, but my arms refused to move. Only my legs would kick, but the movement did nothing. The basement walls pulled further and further away. I was getting nowhere, like I was running on a treadmill underwater. I sank and thrashed my legs to swim up, trying to catch a single breath. I would succeed briefly, only to be pushed down again without air in my lungs. Furniture from our house swirled around me and knocked me further into the dark water.

The panic felt alarmingly real as I shot up, awake, and gasping for air. Gripping my throat, I held myself, fighting back tears. I rocked back and forth to calm down.

Just a dream, just a dream.

There was a hum to the ship now, almost a vibration. We must have gone underway as I slept. I used my hands to cover my face and let myself cry a little, just for a moment while everyone slept. I wasn't sure what the tears were for. I was happy we had made it. I was sad for those that hadn't. Confusion and fear about raising BeLew hung heavy on my mind. I was never much of a crier, unlike my sister.

I took pride in being strong. I fell from my horse and broke my arm - no tears. My brother-in-law hit me in the face - no tears. My sister died in front of me - no tears. In school, a teacher told me crying releases oxytocin and can numb your feelings. A good long cry can heal you, and make you better. Maybe I was crying for relief after all these years of holding it inside.

A gentle hand ran up my back, and I softened. "BeLew, Aunt Row just needs a minute," I sobbed. "Please go back to bed. I love you."

The touch fell away, and I wiped my face with my sleeve. Minutes passed until I braced the wall with one arm and lowered myself back down to bed, still weeping.

Without realizing it, I had curled into Sam's side. When I felt his arm wrap around my waist and pull me to his chest, I froze.

I lifted my head and looked up. His eyes were closed with his face relaxed. In the distance, BeLew had not moved from their position.

Was Sam asleep?

His arm tightened against me, and I rested back on his chest. He was warm and strong. It made me feel safe, even if only for a moment. He may have been delirious, thinking he was in his home. Maybe his subconscious thought I was his girlfriend or wife, and holding me was a reflex after years of sharing a bed.

Whatever the reason, it felt good. I let his arm clutch me and I fell back to sleep. That time, it was dreamless.

A gentle knocking on the door awoke me. I had no sense of what time it was. The boys were curled up on their bunks, still sound asleep. I moved Sam's arm from my waist, and he tensed his grip. His eyes remained closed. I shuffled over him, lifting my right leg up and over his body and setting it on the floor, careful not to brush his injured thigh. His tight hold remained as I squirmed over his chest and slid out. He groaned, and his fingers held onto the edge of my shirt until I escaped his grasp.

There was no peephole. Scared the knocking would wake someone, I opened the door without asking who it was. A woman stood in the hall with a clipboard. Her face was sharp, and she had her black and grey hair in a tight bun.

Lips pursed, she tapped her pencil on some papers and cleared her throat. "Lawson," she clipped.

"Yes," I responded, stepping further into the hall. The woman yanked a cart over, full of supplies. She pulled out a stack of papers and a large bag and thrust them toward me. I took the package and stared at her; my face twisted in confusion.

"We will be back for household fingerprinting and blood draw this afternoon. Be sure to fill out the papers prior. A pen is in the bag, along with some food. There's a map of the ship and your location is starred. Mess hall opens at 0600."

"Thank you," I said. "What time is it now?"

She shot me a look and raised one eyebrow. "It's 1100," she deadpanned. She pointed down the hallway. "Clock's over there. We'll be back in a few hours."

"Is the medical bay open? Or the nurses' station? My... husband, he's injured."

She gave a slight chuckle and started down the hallway with her cart. "No," she laughed. "You're on your own with that." I groaned in frustration.

He'd made it through the night and seemed to have regained some strength, so I gave up on finding a doctor. Infection was the biggest issue now, and I needed to clean his makeshift bandage again. I stepped back into the room and set the bag and papers down on the small table. Sifting through, I saw nothing that would pass for bandages, so I would need to find another shirt.

I ran the water in the sink and collected what I needed. I would have to boil all of this as soon as I had a chance. I washed my hands, singing Happy Birthday to myself three times, smirking at the habits I kept, even under the strangest circumstances.

Placing my supplies on the bed, I moved his right leg out to one side, lifted his left, and laid it over my lap as I sat in between. Lifting the duct tape from his skin was easier than I expected. There was a mix of sweat and blood under the bandage, loosening the glue. The wound looked better today, clean enough, and wasn't hot to the touch.

One spot needed a tug and would have stung if he'd been awake. I held his skin taught and yanked.

"Sorry, Sam," I said to myself as I continued my work.

"It's alright," he whispered back and lifted himself to his elbows with a grin.

My body snapped straight. I moved my gaze to his, mouth agape.

"Who is Sam?" he said.

I tried to make words, but my mouth was dry, and my mind fell blank. The only noise that filled the room was my ragged breathing and the steady drip of blood that tapped the floor.

CHAPTER FIVE

BEAUTY

*H*E'S AWAKE.

"Who is Sam?" He repeated, louder this time while lifting himself to a seated position. He winced in pain, scooting his bad leg slightly back. He reached his hand toward the open hole in his thigh. I grabbed his wrist before he got there.

"Your hands are dirty, don't."

"Okay. I wouldn't want to undo your hard work." His eyes were ice blue. It was the first time I'd seen them fully open.

"Please whisper. The boys are still asleep, and they need to rest."

"Are they okay? Are you?"

I added more antibiotic cream to his wound and held the new bandage in place, thinking about how to respond. My heart pounded hard in my chest. I didn't know if he would ever awaken, yet, there he sat, ice-blue eyes watching my every move. "We're here, aren't we? More okay than others. What do you remember?"

He brought one hand to his jaw, rubbing his stubble and pinching his brow. "I remember pieces of things. I don't remember how I got into your car, but I remember the crash. I remember the boys. You call them BeLew. Everything else is blurry. Where are we?"

I started on the duct tape, wrapping it snug. "Does that hurt?" He shook his head and stared, waiting for my response. "We are on an Island Jumper. I have a close friend in the military. He got us on. Do you know what those are?"

Sam tensed, and he lowered his head. "I know several people thought that was a bunch of conspiracy shit. But, yeah, I know what they are." He rubbed the back of his neck and brought his eyes back to mine. "Sorry, I shouldn't curse in front of your sons. I remember that too," he muttered.

I finished his bandage and placed my hands on his knee and shin, looking down at my work. The way we sat felt intimate, and now that he was awake... inappropriate. But I didn't want to leave the bed. Where would I go in the tiny room if I did?

"I wondered if it was all a hoax too, but I trusted Dean, and I'm glad I did. We will be on this ship for a year. Maybe less if we find a safe-haven, but it's supplied for a year." I stilled my hands and paused.

He bit his lip, taking in the information. I had trapped him on the ship. *Would he be angry?*

"BeLew are my nephews, not my sons," I continued. "My sister and her husband are... they're gone. They passed away. I'm all they have now." My throat closed when the words slipped from my tongue. The memory of my sister with a boy on each hip flashed through my memory. The way she held them like her most precious possessions... so beautiful.

I frowned and pushed the thoughts aside. "Sam is the name I decided for you. My friend, Dean, who got us on the ship, someone he knew had a spot here because she's former military. She's gone, and we're assuming her family's identity."

I exhaled and stared blankly at the opposite wall before I told him the worst of it. My words were falling out of my head so quickly I wasn't sure if he was digesting any of the information. I had to get it all out at once. We could put together any missing pieces later, but for now, I had my nerve.

"To get you approved onboard, I told them you were my husband. Sam, Sam Lawson. Ashley was a friend of Dean's, but you can call me Rowan Lawson. We can say Rowan is a nickname. BeLew are Beau and Lewis Lawson. Do you understand? To stay, you need to go along with this until Dean can think of another solution... which, honestly, may never happen. They are getting blood and fingerprints this afternoon for all of us. For our... our family, for the Lawsons."

My eyes stayed glued to the wall for several minutes, and all I could hear was Sam's steady breathing. His hand lifted, and I felt the warmth of his palm on my back. I slowed my breath until it was in sync with his. His hand moved up my spine to the back of my neck. I flinched at first and then tried my best to relax. He held it there for a moment before he spoke. "Thank you, Rowan. Thank you for what you did."

I met his gaze as my eyes flooded with relief. I opened my mouth to speak, but no words escaped. He rubbed my neck and reached for my other hand, squeezing it. "I like the name Sam," he said with a smile. "I like the idea of... a fresh start."

We sat there, intertwined in silence, examining each other. We were in this together now.

"How about another hour of sleep?" he pleaded, lowering us both to the bed. I eased onto the mattress, resting my body on his chest.

"What's your actual name?" I whispered into the warmth of his body.

"It doesn't matter," he insisted. "I'm Sam. Sam Lawson."

I waited until his breathing became slow and even, then I left the bed. I stared down at him, wondering what happened next.

What the fuck are you doing? Dean's going to kill you — or him.

I couldn't sleep, and I needed to occupy my mind. I paced the small area, wringing my hands. I had paperwork that needed to get done. I dreaded it, but being a problem or on someone's list would make matters worse. I doubted they would make anyone walk the plank for missing documents, but we needed to stay under the radar.

I filled in every blank box I could until I had no choice but to wake Sam again. Most of our information was false, but some items would get tested. We had to inject our story with some truth to pull this off.

BeLew had awoken and started in on the food. I motioned for them to come over. "Boys, Sam is okay to wake up now. Do you want to nudge his shoulders and say hello?" They nodded their heads eagerly. "Please, just his shoulders and be very gentle."

They went to each side of his head and laid their palms on his shoulders with a small shove. His eyes fluttered open, and a smile crossed his lips. "Well, hi, BeLew," Sam yawned.

The boys gave a surprised look to one another.

"He knows us," Beau said, and Lewis covered his mouth and snickered.

Sam lifted himself gingerly and reached his hand out to them. "I want to shake the hands of my saviors. I owe you boys my life, you and your aunt."

They each gave him a shake, practically hopping as their hands moved up and down. They lit up around him.

"Okay, BeLew," I said, standing from the table. "Pick one more snack, and I'll move the wall here so you can play on your own. Sam and I have some grown-up stuff to do. It's very boring."

The boys grunted, grabbed more food, and then climbed into the top bunk. I closed the separator and sat back down at the desk. Sam had shifted upright and was sitting on the side of the bed with his legs on the floor.

"I'd like to stand or at least try to. I'll need some help."

"Okay," I said and rose to stand in front of him. "Do you want me to help pull you up, or... er?" I worried this attempt would be disastrous but so could deflating a man's ego on day one, so I complied.

He reached for my arm and drew me towards him until I was standing just between his legs. He placed both hands on the edge of the bed and gradually lifted with his right leg bearing the weight. He groaned and his face warped in pain. Once standing, he placed both his hands on my shoulders and I held my arms out to his sides, fearful he would sway over.

"How can something feel so good and so terrible at the same time?" he asked.

"I don't know, but I'm terrified you're going to fall."

"Well, I won't go far. This room is only three feet wide."

I held his sides as he bent back down, feeling his muscles tighten with the effort. His grip on my shoulders was firm, but he could partially hold himself if he had something to help support his weight. "It's not quite that bad," I murmured.

Sam rolled his eyes and let out a huff. "It's a shoebox, but it's perfect. Just trying to ease your nerves."

I pulled back to sit at the table, but Sam's grip on my shoulders remained. "I'm just going to get these papers we need to fill out. Are you steady now?"

"Yes, but come sit next to me."

I took the papers from the table and moved to his side. He looked me over, moving his eyes down my body as I shuffled the papers to find the sections we needed to review. His stare made me uncomfortable.

"I'm dirty, I know," I admitted. I had barely washed with the one washcloth we had. I had given BeLew a sink bath in between papers, but I hadn't attended to myself since we got here. My fingernails were black. My hair was in a ponytail, slick from oil. If I had a mirror, I would keel over from mortification.

"You are stunning." His statement came out so even and clear that I inhaled sharply from the words. Red heat filled my cheeks. I continued to stare at the papers like they held the meaning of life.

"Do you also have a head injury?" I deadpanned.

His hand moved to my thigh, and I moved my gaze to his face.

"I'm clear-headed," he said. "I don't want to make you uncomfortable, but I don't know... near death experiences and all. I want to say what I think more. You are a beautiful woman, inside and out. Everything you have done, what you have been through. I'm in awe of you."

He must have hit his head... hard.

"We should do this paperwork. They will be here any minute," I said, monotone. I failed to acknowledge his hand on my thigh, nor did I ask him to move it away. My heart thudded in my chest as I started asking the questions.

"I can enter a middle name for you here. Maybe we should use your actual name, just in case. What is it?"

"My name is Sam Lawson. You can use whatever middle name you like."

"Okay," I exhaled. He had been awake for less than an hour total, and I refused to start this relationship with a fight. I left that section blank, and we could use his correct name later when he came to his senses. "What was your profession on land? What are your skill sets?"

"I have training in engineering. At home, I repaired mechanical equipment. I can also fix up cars, anything with an engine. What did you do?"

I lit up. The more useful we were, the safer our positions. "That's good. I helped run the farm for the past few years. What's your date of birth?"

"September 1st, 1986."

"Do you have any children? Anyone else that might be on this ship or somewhere else?"

"I have BeLew. I have you."

"Seriously, though. Anyone else that might look for you? There is an entire section here dedicated to reunification."

"There is no one, Rowan." His face was stern. There was no invitation to continue my line of questioning, so I moved on without pushing the subject.

I completed the not applicable boxes and moved on to medical history. "Do you have any medications you were taking? Surgeries in your past? Pre-existing conditions?"

He replied no to everything. "I'm very average and very boring. I try to stay healthy," he shrugged.

"You seem like it. I mean, you had t-to be to make it through w-whatever happened to your leg." My awkwardness was shining through, even then. I caught myself complimenting his physique and failed to stutter my way out of it.

"Nice of you to notice," he drawled.

My blushing continued. "I need to put your leg injury on here. Do you know what happened?"

"I don't. I remember running on the trail. The third storm had just hit, and the wind was still up, but not terrible. The next thing I remember is being in your Jeep."

I scrunched my face, trying to describe the injury on the paperwork in front of me. I had nothing to go on, but he was already doing so well. I didn't want us to be a liability, but he could still require medical attention, and these forms would be the start of the process.

"Do you want to ask me anything else?" Sam urged. He had one eyebrow raised and moved his hand over my thigh. "Something that's not on those pages."

We had a year to get to know each other, but there was no time like the present to start. "Where were you going... on the path?"

"Higher ground. My place was completely underwater. I thought I might hot-wire an abandoned car."

"And you lived by yourself?"

"Yes," he paused. "I was married before. I'm not anymore."

"Oh, I see." I shuffled the papers, looking for a reprieve. "I've never been married. I was engaged once."

"Lucky for me it didn't work out."

My eyes widened as I stared back at the familiar place on the wall. A knock at the door offered my desired reprieve from the conversation. I exhaled with gratitude. "Time for more blood," I said, nervously rising to my feet.

Two women entered the small space with a narrow cart, clipboards, and a mission. They never made eye contact with us, completely engrossed in their tasks. BeLew tried to object to the needles, but they had them held down and stuck before they knew what hit them. They stuffed our paperwork away in their files and slammed the door behind them without as much as a goodbye.

The air grew thick with discomfort after their departure. I was aware of myself, my smell, and the man that was in such close proximity. "Do you think—" I began, unsure of how to ask. "Maybe, um, I could try to shower? The bathrooms are down the hall, and I could really use one."

"I'm here with the boys. You don't have to ask, just go," Sam said. "Maybe we can tell each other some stories. I'm sure we will think of something, right, BeLew?"

"Yes!" they shouted in unison.

"Okay, I don't know you really, so I don't know how to do this. I will, I guess, in time," I mumbled.

"It's us now, Row." His face was hard, making his point known. "The four of us. Are you comfortable going out on your own?"

I nodded, collecting the bar of soap, clean clothes, and washcloth. I hugged the boys, and they crawled in front of our bed as the man we would call Sam started a story. I heard his voice boom a tale with enthusiasm as I left and started down the hall.

Small metal slots without shower curtains lined the bathroom wall, but they looked like heaven. I turned on the faucet and felt steam immediately.

Oh, thank God.

The heat felt orgasmic on my skin. The walls and floors ran dark with dirty water, confirming how disgusting I had become over the previous few days. I scrubbed as much as I could with the washcloth before using the soap. We had one bar, and the showers had nothing more to offer. Once I could wash my body with a single layer of suds, I put my clothes on the floor of the shower, cleaning them at the same time.

My muscles ached as I wrung the clothes. I dressed, aware of how empty my stomach felt and looked. There was a mirror in the bathroom that I dared to face, and my reflection appeared tired and gaunt. *How could he think this was beautiful?* I braided my dark hair and secured it with my hairband, inspecting my hollow cheeks and dark under-eye circles. The mess hall opened tomorrow, and I prayed they wouldn't ration our first meals. Everyone had to be starving.

Refreshed, I walked back to my room to find Dean waiting at the door. My elation dissipated when I noticed his demeanor. His arms crossed at his chest and he had a scowl on his face. He paced in front of my door, clucking his tongue. When I came into his view, he tilted his chin upwards and made his stance wide towards me.

"Your boyfriend won't open the door," he barked. "And I-" he stopped short.

And you left your key, I thought to myself.

"Isn't it great he pulled through?" I clipped back.

Not ready for sarcasm, Dean bent down inches from my face and continued, "It might be a good time to remind him who else saved his life."

I gave the door a gentle knock. "It's me, Sam. I didn't bring the key. Could you open up?"

A moment later, BeLew stood at the open door. They waved at Dean, turned, and sat back down next to Sam.

I stepped into the room and arranged my things while my hands gave a slight shake. Sam noticed and furrowed his brow. Dean strolled in behind me, arms still crossed. He slammed the door with his foot and glared at Sam.

"Sam, this is my friend, Dean. He's the one that helped us get on the ship," I said. "Dean, you remember Sam."

"Oh, how could I forget?" Dean hissed. "The man that I allowed on this vessel, then carted to this very room, and the one I just signed intake papers for. Intake papers that are full of lies. Lies that could get me killed. That Sam?"

"I'm sorry, man," Sam calmly replied. He wasn't defensive or upset. Dean's aggression had no effect on his demeanor. "I didn't know who you were, and these boys are my responsibility."

"And Rowan isn't? You let her go to the bathrooms by herself on the first day here. We don't even know how many psychos made it onto this thing."

"Wait a minute," I interjected. "You don't think it's safe for me to pee by myself? You left that out in your, *that's all*, speech last night."

"All I'm saying is you're picking and choosing how to protect your newfound family," Dean snapped, keeping his eyes on Sam.

I moved next to Dean and gently placed my hand on his bicep. "And all I'm saying is you are picking a fight right now over nothing. We appreciate what you've done, Dean. Sam's sorry you had to wait outside."

"I am sorry, Dean," Sam affirmed. "I owe you my life. The last thing I would want is to offend you."

With that, Dean uncrossed his arms and put his hand on top of mine. Bringing me to a hug, he kissed the top of my head. "I'm short-tempered," he whispered into my hair. "All that matters is you and BeLew."

"And Sam," Beau added.

Dean cleared his throat but didn't comment. He took out papers from his back pocket and handed them over to me. "I started your assignments and got the boys enrolled in school when I saw your forms come over. I can get us to the mess hall now and we can go over them. It isn't open to the public yet, and it will be quiet enough."

He turned his head to Sam and gave him a sideways smirk. "You have to walk there, so it will just be us for now."

"Not a problem," Sam said. "I'll rest. You need to eat, Rowan. I can hear your belly growling from here."

BeLew grabbed at Dean's hands to yank him towards the door. Fully rested, the boys needed to escape these four walls and stretch their legs.

"I'm right behind you," I told Dean. "Start with them, and I'll run-up. I just want to check on Sam's bandage, okay?"

"We'll wait at the end of the hallway unless we're still afraid of hallways. We might have big problems if that's the case." Dean gave the boys a wink.

"We aren't afraid," Beau announced, stepping towards the door.

"We are like Captain America," Lewis added.

Dean left with the boys bouncing at his sides, and I sat next to Sam on the bed.

"You just changed my bandage. I think it's fine."

"I'm sorry you can't come to the mess hall, but I'll bring you back something to eat. I just feel bad leaving you here by yourself. And after that weird interaction with Dean..." I trailed off.

"Don't worry about it, Row. I'm completely fine to rest more. My body is telling me to do nothing but sleep right now. Well, mostly sleep." He gave a slight grin.

"Right, okay. You won't even notice we're gone, and I'll have food for you when I get back."

I was unsure how to leave Sam just then. My hands twisted in front of me and I crossed and uncrossed my legs. Determined to stop fidgeting, I stood and gave an awkward wave. Sam reached for my belt loop and drew me back towards him.

"I'll notice you're gone, Row. But please, eat, you need to take care of yourself. I'll see you in a few hours."

I bent over and hugged him. "Don't try to stand without me."

"I'll be good," he breathed into my hair. I pulled back, our arms still wrapped around each other, face to face. Our noses almost touched, and I stilled myself, unsure of what to do next. Sensing my awkwardness, Sam moved his lips to the side of my cheek and gave me a quick kiss. I stood, and he sank back down into the mattress, eyes heavy.

I walked in a rush down the hallway after Dean. My cheek was on fire where he had given me a quick peck. My heart fluttered, and I almost passed by Dean in my trance.

"You must be hungry," Dean said, in step after me.

"Yes, I'm starving. Thank you for getting us to the mess hall tonight. I'm glad for your help with our assignments too."

"Well, we have a lot to go over and figure out," Dean huffed. "Especially now."

We started on the stairs. BeLew took them two at a time as I struggled to keep up. "What do you mean, especially now?" I asked when we approached swinging metal doors.

Dean opened a door to the mess hall, showed a badge, then led me in by my elbow. The smell of food filled my nostrils, and my stomach cramped in response. He moved his arm fully around my waist and whispered in my ear, "Now that we have to get rid of your new husband."

Chapter Six

Persuasion

THE ONE THING DEAN taught me was how to manipulate people. His influence on others was something I almost admired. He must have been born with it because I couldn't remember a time that I wasn't under the direct influence of Dean Riggs.

In school, teachers hung on his every word. He would run his hand through that charcoal hair and beam at you with those deep brown eyes, and they forgot their point. Maybe he needed an extension on a paper or a curve for the class. He may have just wanted to fuck with them. Whatever the reason, he left satisfied and victorious every time.

Having a close relationship with a manipulator lulled me into a false sense of security. I had every reason to believe that Dean would never exploit me. I was in control of my decisions and actions, right? When he talked in circles, it wasn't to sway *me*, to make *me* forget the whole reason we were talking.

Right?

But Dean's mastery of manipulation extended to every person in his life. Of course it did, and I realized it with some distance. Dean's time away from me while he was enlisted was his downfall. It made me realize his manipulation stretched on for years, infiltrating every thought and feeling I thought I owned.

His father kept watch over me, but he didn't have Dean's cunning presence. I caught on quickly when he stopped by the farm or accompanied me to town while Dean was away. He would pick and pry for information that was then fed back to Dean.

Dean would visit, and I would fall back into the trap, back into his bed. Then, shortly after his departure, his father would casually stop by to check on me. It took me too much time for the tactics to come into focus. But once I saw it, everything was clear. Denial was a manipulator's best friend.

It took one year of separation to see the cycle. It took my sister's entanglements to realize that despite Dean's tactics; I needed him. I *still* needed him, and I feared I would forever be indebted to him.

Regardless of his selfishness, I loved Dean Riggs. He would always put himself first, but true love meant accepting the worst things about a person and loving them in spite of that. Knowing that fact about Dean, being aware that every move he made would always benefit himself first, allowed me to love him properly. It didn't disappoint me anymore when he made a decision that helped himself over others. It was simply nature: a wild animal bit, and Dean Riggs lied.

He saved our lives by getting us on the ship. He maintained he risked his life in doing so, but he had motivation behind his actions that I didn't understand yet. He needed me here. He wanted Sam gone.

The mess hall was full of boxes stacked high to the ceiling. I imagined they haphazardly dropped everything, knowing they would handle it and unpack the contents once the ship was moving. A few tables stretched out in the metal room. They reminded me of high school folding tables with their fake wood and circular seats. As we made our way inside, a few men gave Dean a salute. BeLew followed suit, beaming with pride.

A young woman, early thirties maybe, crossed the distance of the mess hall and met us at the table. Her steps echoed in the empty room. "Lieutenant Riggs," she spoke with apprehension. "Is this your family? Will they be joining you?"

"Yes, Smith, but don't trouble yourself with us. We can manage ourselves," he answered kindly. She visibly relaxed and gave a tight smile. "I don't have much made at the moment, only crew food."

"That would be wonderful. I'll venture in and get us some plates. Are your sons here?"

Her back straightened, and her eyes shifted down to the floor as she answered. "Yes, Lieutenant. I didn't want to leave them alone."

"I completely understand. Where are they exactly?"

She pointed to the far corner of the room. The expanse was so great, I couldn't make out any children in the direction she motioned. "They are playing in the empty boxes over there, building a fort."

BeLew gasped and gave Dean a pleading look. "Go on," he said. "We can bring plates back to the room later. Your mother and I have to talk, anyway." He turned to Smith and put his hand on her shoulder, leading her back to the kitchen. "I'll be right in to make us something. You have work to do. I won't keep you."

She nodded and sped off back to her duties. Dean turned to me and gestured for us to take a seat. "I'll head in there and get some food for you. Start looking through the assignments." He then gave my chin a quick pinch and sauntered over toward the smell of baking bread.

The prickling on my skin took hold, and I knew this was the start of his plan. He wanted something from me. His mannerisms gave him away after all these years. The way he would subtly flirt and act on someone's needs. Innocent to most, but I knew him better than that.

I took the pages and skimmed their contents.

Assignment—A. Rowan Lawson
Division—Agriculture—Seeding/Sowing/Harvest
Subdivision—Chemistry
Leadership—Yes
Direct Reports—Yes, 27
Intake Date—Immediate

We have assigned deck sections 900 to 1300 to A. Rowan Lawson. Introductory planting has yet to begin. The mandated outcome is one completed growing cycle. Direct report to Lieutenant Dean Riggs.

The rest of the paper was military confusion. Dean may also need to school me in the jargon, considering Ashley Rowan Lawson was honorably discharged and would have been well versed in what all of it meant. I sifted through to the other assignment.

Assignment—Samuel Lawson
Division—Janitorial
Subdivision—Sub Decks 4200-4800

Leadership–N/A
Direct Reports–N/A
Intake Date–Undetermined

Samuel Lawson currently cannot perform assigned obligations because of an injury. The desired outcome is 1-2 weeks of recuperation. Direct report to Mary Vislow.

There was no need to read more. Not that it would make sense to me, anyway. Dean was an asshole. One to two weeks was not nearly enough time for Sam to recover and perform a physically demanding job, and janitorial work was a waste of Sam's skill sets. They could use him for other tasks that would benefit us all. I had a few minutes before Dean came back. I sat up straight and turned the pages over, thinking my way through his tactics.

He wanted me in chemistry. I had no skills for that, so he had a reason that suited his needs. Agriculture made sense. I'd never been in leadership, yet I was assigned twenty-seven direct reports. That means *he* wanted more direct reports. He wanted Sam separated from me, in a demeaning role. He wanted Sam tired and to appear unable to pull his weight on the ship.

I had my key points to stick to when Dean sat down at the table with overflowing plates. I drooled at the sight and moaned as the food hit my lips. Dean watched me eat as he took a few bites.

"You look like you just had an orgasm," he smirked.

"Well, you would know," I shot back, playing his game. He wanted me agreeable and uncomfortable. We had spent too much time apart. He didn't know the woman I was today.

"Might be hard to refresh my memory with your husband around, but it's a big ship," he replied with a devilish grin. "I still need to give you the grand tour." He moved his eyes to my body and licked his bottom lip.

"This must be the epitome of lack of options, right?" I snorted. "I mean, you only have so many women to choose from. We are on a floating island. I never figured you for low-hanging fruit first. The Dean I knew loved a challenge."

He frowned and sat back. "You consider yourself easy prey?" His eyes flicked from my breasts to my face.

"No, but you do. You think I'm weak from the past month and the trip. You think I owe you something because of Sam. Shit - you think I owe you something because I'm alive. It's more than sex you want, but you'll start with that, won't you? You'll fuck me and then you'll fuck me over."

Dean's jaw tightened. He stabbed his food and took a bite, chewing audibly. He hunched over his plate and looked up at me, moving his jaw from side to side as he ate. I had him.

"Great way to say thanks, Row," he sneered.

"I'll say thanks anyway you want. The boys are what matter. If I have to pay a penance for that, I will. Whether that's with my body or other ways."

His eyebrows lifted. "Other ways?"

I stayed silent for a moment, eating mindfully. Each bite of food gave me strength. I felt more like myself, more in control.

"You don't have to tell me why you want me in chemistry," I said. "I've trusted you my entire life. I'm not stopping now."

"Row, please," he started, but I shot my hand up to his face.

"You don't have to give me a bullshit reason either," I continued. "Honestly, I couldn't care less what your intentions are. All I care about are the boys."

Dean slammed his fork down on the table. "That's all I care about, too. You and BeLew."

I bit the inside of my cheek. That's what he wanted to believe. He may have even tricked himself into thinking that's true. We mattered to Dean, but the most important thing? Not even close. "You're ten steps ahead always. You know there are dangers on this boat. You gave me shit for taking a shower by myself."

"That's why you will work in the agriculture unit and report to me. I need to make sure you're safe," he added.

"Yes, I know." I reached for his hand and interlaced our fingers. "I assume you will work an opposite shift than me though, as I'm in leadership."

Dean nodded, giving me a quizzical look. "We will probably cross a few hours, though. We won't be on the overnights. You can be home with BeLew every night, have every dinner with them."

I crossed my legs and hovered my body over the table, moving closer to him. "Sam does us no good in the lower decks, scrubbing toilets. Think with your head and not your heart or your dick. You want my allegiance, you have it. You want him gone so I can't pull away from you - don't be ridiculous. You know this ship is dangerous. You want me and the boys safe. You know he has experience in mechanics and engineering. He owes me his life and will do what I ask to pay that debt. Put him on nights. He won't be in the room when we sleep and you will have another ally - another set of eyes helping you."

Dean opened his mouth, ready to rebuff, but snapped it shut.

"Focusing your energy on getting him away from us is a waste of time. We need to create a support system here. He's an easy addition. I can handle him," I added.

Dean's eyes moved side to side in thought, and I took advantage of the moment. "What's her name, Smith?" I asked, pointing to the kitchen. "I'll go ask her for to-go plates. You let what I said marinate."

I hurried across the empty room toward the steel appliances, my heart thudding in my chest. I didn't have Dean's caress for debate, but I had solid points. Smith met me at the door with a soft smile. I imagined it was because I was sans Dean.

"Hi. Could I bring a tray back to my quarters? You know how boys are," I said.

She laughed and agreed, then showed me around her workspace, proud of all she had accomplished. I was happy about the tour so Dean could mull things over.

She filled reusable containers to the brim and then emptied an entire tray of rolls into a large plastic bag. "Boys are bottomless pits," she chuckled, handing me the food. "If you need anything at all, please come see me. Just bring those back rinsed."

I thanked her and headed back. Dean stood, slightly bent over the table, resting his hands next to his plate. He didn't turn when he heard me coming, and I sat and continued eating my meal until he was ready to talk.

He left to go check on the boys, circled the room once, and had another conversation with Smith before he resumed our discussion. It was a power play, his game to see if I would beg. I kept my resolve.

"Nights it is," he clipped, knocking on the table twice. "He needs to prove his loyalty to us. I hope you are right about him." He took our assignments and folded them back, shoving them in his pocket. "I'll be back tomorrow morning to take you all to breakfast and bring you updated papers. I expect to be let in this time."

"Yes, I understand. Will he start immediately?"

"Two weeks," Dean answered. "He can do a lot from a chair if needed. I have to go. Can you find your way back?"

I set down my utensils and rose to my feet. "You are making the right decision." I circled the table and brought him into a hug. He *was* making the right decision, and not just because it was the right thing to do. I knew in my gut we could trust Sam.

He snaked his arms around me and buried his face in the crook of my neck. "I'm not letting you off the hook on the sex," he joked. I could feel his laugh rumble in his chest, but I knew he was partially serious. He pulled back and brushed his lips against mine, then tilted his chin upward and kissed me on the head.

As he walked away, I mumbled, "I love you, Dean," mostly to myself. I had love for Dean Riggs, and I hoped I still would when this was all over.

The boys played happily with the Smith kids, and I hated pulling them away. I stopped by the kitchen before I left to see if I could set up a time to get them all together again. I waved hello and Smith came back over.

"I have to go, but our boys seem to enjoy each other's company quite a bit. I'm Rowan, Rowan Lawson. Do you have a first name I could use?" I asked.

"Lori," she beamed. "Please Rowan, Lori is perfect. I'm so happy to get them together anytime. Are they starting school next week?"

I bit my lip and leaned against a counter in her kitchen. "Um, I assume so. I'm just a bit all over the place at the moment." The truth was, I should know. Had I been military, I would understand the inner workings of this ship. The intake papers had information about the boys' enrollment, but I had become focused on Sam's assignment. Lori was unphased by my comment and continued to shuffle around pots and pans.

"Well, there are far fewer children than they expected," she said, sliding knives into open slots. "I know because I heard a few teachers pissed about their work orders. They moved them to agriculture because we didn't need as many. They need to get over it. We are lucky to be here. Maybe they should take a moment to grieve why they don't need as many teachers."

A lump formed in my throat, and I felt a pang in my heart. "Right," I choked. "We all need to keep some perspective."

The sound of running feet became louder until all four boys stood in front of us, panting. "It's time for us to go BeLew," I said. "Let's get Sam's food and head out."

They gave visible pouts and lowered their shoulders. "But tomorrow your mom and I are going to let you play on the deck after lunch while we take a walk in the sunshine," Lori added. They gasped and jumped up and down. Lori's boys gave each other a high five, and I winked at her in thanks. Her sons looked a bit older, but BeLew were tall for their age and all four children stood at almost the same height.

Already, the layout of the ship was familiar to me and the boys. They left the vastness of the unoccupied room and took a left without being directed. I wondered how many mess halls were on the vessel. I only had a murky image of the size of our floating home, but in my mind, this ship went on forever.

Ten minutes later, I announced, "Honey, I'm home," in jest, setting the food and rolls on the small table. The front bed was empty, which meant he had done the exact thing I asked him not to do. This was not boding well for the *I can control him* promise I just gave Dean. The divider was closed, and Beau yanked it open.

"Why would you get up without me? I asked you to wait one hour, and you said you would sleep," I bellowed, but when the wall collapsed to one side, there was nothing.

Sam was gone.

CHAPTER SEVEN

CAUTION

A RUSH OF ADRENALINE filled my veins. My fingers tingled and my ears burned. There was nowhere he could hide from me, but I turned over blankets and lifted the beds, desperate to find him. He could barely take a step, let alone walk out of the room on his own.

My mind spun with possibilities, but there was only one plausible explanation. Dean had left before me and had come straight here.

Has he played me that well? Is he proving a point with an iron fist?

"Where's Sam?" Beau asked calmly.

My hands shook while I lowered their beds back down. "He's with Dean, having some guy time."

They frowned, and I directed them to their bunks to play with some small gadgets they had brought. I closed the curtain and sat on our bed, staring at the familiar spot on the wall.

Our bed.

I would not leave the boys, so the furthest I could search was the hallway. I knew the ship well enough to make it to the showers and mess hall, but that wasn't far at all. An exploration with our pathetic map was out, and what if Dean found out? He would think I had developed feelings or lied about my relationship with Sam. No, all I could do was sit there, helpless.

I had an electronic reader with a full charge I had kept turned off for a month. It would last hundreds of hours without a recharge, but how many hours are in a year, thousands? I knew once it died, it would break my heart. I'd probably never get to charge it again, but I needed a distraction.

I resigned to staring at my reader rather than the wall, but I read several pages repeatedly. My focus was shit. All I could think about was Sam. My brain went to the worst potential scenarios. What if he had died, and they had removed him from the bunk? What if Dean had killed him, reported he died, and then removed him from the bunk?

I asked the boys to sit with me, and I read Harry Potter until they fell fast asleep. I lifted them one by one to the bunks, nudging them both into the bottom bunk when the weight of them was too much for my exhausted arms to push overhead.

Then I lay on my side, staring at the spot on the wall. When I fell asleep after hours of worry, I dreamed I was in the water again. This time I was alone, staring at the side of a ship, unable to move my arms, so I kicked my legs to stay afloat. I still sank into the darkness, yanking and pulling my body, trying to free my arms. Strangers dove into the water all around me. They sank with me, their faces stricken with panic and fear. They looked at me for help, but I did nothing. We thrashed and jerked as we drifted lower.

When I awoke, I tried to grab my throat as I gasped for air, but something pinned my arms down on the bed. Unable to realize I was no longer dreaming, I coughed and choked and shook until I saw Dean. He had my hands pinned above me and was inches from my face. I could smell coffee on his breath with every sharp inhale.

"Rowan," he barked in my face. "Rowan, wake up. You're having a nightmare. Wake up!" Beads of sweat spread across his brow, and veins protruded from his neck. *How long have I been dreaming?*

I stilled my body as his words registered. I could see BeLew to the side, and I turned my head to them. They were flush against the wall, holding hands, eyes wide. Lewis whispered something in Beau's ear with a shielded hand.

"Rowan, say something," Dean repeated. He loosened his grip on my wrists and ran his hands down my forearms.

"I'm sorry, I'm so sorry, boys," I cried. Dean reached behind my back and lifted me upward. "I've just been having these terrible dreams. They feel very real. Boys, I'm just fine. It was just a dream."

They nodded and shuffled back towards their bunks. I watched them in horror, my sisters' voice chastising me in my thoughts. Dean closed the divider and moved back to me. "What's happening in the dream?" he asked. "You're sweating and shaking. It seems more like more night terrors again."

I rubbed my wet palms on my pants and clenched my teeth. Dean rested his hand on my shoulder, encouraging me to explain.

"It's hard to describe, really, like most dreams, I suppose. I'm drowning in my dreams. I'm always drowning and I know this sounds crazy, but it feels like if I don't wake up, I might suffocate, like my body is shocking me awake when I'm out of breath. I feel it, Dean, the lack of oxygen. It's terrifying. I come out of these nightmares desperate for air. I don't know what else to say. No one knows they are dreaming in dreams. It feels very real."

Dean moved closer, resting his chin on my shoulder. "I need to know what happens in order to help you. Who's with you, when you are drowning?"

"I'm fine. It's just a dream. You have helped us enough already."

He inhaled deeply and I could feel his breath on my neck when he let the air out. "Well, I guess the arrangement works out with Sam. I don't think you should be here alone for too long at night if you are having these night terrors."

I had forgotten about Sam for a moment. My body tensed, and I wondered if Dean could feel it. He pulled me closer, kissed my neck, and then stood up to face me. My eyes met his, and I considered what to say next. My most horrible thoughts about Sam's disappearance hadn't come to fruition. He was alive, but asking about him meant I cared. I needed to appear indifferent about Sam to Dean.

"Thank you for waking me, Dean. I hate how I scared the boys. I'm glad you are here."

One side of his lips lifted, and he moved to grab a bag from the table. "I'll always be here for you all. You can depend on me not to vanish." He pulled out two small containers and steam puffed in the air when he lifted the lids. He handed me one and then stuck a spoon in the hot mush.

"Oatmeal?" I asked, stirring.

Dean raised his eyebrows and nodded. "Get used to that. It's likely an everyday thing."

I started in on the food, deciding not to take the bait when he alluded to Sam's departure. I would address the situation once Dean felt in control.

After a few bites, and a few tense minutes, he shrugged his shoulders and let out a huff. "Sam's now on nights with the Ag unit. Nights are a late second shift. No one works from three to six in the morning now. It's a full blackout for navigation and communication during that time. We're having difficulty with comms. He'll be here until you get up with the boys around seven, so he can smack some sense into you the next time you wake up like that. The turn of events with his scheduling displeased me, but seeing you this morning..." he trailed off and squared his jaw.

"Seeing you this morning, it may be best to have another adult with BeLew. I've never witnessed someone have a night terror. How long have you been having these dreams?"

I was reluctant to answer him. My sister was the only one who had experienced this with me. It had happened when I was a child more often than I could count. It stopped completely in high school but started back up a few months before the weather turned against us. When I was little, the dreams had petrified me. They confused me.

And then I experienced the visions in real-life.

When my sister and I noticed a pattern with the dreams, the fear took hold. She promised never to tell anyone my secret if I swore to tell her every dream. I kept my word in my younger years, but when I dreamed of the storms and the world today, I couldn't bear to tell her what I saw. I knew what it meant and what it would do to her. No one wanted to know they were dying. No one wanted to live in fear.

We hadn't referred to them as night terrors. We'd called them premonitions.

"When I was young, I did. It's been a hard year, so I'm sure the trauma has brought them back." It wasn't a lie, but it wasn't the whole truth.

"Brought them back exactly when? What else have you been dreaming?"

"It's just a stupid dream. When things become more routine, they'll stop."

Dean lowered his shoulders and shoveled another bite of food into his mouth. He chewed, letting the silence build between us before he spoke again. "You're probably right, but let me know if you have another."

"I will, but I don't want you to worry yourself with it. I'm okay. I'm adjusting."

A light knock on the door diverted our attention. "Ah, your husband is back." Dean opened the door and stepped outside. I could hear hushed voices through the wall. Someone let out a grunt of pain, and I considered barging into the hall, but I restrained myself. I wanted him back, preferably in less pain than when he left, and he was so close.

The door opened, and Sam appeared on the arm of another large man. They were both dressed in blue scrubs, and I could tell he was getting around better. Sam's face tensed in pain, but he was walking, or rather shuffling. With his arm wrapped around someone else, he could make it from point A to point B. The only issue was both bulky men would never make it through our narrow doorway.

I rushed over to him and his face lit up. "Hey, Wifey. Sorry to bail on our honeymoon."

Sam moved his grip to mine with the grace of a linebacker. Huffing and grimacing, we made it to the bed. He kept his eyes on me the whole time, and I made a mental note to go over future Dean etiquette. If he called me beautiful right now, Dean would send him straight to cleaning toilets, tonight.

He lowered to the bed with a thud, and I covered him up, grabbed my oatmeal, and went to the hallway with the men. "He looks better." I shoved a bite into my mouth. My heart fluttered now that I knew where Sam was and that his disappearance didn't appear to be ill-intended.

"He looks like shit, but at least he's clean and so is his wound," Dean snapped.

"I did the best I could," I mumbled through bites of food.

"You did a magnificent job," the other man chimed in. "If you'll excuse me, I need to get back to the clinic." He left, pushing an empty wheelchair, and I thanked him as he strolled away.

"You did a great job, but he needed to get checked out. I pulled a few strings and got him seen. You weren't worried I hope." I stayed silent, pretending to chew oatmeal. "You were right about the severity. The gash scraped the bone. It's going to take months to fully heal, and even then, he may have a limp."

"Well, I appreciate you taking care of him. Again, the right thing to do. Thank you."

"Well, I'll leave you to it then. I'm sorry I forgot to leave a note that I took him down there earlier. I got wrapped up with the effort to get him up and out of the room. You understand?"

"Absolutely, no big deal. Should we meet in the mess hall for dinner today since our breakfast plans got a little shuffled? I'm having lunch with Lori, er, I mean Smith, and her boys."

Dean rocked back on his heels. "Making friends already, I see. Yes, dinner at seven in civilian time. You'll need to learn the military clock."

"I figured it out, 1900. And I could use a female friend. Plus, she manages the kitchen. She's an ally we need to have. See you then, Dean." I turned on my heel and headed for the door. I heard Dean's footsteps without a goodbye and took that as a good sign. He went along with me seeing Smith. I believed I passed his little test with Sam too, but only time would tell.

When I got back into the room, I shut the door behind me and leaned my body against it, letting out an audible sigh. I chucked the empty cup in the garbage can and lowered my hands to my knees, my head hanging low.

"That distraught over losing me for an evening?" Sam quipped. He propped himself on his elbows with his chest on display. The sheet crept down to his waist as he lifted, showing off his chiseled chest.

I averted my eyes, but they kept flicking back to his body. "Where's your shirt?"

"It itched. That fabric is awful. I had a very odd few hours, but I'm feeling better now."

I walked to the divider and heard the boys playing, so I plopped into a chair at our table, ready to hear about Sam's adventure. Sam reached out his arm, gesturing for me to sit on the bed. I gave him a sideways smirk and complied.

I wiggled in between Sam and the wall and covered myself with the sheet. I had a full stomach and hours to rest before I visited with Lori. I had a feeling that relaxation was going to be short-lived soon, so I took advantage of it. "So, they took care of you? Helped you have less pain?"

"Hell no. I thought they were trying to kill me."

My eyes narrowed in confusion, and I reached for Sam's arm. "What do you mean?"

"Your friend Dean, he came in saying something about going to get medical treatment. And treat me, they did. But there's no anesthesia, nothing to numb the wound." Sam swallowed hard and cracked his knuckles. "Silver lining is I passed out quickly from the pain, and when I woke up, it looked a lot better."

My intense grip on Sam's arm caused my knuckles to go white. I tried to keep my fury hidden, but Sam knew. He reached his hand over mine and unclasped my fingers, interlacing them with his. "We can't have my arm bruised up too."

I softened and murmured an apology, folding my arms across my body. "Sam, you need to be careful with Dean. Don't, um, touch me around him. He's not someone you want upset."

"He's certainly a peach. I hope I won't be seeing him too often. It's nice he got me fixed up, but he watched the show at first. Seemed like he got some amusement out of it."

"Oh, I'm sure he did, but you won't be getting your wish. We will all be working together on the decks in agriculture. We report to Dean."

Sam's face turned from shock to a wide smile. "So, I'll be with you all day and night?"

"Not exactly. Our shifts won't align. We will be together overnight for a bit, but that's all. But at least you aren't cleaning toilets."

Sam chuckled. "Right, that would be awful."

I remained expressionless and nodded. "Oh, God. He was going to have me do that, wasn't he?" Sam gasped.

"Again," I said. "Be careful with Dean. We want to keep him happy. He needs to feel like he's in control."

BeLew made crashing sounds on the other side of the divider. Their laughter could brighten any situation, even the prospect of cleaning thousands of toilets.

"We're in this together." Sam glanced toward the divider. "Whatever you say, Row. We'll do what we have to, okay. What do we have left, three hundred or so days? That's nothing in the scheme of things."

I exhaled and flopped on the bed at that thought. None of us knew how long we would be on the vessel with nothing to see but the ocean. I didn't even know the name of the ship and cursed silently, hoping that wasn't bad luck. I knew there were about two dozen island jumpers, but who knew how many people made it aboard or if they all survived the first few storms.

We had known the weather was getting worse for years, but no one could have imagined what the storms would bring. It seemed the coasts around the world were getting battered again and again from the unrelenting hand of God or whatever you believed. Just when we thought there was a break in the onslaught, we saw the line of hurricanes coming up from the Atlantic. The typhoons and cyclones were eating up the other side of the world at the same time. They were relentless in their attack, each one bigger than the last. No one would survive in the end, so people fled inland, hoping for refuge. They had said we had done it, the people of Earth. We'd changed the natural order of things.

After the first storm hit, the tornados and floods proved no place was safe from the devastation. People designed several escape plans and safe havens. Underground cities, civilizations carved miles into mountains, and ships to dodge the weather patterns and deposit souls in a new home.

I considered myself lucky we landed anywhere when millions had been left out in the dangerous open. Dean had gone to the ships, so that was where we followed.

One year.

One year and the earth had a reset.

One year and no one left on an island would have survived.

That's where these ships would go. A place to rebuild and restart. Chances were, some people would endure on the continents, but what would that look like? Those left would ravage our supplies. Survivors would take our weapons and our food, killing anyone in their way. Island hoppers isolated those that were left. There was safety in that isolation.

"Three hundred or so, yes," I muttered. "You will need to trust me for all of them. Every damn one."

Sam turned on his side, letting out a groan as he moved to rest on his elbow. "We'll trust each other. How about you start by telling me who Dean is to you?"

I turned to Sam, mirroring his position, propping up on my elbow and letting my hair fall to the pillow. "How about you start by telling me your real name?"

A silent standoff. Or would it be a lay-off as we both were chest to chest in the small bed? I could feel Sam's breath on my forehead as he gazed slightly downward into my eyes. His Adam's apple rose and fall as he swallowed and let out a rough breath.

"I would like to be Sam, but my last name is Rivera."

"That's enough for me, for now." I lowered my elbow and rolled onto my back. Sam cleared his throat, waiting for my end of the bargain.

I inhaled sharply. "Do you remember when I said I was engaged once, and it didn't work out? Well, Dean is my ex-fiancé. And we need to be careful around him."

CHAPTER EIGHT

DRONES

THERE WAS SILENCE BETWEEN us after I revealed that part of my past to Sam. He didn't ask questions, just sat still beside me, taking it in. We were strangers, but I knew the information upset him. A few long sighs left his chest in somber thought. The air felt heavy between us, and I waited for him to speak.

I thought he had fallen asleep until his hand touched my cheek, turning me to face him.

"He has a key, Row," he said.

"Huh?" I replied.

"Dean has a key to this room. It's how he got in yesterday. I saw him use it. He must have taken one when he took me, or maybe he had it all along."

"Oh." I rubbed my temples with my hand and thought for a moment. "I know, and I'm not surprised. It's good to keep that in mind, but there isn't much we can do about it."

Sam sat up and scanned the room. We could hear BeLew playing on their side. He reached out and gave the edge of the table a gentle tug, and it moved away from the wall. "We can wedge this between the edge of the bed and the door. It will fit and keep the door jammed shut." He pushed the table back to the wall and lay back down.

I considered what he said, but it confused me. "Why does it matter so much? Dean won't hurt us. I-I mean, I know he took some sick pleasure in your suffering the other day. But he fixed you up, and trust me, he didn't have to."

Sam's eyes darkened. "You said I can't touch you around Dean. How will we sleep at night, knowing he can barge in whenever he wants? I have to hold you or someone falls off the bed."

"I guess you won't," I stammered. I felt my cheeks flush. "The bed is small, but I can sleep with my back to you." I turned away from him and pushed my hips flush to the wall. Our entire bodies still touched, but if Dean walked in, he wouldn't think much of our embrace.

Sam cleared his throat and said nothing. I scaled the wall a bit to lift myself. It was awkward and ridiculous. I wanted Sam to hold me at night, and I didn't know why. I wanted him to hold me right now, but it was time to leave soon and meet Lori.

God, I need a watch and to get my head on straight.

"I'm heading to meet with a woman named Lori. She runs the mess hall, and she has two boys. We are letting the kids play."

"That's good." Sam's tone was short. He didn't offer to move as I tried to shift my body over him to exit the bed. When my right foot hit the floor, he gripped my hips as they hovered over him and pulled me down. If Dean came in and saw me straddling Sam, there would be nothing but toilets in Sam's future.

"Sam," I whispered. "We have been through a traumatic event. That can, um, alter your view on things."

"Do you want me to touch you, Rowen? Do you want me to hold you?"

I remained silent.

I wanted that more than anything.

A rush of heat filled my body. It made my skin prickle and my nipples harden. I closed my eyes and for a moment, imagined what it would be like to give myself to Sam, to start over with this new family. It was a fantasy and a damn good one.

I knew so little about Sam, but I felt the chemistry between us. Mysterious and attractive, everything about him drew me in. Both of us had a past we were happy to forget. Both of us felt protective of each other. Both of us had to sleep in this very tiny bed and pretend to be married.

"I have to go," I argued, pushing his hands off my body. His face hardened, and he turned away from me, covering himself with the sheet. No one liked rejection.

"BeLew, it's time to go." I opened the divider and grabbed a key. "I'll bring you back some food." We left the room as he muttered, "Thank you," and I shut the door behind us.

That was how I showed I cared for him. Keeping him at a distance kept him safe. Explaining what Dean had done in the past, what he could do to our future, would only entice Sam. Even though I knew very little about him, I recognized his type. He was an alpha, someone who didn't back down from a fight. The kind of man that ran toward a fire or someone's cry for help. I needed to extinguish the flames, not fan them.

BeLew knew the route to the mess hall, but I had studied the map of the ship during my sleepless night without Sam. I wanted to try another route and get a better layout of where we were, and we had time. I ushered the boys to follow me and they trotted along, happy for an adventure.

I sprinted to the first window I had seen in days. It was a small porthole, but the sun shone through, and I lifted the boys to look outside. We were high inside the ship, the water far beneath us splashed on the sides, causing white sprays of mist stories below. We moved quickly from what I could see, yet I felt nothing as a passenger.

Almost everything on the floors appeared to be closed metal doors and corridors to more of the same. There were numbers and names on each one. A few restrooms and a maintenance room were the only change in scenery. We all made it to the mess hall on time without getting too turned around.

Lori rushed out of the kitchen when she saw me and untied her apron. "You have impeccable timing," she beamed. "I just set out some sandwiches for everyone. The boys are washing up."

We ate together while the boys discussed the start of school. I let Lori talk, taking in the information as if I knew it already. The school was in the Classis rooms. We would walk by them on our way to the top deck. They started the week with assessments and then divided classrooms by skill level rather than age. Someone would be available in all Classis rooms at 0500 hours until 1900 hours.

When our stomachs were full and the boys couldn't sit still any longer, we cleaned up and headed out. More stairwells, but at least I would have an amazing ass after taking the stairs everywhere I went for a year.

Lori shoved open a large door that squeaked like a cattle gate. It thudded as it slammed to the side, and we stepped out into the sun. If I had known this woman better, I would have stripped down to my underwear and run around the deck, letting the rays touch every inch of my skin. As thankful as I was for a bed, food, and safety, the darkness was hard to ignore. It sucked me into a void, but the sun awakened my senses again.

I was right about the movement of the ship. The wind whipped around us as the vessel sped along the water. "Do you know where we're going, or where we are?" I asked.

Lori shrugged her shoulders. "Not a damn clue," she responded. "We're getting somewhere fast."

I thought for a moment. "They have to outrun the line of storms and any other boats. We are either going far out to the middle of nowhere or hauling it to the Panama Canal."

Lori shot her head towards me, and her eyes squinted. "That's intuitive. Or do you have some inside information?"

"Those are just my thoughts. I know far less than you could imagine about this ship."

"Oh, I can imagine quite a bit. You're connected to Lieutenant Riggs somehow. Care to share?"

I should have known part of this stroll would be a fact-finding mission. The boys were running in circles, enthralled with an energetic game of tag. "I've known him my entire life," I admitted.

Lori gave a small grunt. "So sorry to hear that, dear," and we both laughed. "I've worked with Riggs for the past eight years. He's something else."

"He has a way of getting what he wants."

Most of the decks were open, with occasional stairs leading you up or down a few levels. The end of the ship was nowhere in sight. Its size was still a mystery. We stopped in front of ten-foot-high gates wrapped in barbed wire. Armed soldiers stood on either side of a wide steel door.

"This is foreboding," I sputtered.

Lori moved closer to my side. "This is the agriculture department."

"What?" I muttered under my breath. Several cameras were lining the gates and murky plastic covered the walls from top to bottom. I couldn't see through, but beyond the top of the barbed wire, I could make out the roofs of greenhouses. The place gave me the creeps, and I had to work there.

Lori crossed her arms and kept walking. I shuffled behind her, craning my neck to spot a view of the inside. "You'll be in there soon enough, right?" she said.

"Oh, did I tell you my assignment?" I asked, knowing damn well I didn't.

"No, but I know Riggs runs the ag unit. I'll get all my produce through him."

"Okay," I responded. That wasn't an explanation of how she knew my assignment, but I always found it best to let people sit in their silence - a trick learned from my dear Dean. They usually spat out more than they intended.

We walked in peace for a moment, watching the boys continue to sprint around, unaffected by the wire and guns and strangeness of it all.

"I like you," Lori admitted. "There's something about you. We're going to be friends."

"I'd like that," I said. That was true. We were similar in age and both had young children to care for, but it was more than that. I felt at ease with Lori. Maybe I didn't trust her yet, but I saw myself getting there.

"You know, maybe it's the fact that you look at Riggs like I do. You respect him, but you despise him a little too. I watched you the other day. You're careful when you speak to him because you know what he is. You know what he's capable of. When he came into the kitchen, he said you've known each other since you were children. I take it you saw him become what he is today."

"And what is that?"

"Someone who is running agriculture, but spent his whole military career with drones. Someone who has lined up every person he has any connection to in that agriculture unit, even if their experience was puppetry or underwater basket weaving."

"Well, we are all learning new things to survive. We have to get back to basics to have things like food. He's chipping in."

"He has automatic weapons by tents of seeds and soil – armed guards and cameras over lettuce."

"What are you saying?" I grumbled. Lori had a point, and I needed her to get to it.

"I'm saying they aren't growing just vegetables in there. But you're a smart girl, right? You'll take care of yourself, stay out of his way. Keep those boys out of his way."

I bit my bottom lip and stared off into the distance. There was nothing but a vast ocean as far as I could see. That would be my view for months to come. There was no escape from this boat and Dean Riggs. The realization hit my gut, giving me pause about my decision to come here. *What other choice did I have, though?*

Lori could be a friend, or she could be another set of eyes on me, another test.

A clamped my jaw tight and turned to her, giving a tight smile. "I'm sure he's just being overly cautious. Scarcity is terrifying. Dean has his reasons for protecting the food supply."

Lori let out a sarcastic chuckle and clapped her hands together. "Sure, he does, but hey, at least he's still using that drone knowledge." She looked upward, and I followed her gaze. A black drone hovered maybe twenty feet above our heads. It was completely silent, and if she hadn't said anything, I never would have known its existence. It swayed left to right, then sped off towards the agriculture gates.

Lori touched a gentle finger to my chin and turned me eye to eye with her. "Be smart, Rowan. He's always watching."

CHAPTER NINE

THE SIX

T HE NEXT FEW NIGHTS, I slept with my face and body crammed against the cold steel wall of our home, intent on keeping myself unavailable to Sam. I stayed on my right side and refused to turn and face him. Ironically, it wasn't the most physically uncomfortable I had ever been. I had slept on an air mattress in a flooded basement during a category five hurricane not too long ago after all. It was, however, the most emotionally uncomfortable I had ever felt.

Every night, Sam tried to talk to me, get me to face him. He would brush a hand up my back and I would stiffen or shake him away. He felt dejected, and I was losing my resolve. I even tried to sleep on the back bunks one night. Only five feet long, I had to stay scrunched in the tiny bed with a small human almost suffocating me with his stuffed duck.

Forced to cram my body in between a handsome man and icy metal, part of me wondered if I had died in the storm and if this was my purgatory. My first day of work was Monday morning. I only knew it was Sunday by the large calendar drawn in chalk on the mess hall wall when

I went to get breakfast. Every day I would walk the halls of the ship, get Sam food, and try to get the boys outside.

BeLew started school on Monday too, and I needed to get them on more of a routine. We had created a schedule, but there was nothing in it. Walk, bathroom, eat, walk, shower, eat was all we had to do. I also had the fun task of avoiding eye contact with my pseudo-husband.

I knew I took it too far, but fear led my actions. Days ticked by, and each time I saw Sam care for the boys, struggle with his pain, or put his warm hands on me at night, I fell for him a little more. Avoidance was stupid and immature, and it wouldn't last much longer. I was falling for him a little more each day, and I craved his touch, but Dean watched nearby. I never saw him, but I knew his eyes were on me somehow.

For the next few days, Lori acted as if we were lifelong friends. She remained comfortable around me, and I enjoyed our time together. I decided our conversation on deck was a warning and not a threat. Fond memories of Dean were few and far between. She alluded to some of her own experiences with his manipulation that mirrored mine. She knew his military life, whereas I knew the home life of Dean Riggs. If we were on the farm, I would have some insights for her, but this was their territory.

After another stiff night's sleep, I took the boys to the mess hall for breakfast, and to my surprise, Lori and her boys joined us without her uniform or apron. "Off today?" I asked.

"Yes, the first day since we got here. Not that I can enjoy it," she whined. "My friend is a teacher, and I promised I would help her get some rooms and tests ready for tomorrow. I get to spend time with her, but I would rather sleep."

"Do you need help? It would go faster with two more hands." I waved my fingers in her direction.

"It would, but I have a better idea. How about I take BeLew with me to the school and the boys can entertain each other? Then tonight you could watch them for dinner and walk the deck with them. It would give me two to three hours by myself, which is what I want more than anything. And BeLew can see the classrooms, get more comfortable."

"That sounds fabulous," I beamed. Lori worked hard, and once everyone's jobs started in full swing, hers would only become more difficult.

Lori let out an exhale and lay her body on the table like she was fainting. I giggled at her dramatics. I decided she was right, and we would be good friends.

The boys were all too happy to leave with Lori. They would get to play and meet a new teacher, and I would, what? I could take yet another walk around this ship. I'd done that so many times, that I was memorizing the names on the silver doors of the hallways. I would memorize the faces with those names if I saw them exit or enter their room. Why? I'm not sure. Nothing else to do, I suppose, but it kept my mind occupied.

I headed back to my room with Sam's food. "Order up," I announced as I opened the door. "Oh my God, you're up!"

Sam was standing. His broad chest puffed out with accomplishment, and he took a few limping strides toward me. This was a turning point for him. I could see the resolve in his expression, in his eyes. The man he once was standing before me, strong and resilient.

"I'm up and better than ever," he said and reached his arms to me. I stretched toward him, fearful he needed support, but he drew me into his chest. I tried to pull away, but my body would not budge once it was wrapped in his powerful arms. I exhaled and let myself rest on him - giving into his warmth, his scent.

A lump formed in my throat, but not from sadness. From relief. The entire time we'd be on the ship, I feared he would take a turn for the worse. That a small kit of antibiotics wouldn't be enough, and without time to prove his worth to Dean, he would be as good as dead. Dean had given him a chance, but until he thought he needed Sam, that was all he would give.

I had said silent prayers for the moment we shared then, for his recovery. Every night I would awaken from either night terrors or the fear in my gut that Sam had stopped breathing. I would lick the inside of my hand and hold it to his mouth, waiting to feel the air. Then I would will myself to sleep again, hoping he was getting better - telling myself he just needed time.

Standing in his arms was proof of his turn for the better. It was the sign that he was going to make it, and I wouldn't be alone on this ship. I held him, smiling into his chest, hiding my expression from him.

"Where are the boys?" he asked, rubbing his hand up and down my spine.

"Oh, they're with Lori. She's helping set up the school with a friend. They will get familiar with the space, and I promised to take over later so she could have some alone time." I felt Sam still and hold his breath.

"It's okay," I continued. "I trust her with them, and it will be good for them to get a look at the school."

Sam moved his head back and grabbed my chin with his hand. The boys were the last thing on his mind. He had a fire in his eyes, and I realized my error. He wasn't worried about the boys' safety. He trusted I could leave them with Lori and they would be fine.

He knew we were alone, and he wanted to take advantage.

And I want him to.

With one hand, he pulled the table from the wall and shoved it in between the bed and door, never breaking our gaze.

I remained frozen. My body had begged to be closer to him, but my brain was forbidding it. The push and pull made my feet feel like they were wrapped in cement as I stood there saying nothing, eyes wide.

Oh, God.

Sam brought both hands to the sides of my face. His stare was intense as he moved his lips closer to my mouth. The thoughts in my brain sounded something like: *No, we can't do this. This is wrong. I just told you that Dean was a threat, and he doesn't want us together.*

Except my body refused to listen to anything my brain said, and those words never left my lips. My body felt him push up against me, showing me he was ready for me. His lips took mine, and I moaned in response, opening my mouth to his. His hardened length pushed against my stomach as his tongue invaded my mouth.

I ran my hands underneath the back of his shirt, feeling the muscles tighten. We were ravenous, desperate after days of avoiding the inevitable. This was unavoidable. An attractive man sleeping next to me every night. A man who thought I was beautiful on one of the worst days of my life. Eventually, we had to come together this way. There weren't a lot of joys on this boat, but I guaranteed there was a lot of sex. Anybody could sense the tension walking through the halls. People needed an escape.

His hands moved down my back and then slipped underneath my pants, cupping my bare ass. I pulled him closer to me, and he groaned. We continued to kiss for several minutes until my lips swelled from the force and pressure. His tongue danced in my mouth and sent shivers through my body. I trembled in response.

He broke away for a moment and placed one hand on the bed. He carefully lowered himself down with a firm grip on my ass. He grunted with discomfort but recovered, pulling my body down to him. I followed his movements and straddled his lap, careful to lean on his uninjured side. I yanked my shirt over my head as he did the same with his.

Skin to skin, heat radiated from his body to mine. Our heavy breaths joined in unison as we rocked together, desperate for more. He moved his lips down my body, nibbling my neck and biting my clavicle. I ran my fingers through his hair as he took my nipple in his mouth, and I whimpered. He sucked and nipped until I cried out and begged. I wasn't sure for what, but I could hear myself saying it. "Please, please, Sam. Oh God, don't stop."

But life had a terrible sense of humor. The moment his hand found its way lower, hovering at the clasp of my pants, ready to open them, the room went dark. A loud buzzing blared from the hallway, and after the alarm sounded a few times, he stopped. We panted with our faces inches away from each other, trying to register the turn of events. A red beam of light blinked underneath the doorway and the noise was so loud it vibrated inside my chest.

I rose from Sam and looked for my shirt in the darkness. "Can you walk some?" I snapped. My temper and confusion were bubbling to the surface.

"Yes," he panted. "I can walk enough. Walk where Rowan?"

"I don't know," I shrugged, still topless.

I was half blind with the blinking light as my only guide to finding my shirt, but I felt Sam's eyes on me. "It's hung on the chair, but I prefer you this way."

I huffed a laugh. "I think the party's over." We both put our shirts back on and I wrapped my arm around his waist to help hoist him up.

"For the moment," he teased in my ear as we lifted. Goosebumps covered my body, knowing he'd keep his word.

I could hear footsteps in the hallway and thought it best to follow the crowd. I was unfamiliar with the protocol, and I should have been if I were truly Ashley.

Sam walked with a slight limp and minimal weight on me. I encouraged him to put more on my shoulders so he could make it however far we were going. The boys were with Lori, and she would take care of them. I was sure of that but anxious to have them back with me. I clenched my jaw in frustration and quickened our pace. *Is this what mom guilt feels like?*

A herd of people flowed through the hallway, and the terrible memory of our first day here resurfaced. This time, everyone walked with a purpose without running or pushing. They were heading upstairs to the upper decks.

"Stairs," I hissed to Sam.

"It's fine," he responded. I couldn't see his expression with the red lights blinking and blinding my vision. It was daytime, but the thick hull of the ship created a perpetual night when everything shut down. I made a mental note to find a flashlight in case we were ever in this situation again.

The first steps Sam took with ease, but by the time we were on the sixth flight, I could feel myself pulling him with me. He grunted and huffed through each step, and I was sweating, holding his weight as we continued.

"Two more flights," I grumbled, and I felt his head nod in response. Our path led to the top deck, and as the last flight of steps emerged, light beamed from the open doorway. "Almost there," I continued. I saw a spot of blood on his leg had formed. This had been too much for him, and I instinctively kissed him on the cheek. Whether it was for my comfort or his, I wasn't sure.

"I can do this. We can do this together," he said, assuring me.

Stepping out into the daylight, the contrast from the dark halls blinded me once more. We made our way through the crowd, where everyone had formed lines across the width of the hull. It looked to be a thousand people. Some were standing and others sat, but there was a logical formation from one end of the boat to the other. We moved into the line and Sam collapsed to the ground. He shook, and the blood trailed down his leg. I looked him over and frowned.

"Don't worry," he demanded, gripping my hands. "I'll be fine."

"But what is this?" I asked, gesturing at the crowd. More people formed behind us, and the alarm continued in the distance. "I need to find BeLew."

"Go, I'm good."

I hesitated to stare once more at his leg. The stain of blood stopped growing, but the journey up to the deck was a setback. His lips formed a tight line, trying to hide the pain.

"I'll just be a moment. I'll be right back." Again, I had no clue if my words were to comfort him or convince myself everything would be okay.

He placed a hand on my stomach and nudged me. "Go. We're in this together, and by together, I mean with BeLew. Find the kids."

I nodded and jogged off to the edge of the boat. As I made it to the front of the lines, I saw a small platform or stage. *Is this a performance or a genuine emergency?*

I inspected the rows. The school was closer to the deck, so Lori and the boys would be near the front. I heard them before I saw them. "Row!" a yell came from deep within the crowd. I couldn't find them. Too many people were still standing and blocking the way. "Row - Mama!" louder this time. The sound was moving towards me. It was BeLew. They had never called me mama, but yelling aunt would have gone against our cover story. Whatever the reason they said it, my heart melted in response.

"Come to me. I can't see you," I screamed. "BeLew, please come to me."

Their tiny bodies broke through the crowd and leaped into my arms. I gripped them close and checked them over. Lori popped behind them. "Do you know what's going on?"

"Not a clue," I answered through Lewis's hair as I squeezed him tight. "Sam, my husband, he's back there. I need to get back to him. Thank you for taking care of the boys."

Lori nodded and rushed back to her family. I held BeLew's hands in a tight grip, dragging them back to Sam. They were silent and looked down. Not much phased the boys, but this affected them, I could tell. Their little legs jogged when they saw Sam. He reached his arms out towards them and they smiled, hugged him, and then sat at my side. Then we waited as the lines formed behind us. People were strewn on the deck as far as I could see. It must have been over an hour before we heard the tapping on a microphone.

"We need everyone's attention and all to sit," a loud voice boomed from all around us. As people lowered to the ground, I could see a line of military personnel on the stage up ahead. Dean stood next to the microphone but wasn't the one speaking. He had to be looking for me. His head moved from left to right. Everyone obeyed and the only sound was fidgeting bodies and the wind. We waited for the voice to continue.

The man at the microphone looked older and well built. He was dressed in full uniform, which included a sharp haircut and a sharper jawline. He looked at Dean and another man. They nodded, and he continued speaking.

"Hello, quadrant C. We understand several of you are confused and maybe even frightened. Everything is fine, and you are safe."

Fuck yes, I was frightened, but I wouldn't dare show it to the boys. I looked at Sam. His face tensed in pain with one hand resting on top of his injury.

"I'm Captain Matthews. I hope to meet you all as we journey together this year. After decades in service, I don't have the time or patience for niceties, so I'll get right to the point. We must have honesty and transparency on this journey. We had an event today that created the need for a red out. As quadrant C is a family unit, let me clarify what's happening."

Sam's hand shifted to mine. Dean couldn't see us from where he stood, so I entwined our fingers and noticed I was trembling. I wrapped my other arm around the boys, scooting us all together, waiting to hear more.

"A red out will occur when everyone needs to move to the deck immediately. There will be alarms and red lights. Your cabins are currently being searched and re-stocked. You will return with toiletries and possibly medications if we have deemed it necessary. If you are curious about what we are searching for, then you have nothing to worry about. For all others, let me clarify the next steps."

Sam's hold tightened around my fingers and I felt the uniform shuffle of a confused crowd. *I'm not curious. I'm scared as hell, Matthews.*

"In the chaos of boarding, we understand individuals not cleared to be on this vessel may have gained access. Some of you may have taken additional family members with you. We aren't saying they can't stay, but we need the honesty and transparency I spoke of earlier. While the kitchen crew was taking a much-needed day off, we discovered several passengers attempting to steal food for others they had smuggled aboard."

I saw Dean's neck crane again, searching the crowd, searching for my eyes after hearing those words.

I hadn't stolen and Sam couldn't even walk to the mess hall to get food for himself, but we didn't belong on this vessel. We weren't cleared to be here, and Dean stood next to Matthews, knowing that fact. My fingers numbed from Sam's grip and I wiggled my wrist, signaling for him to loosen his hold.

"We need an accurate roster of travelers to succeed on our journey. We don't have room for waste or excess. If you're fat, expect to succeed on that diet you've failed at over and over again. There's nothing extra. There's not enough if we aren't successful in growing food, so we will not tolerate theft. If you're one of these uninvited guests, or there are some in your cabin, come to Lieutenant Lindell immediately, and he will direct you. You need not be afraid if you are candid with your situation."

A large red-haired man stepped forward and jumped from the stage. A few others followed, making their way to his side.

"If you don't comply, we won't keep you on the ship," Matthews continued. "That means exactly what it sounds like. Please see Lieutenant Lindell now."

Bodies shuffled around us in hushed voices. Sam moved my hand to the floor and held it down, a gesture to say we were not getting up. No one got up yet, but it was statistically impossible everyone here had a ticket. Someone besides us had to have sneaked aboard.

Dean left the stage and walked down the lines of people. He scanned the crowd, looking for me.

Captain Matthews cleared his throat in the microphone. "You have thirty seconds to come forward if there are individuals in your cabin that aren't on the manifest."

I was holding my breath, and Sam had such a tight grip on my hand I could feel my pulse beat through my palm. The boys stared at their shoes. A few people had risen and trudged towards the front of the rows. I could hear people behind us murmuring. Sam's hand pressed down harder.

The thirty seconds turned into minutes as a small crowd huddled by the Lieutenant, and my head spun with thoughts. I felt like I was floating out of my body. I looked down at my hand, still pinned by Sam. My fingertips were white as he pushed them to the floor.

Matthews continued, "We have located the rest of the individuals stealing and hoarding food. Unfortunately, their family has not come forward. We cannot tolerate this."

I heard screams from the crowd coming from our left. Two soldiers carried over a man and woman as they kicked, screamed, and cursed. They brought four others to their sides and the six of them stood together, wide-eyed. Panic and fear filled their expressions, and the surrounding crowd looked at them in shock. My breathing stopped when they pulled their hands together, zip-tying their wrists behind their back.

"Don't look," Sam said in my direction, but I couldn't pull my eyes away. I watched them with eery familiarity.

I watched their rage turn to pleas for their lives that fell on silent ears.

"If we don't work as one to survive together, we die together. If you work against us all to survive alone, you die."

With that, Matthews' men lifted the six souls over the bars of the boat and threw them over. A gasp filled the crowd with a few sharp cries. I went to cover BeLew's eyes, but Sam had already moved to them and pressed them against his chest. His face filled with agony as he looked back at me. I floated back down into my body, into the reality of what had just happened. It hit me like a train, and I exhaled a harsh breath and curled my numb fingers to my chest.

I dreamed this.

I felt the souls without the use of their hands sinking into the darkness.

I knew their hysteria as they sank deep into the black waters below.

My bottom lip quivered as I turned back to the edge of the boat where six souls once stood.

Dean stared back.

CHAPTER TEN

EPONYM

I CHECKED MY NEW watch for the hundredth time. It glowed a pale yellow in the darkness of our cabin, telling me I had two hours before I reported for work. Someone had left it in the center of the bed, along with fresh bandages, toiletries, and schoolbooks for BeLew. The boys had shoved them to the floor and gone to sleep when we'd returned from our horrible day.

After the event with the six, we had moved to the edge of the deck, waiting for a break in the crowd. The journey back would be just as challenging for Sam. Passengers at our heels would only make it harder. Dean walked through the crowd, and his face had spoken volumes. I was to stay put and stay in line. Betrayal meant death.

BeLew had remained silent, and I had no words for them. My sister would have known how to comfort them. Instead, they sat on either side of Sam as we waited, their faces nuzzled underneath his arms. Dean passed us and grabbed my elbow briefly as he walked away, another silent signal he was watching me.

"It won't be us, Row," Sam mumbled into my ear as he held me that night. He knew what filled my thoughts, and it had to be on his mind, too. "It's one year. We can make it." His arm tightened around me as he spoke.

"It won't be us," I vowed, not sure if I was reassuring myself or Sam. I pulled his hand up to my lips and kissed his palm. "Dean won't let it happen." He stiffened at the sound of Dean's name.

"We won't let it happen," Sam corrected. He nuzzled into my neck, pulled me closer, and went to sleep. *Will Dean protect us?* I felt I had no choice but to board this ship, but now it trapped me here, under Dean's thumb, again. *Should I have stayed in his shelter?*

I slept in bursts, terrified to dream. Not dreaming wouldn't stop the things to come, but I preferred to stay oblivious. I had seen the bodies in the water without the use of their hands before it happened. I had felt their panic while they sank into darkness.

The premonitions were with me here, on this vessel, in this bed.

After another hour, I roused Sam and told him I had to shower. We agreed to take the boys to school together on their first day, even after I protested, arguing he should rest instead.

"It looks normal for Dad to see them off, don't you think?" Sam had countered. I'd agreed, but the setback with his injury worried me. His leg still bled through the sheets at night.

I showered in a haze and returned to find everyone ready for breakfast. The boys seemed better today, with faint smiles. Eager to see Lori, and to thank her for taking care of the boys, I helped Sam to his feet.

The thought of us all together healed my soul a bit. We would never forget yesterday's events, but we had to move on and pretend to be normal. We had to act like we had nothing to worry about.

I am Ashley Rowan Lawson, and these are my sons and husband. We belong here. It was the answer I'd give to each question about our existence.

Sam did his best to hide his pain during our walk, and when we found a spot to sit, I took Beau with me to get plates for us all. It was oatmeal or oatmeal, so I was back with the food in no time. Sam ran his hand down my thigh under the table, and I let him. He was my husband, after all. When I saw Lori cross the mess hall, dragging a cart of trays behind her, I excused myself to speak with her.

"Need any help?" I asked from behind her overflowing cart.

Lori turned and wrapped me in a hug. "Are you okay?" she asked.

"I'm fine," I lied. "What about you?"

"I'll be blunt. I expected what happened yesterday, or some form of it. I just thought it would be six months down the line. Or the crime to be something much worse to create that pirate show, like breaking a law or, I don't know, something unforgivable." Her eyes drifted to her shoes, and she frowned. "I caught them - stealing the food. I reported it."

"As you should have. Resources are limited. The food they stole was basically out of your sons' mouths. That's breaking a law. I'm not saying the punishment was just, but you aren't to blame."

"That's kind of you to say."

"That's reality, Lori. That's our life now."

She looked up and studied me for a moment and gave a sharp nod to the kitchen. I followed her and she led me to a pantry in the back, pushing the door closed behind us. It smelled of metal and flour, and dim lighting cast over her dismal face.

"I heard they found over two hundred stowaways," she confessed.

My eyes grew wide. "Okay, so they killed six. What about the rest?"

"I heard..." Lori paused, fidgeting with her hands. "I heard they transferred them to agriculture. Dean pledged he would put them to work and said we needed the hands. They've moved them to the lower levels. They sleep on nets down there, but the alternative is the bottom of the ocean, so who could argue?" Lori shifted her weight from side to side, waiting for my response.

"Okay, well, that's true. They should help us grow the food that they're eating. It makes sense. Everything will be fine. You did the right thing." I presumed Lori had more to say, but she wasn't ready, so I changed the subject. "How are your boys?"

"The boys are acting tough, but they watched the whole thing yesterday. They know there is no chance for that to happen to us, but it's frightening. Will you walk them to school with BeLew? I'm buried here with all the extra shifts today."

"Of course. Thank you for telling me about the two hundred others. I won't say anything, Lori."

We hugged again. I went back to Sam and BeLew with Lori's boys in tow. We took our time walking to the Classis rooms so Sam could keep up. They were all excited about school and although the trauma of yesterday was still there; it had started to fade.

"Now remember what I told you, boys?" I asked.

"Don't say shit," Lewis responded.

"Or damn," Beau added.

"Seriously, BeLew?" I shook my head and poked them in the shoulders. "Do your best and have fun. Listen to the teachers. Make new friends. Any of that ringing a bell?"

They poked back, tickling my sides, and I knew we were on the mend. "They aren't wrong," Sam added. He touched the small of my back, leading me down the hallway. His face relaxed when he looked at me, giving me a smile. We were happy together. We were in this together.

The rush into the school rooms felt like a whirlwind of a drop-off. They ran us through like cattle, and in less than five minutes, we were child-free. I thought there might be some tears or an orientation, but we were lucky the door didn't hit our asses on the way out.

That left two whole hours before I had to report to the top deck. The first day of school started early, while the first day of work started late.

I wrapped my arm around Sam's middle to help steady his walk. "Do you want some more coffee?"

He shook his head. "I would like to lie down. I only have another week until I start my shifts, and I need this leg to be better. I don't want to start in a chair."

"Are you insane? Eight to ten-hour days on your feet, no way. Please be reasonable."

Sam rested an arm on the wall and stopped for a moment, wincing. I rolled my eyes and continued. "You can hardly walk for ten minutes without a break."

His face fell. "My brain tells me I'm fine and I can do these things. My body won't agree. It's infuriating."

"Come on," I said, pulling him back up. "Only a few more minutes to go, and then I'll rest with you. We need to check out your bandage too." I had changed it late the night before after the wound re-opened, and I worried about the setback in his healing. When we got to the cabin, Sam dropped his pants and sat sideways on the bed.

In any other circumstance, his familiarity would put me off, but it felt like we were a couple. Not exactly married with two kids, but my slip up with him the other day changed things. I permitted myself to say yes to him. He understood we were still in danger, from the weather, from our lies, from Dean. He also knew I wanted him. It united us.

His leg looked good. Better than expected. As I worked, he took off his shirt, and I raised one eyebrow at him.

"Presumptuous?" I smirked.

"Dirty," he replied. "I'll give myself a sink bath when you head out. Do we know when laundry opens?"

"I imagine it's underway for crew and starts for all others this week. Everyone should start work by Wednesday. I'll find out, and I'll grab your work clothes today too, if I can, so you'll have something clean."

I rinsed our washcloth in scalding water and brought it over to Sam, placing it on his neck.

He placed his hand on top of mine, stroking it back and forth. "I'm that gross you need me to start now?"

"Not at all. I just thought it would feel good," I said.

"You know what else would feel good?" And he crashed his mouth to mine before I could object, not that I could refuse him anymore. I slept next to him, every night, and wondered... how would he feel inside me? How would his mouth feel in my most intimate places? I longed for that connection again, even though I tried to ignore it, to fight the need. It remained in my thoughts. Heat filled my body, and I lost any resolve I had left.

He threw the washcloth to the floor and took hold of my waist, lifting me to his lap again, picking up where we left off. I felt the blood from his leg slick under my thigh, and I tried to push myself away, afraid of hurting him. He pulled me back with renewed intensity. A growl left his lips, echoing from his chest, which pressed against my peaked nipples.

Our lips moved together in rhythm, and my body rocked with the pace. His hands pulled my shirt over my head, and his mouth dipped to my breast before the clothing hit the floor. I whimpered, gripping his hair, and pressed him tighter against me. I lost control at his touch. His powerful body held mine, and he pushed his hard cock against my center.

"The table," he breathed as he licked and sucked. "Move the table."

The thought of separating our bodies made my skin ache. If I left his embrace too long, I may come to my senses. I couldn't twist around to throw the table between the bed and the door, so I was forced to get up from his lap. Sam hissed as I left his clutches, and his fingers pushed into my slick skin, clawing me back to him before I could get too far. I escaped and wedged the table in place, and when I turned back around, I found him naked.

"Take your pants off," he commanded, stroking himself.

Fuck, he's beautiful.

Every muscle in Sam's body stiffened, misted in sweat and carved from stone. Even injured, strength permeated from every inch of his form. Just the sight of his rigid cock made my jaw drop. I stood in front of him and gasped, staring at what waited for me.

One side of his lips rose in a smile. "I said, take your pants off."

I obeyed, keeping my eyes on his length. My heart beat erratically as I stilled, standing nude in front of him, my body trembling with anticipation. I opened my mouth to speak, but nothing escaped. I heaved each breath, my mind swimming with what was about to happen. There was no turning back now, not with that massive cock promising to make me feel so damn good. I deserved to feel good for once. I *needed* it.

"Come over here," he commanded. I took a step forward, and he drew me back into his arms. He hooked his hands behind my knees, one at a time, until I straddled him. I could feel him, hard and ready beneath me, and I whimpered. His hand moved around my back and down... lower, running a palm over my ass.

He made his way further, until his fingers stroked my center, spreading my wetness up to my clit. I cried out, and my body jolted. He grunted and adjusted his injured leg. "I'm sorry," I murmured, rocking my body against his touch.

"Don't be," he said, but I could feel his leg clench beneath me and the slippery feeling of blood.

I tried to push off, afraid of what damage I could do. "I'll hurt you. Your... l-leg."

"Get back down here," he ordered, yanking me back flush with him. "Sometimes a little pain mixed with pleasure is good." His eyes were playful when he spoke, and full of lust.

Pressed flush against him, he didn't hesitate to slide one finger inside me while licking and nipping the side of my neck. My entire body quaked in response, sending goose pimples across my skin.

Another finger stretched me and pushed further, filling me with his touch.

"Sam, I'm not on anything. We don't have anything," I gasped. My words didn't stop me from grinding down with every stroke of his fingers.

"I could do this until you come on my hand. Or I could bury my face between your legs," he answered. Each word was calm and self-assured. My voice cracked and stuttered while he remained in complete control.

Another finger, and a deep moan left my lips. It was pleading and loud and escaped a woman in the throes of ecstasy. I grabbed his wrist and rode his fingers while he kissed across my shoulder and chest, dragging me forward and back.

"You know what I think," he growled. "I think you're my fucking wife." He removed his fingers and slammed his length inside me in one motion. I gasped and dug my nails into his shoulders, piercing his skin. My shallow pants turned into cries as he clutched my hips, pumping himself in and out.

"Fuck!" I screamed over the slap of our bodies. Sam filled me with every glorious inch, hitting all the spots that sent tingles of pleasure across my skin. I felt my core immediately tighten, squeezing against his shaft. He grunted, pulling my hips up and keeping me there, hovering with just the tip of him inside. His strength in that moment, even after all he'd endured, filled my heart with admiration.

"You feel... too good," he moaned and brought me back down in a slow stroke. "So good."

Lips barely touching, our breaths were heavy, exchanging air between our open mouths. We stared into each other's eyes as he continued to thrust. It was both intimate and terrifying, and I wished the feeling would never end.

I wrapped my arms around his back as he continued pounding into me. He closed his eyes and kissed me, slower, harder. His tongue invaded my mouth with deep strokes. He kissed me like we had known each other for years. It felt familiar and right, and I lost myself in it.

My body had taken over, desperate for the climax. I tried not to scream out again as the heat grew in my center and burned through my veins.

"I'm coming," I panted into his mouth. He tensed as I felt him thicken and stretch me further.

"Good, baby. I—I can't..." he gasped.

When he exploded inside me, I went over the edge, convulsing in his arms. I moved my mouth to the side of his neck, tasted the salt of his sweat, and let his skin muffle my endless moans of pleasure. My release took all my strength, and I went limp in his arms. I smiled against his skin and enjoyed the moment of peace, of bliss.

I kept myself wrapped around him until I felt chilled from my nakedness, and even then, I had to make myself get up. As I separated our bodies, Sam watched me with hooded eyes. His gaze rose to mine with a close-lipped smile.

"God, you're sexy, Row. I could have you again if you let me."

I grabbed the washcloth off the floor and tossed it into the sink with the soap. I needed to clean myself up before work. I smiled back at him, unsure of myself and how to act at the moment. I didn't have the immediate pang of regret that I'd felt before after giving myself to a man, but I was uneasy.

He grabbed my arm and sat me back on the bed, wrapping me in the sheet. "Are you okay?"

"Yes, I'm better than okay. I wanted that. It's just... we weren't careful," I answered. My head registered the immediate thoughts of guilt. I had decided long ago to never have children, and I was always vigilant about protection. This place made me careless. *Or maybe it was this man?*

"I meant to pull out," he admitted. "I just couldn't separate from you. Whatever happens, happens. We're in this together. Especially if there is another one of us."

I stiffened immediately and clenched my jaw. Sam sat up straight in response. I could feel the pain in my heart, with a mix of sadness and anger. This environment made every emotion and feeling rise to the surface.

"Row?" he questioned. "What's wrong? Am I making you panic? Everything we have been through and no condom fills you with dread?"

"What's your real name?" I spat. "I'll call you Sam, but tell me. I need to know if we're having sex."

He gave a half laugh and smiled, then realized it was no joke. "Rowan, I need to be Sam."

I shook my head in response and pushed him away from me. There were so many things I needed to say before I lost the courage. I hated to bare myself and my secrets, but I'd decided that already when I let him inside me.

"As I've gotten older, I've realized that being with someone, being intimate with them... it's the most vulnerable thing you can do in this life. Having that connection opens up every wound, every fear, every feeling, and leaves you exposed to all the pain."

"I won't hurt you, Rowan. We're in this together."

"What we just did, opening myself up to you like that, it's already unlocked wounds."

Sam tilted his head and remained quiet. I spoke in riddles, and he didn't understand. I had to make him understand.

"You can talk to me," he said. "I want you to talk to me. I want to be what you need."

"You don't need to *be* Sam. You need to *know* about Sam. You need to understand what Sam means to me and where your name came from."

CHAPTER ELEVEN

MEMORY

N OT EVERY DREAM I had when I was a little girl made sense. Sometimes it would be years before I could piece together the images that had permeated my mind. There were so many misunderstood stories in my head that I would forget about the forewarning until it happened in front of me.

Not that I could do anything about it.

Not that my remembering changed anything.

What was going to happen was already in play. Nothing I ever did ceased it from coming to pass.

Once in a dream, my cousin stumbled from a car with his face covered in blood. His eyes were blank and lifeless as he staggered towards me. It haunted me for countless nights. I awoke with the taste of copper in my mouth, and a sense of death filled my bedroom. When I confided in my sister, she insisted we take action.

I forbade him from driving his entire sixteenth year. He, as expected, continued driving, so my sister and I pleaded with our mother and his, quoting deadly statistics about inexperienced drivers. Our attempts to scare them worked. They forced my cousin to walk every-where, but I still dreamed of his face and the blood.

One summer night, he was walking in town when a school friend ran her car into a metal barrier. He ran to the scene, climbed into her car, and tried to un-wedge her from the collapsed steering column. She died in her seat, bleeding out. The local newspaper printed a picture of him exiting the car, covered in her blood. That look from my dreams, of his emptiness and dread, filled his eyes in the black and white shot. My attempts did nothing to stop the unavoidable.

The night I gave birth to Sam, he was almost out before I remembered the dream from my childhood. The pain and exhaustion I had felt during his delivery morphed into intense fear. I turned to my sister in terror and told her what I recalled. The broken cuckoo clock that went off every ten minutes and drove me insane for the whole delivery. The three feet of snow that had come out of nowhere in March. Our neighbor who had dropped the teapot and burned her right foot.

She gave me a solemn nod as tears steadily fell down her cheeks. She had known the entire time.

She remembered.

Samuel Riggs was born at five in the morning. Seven pounds and four ounces, with charcoal hair like his fa-ther. He came out without a sound and despite every-thing we did, I never heard him cry. When the para-medics came, they wrapped him in a red blanket, just as I had dreamed. I held him until mid-day when Dean pried him from my hands while I screamed and clawed to get him back.

That was the first and last time I saw Dean Riggs cry.

As I told the story in our cabin, it was also the first time I saw Sam Rivera cry. His sympathy was tangible when I told him of what I'd lost, of what Dean and I had grieved. There was no jealousy or judgment – only sadness from Sam and his efforts to comfort me as the story fell from my lips.

I loved my son every second of every day, from the moment I found out about the pregnancy to the moment I spoke the words to Sam about his death. When the men at the dock asked me for my husband's name, I gave Sam because memories of him always hovered near the surface. Sam Riggs occupied every thought.

I believed I wouldn't survive anything like that again, and I promised myself I would never have any more children. A heart can only break so many times before it can no longer heal and love again. I saved my love for BeLew, and I hoped there was enough left for Sam.

I got ready for work in silence. Sam didn't have words of comfort, but he reached for my hand anytime it was free. I kissed him before I left and reassured him we were fine and we would get through this. I just needed him to know, especially because I suspected it gave Dean an aversion to him.

"Rowan," he stammered as I walked towards the door. "It's Nico. Nico Rivera."

"Thank you," I mouthed to him. He looked to be in agony when he said it, like it physically hurt him to admit his true identity. No one knew him on this boat that I could tell. He trusted me with the information, and that was all I needed for now.

"I need to be Sam, okay. I'm your Sam. You're my Rowan."

"In this together," I said, and I turned and left the cabin.

I knew better than most that not much happened by chance. The universe had a plan, and — fortunately — sometimes I saw that plan before it happened. And yes, sometimes that plan tore me into a million pieces and broke me, but, no, not everything was by chance. Nico was sent to me — he was here for me. I left the cabin fully aware that it wasn't a coincidence or my fear of loneliness that drew me to him. My faith in that bound me to him, always.

The agriculture unit was as foreboding on the inside as it was on the outside. Wire fences topped with barbs sectioned off several greenhouses and planting sites. Men with automatic rifles paced the makeshift hallways, and they dressed us in prison uniforms. *Well, they look and feel like prison uniforms.*

During orientation, we were all given jumpsuits to wear over our clothes. Except many of us desperately needed fresh clothing, so we opted for the jumpsuit only. I could take two suits for Sam back with me as long as I signed for them.

I found out laundry started next week. This week's focus for the garment area was making work attire and school uniforms. Another win because BeLew needed something not washed in a sink.

Changed and crammed in between gates, unsure of where to go, I heard a voice from the front of the crowd speak. "We want to stress the importance of your being here and being successful. It's a fact that we will run out of food if we cannot farm on the boat." The voice was

Captain Matthews speaking again. It sent a shiver down my spine.

I sifted my way through the crowd. My jumpsuit boasted the insignia of leadership, so most obliged and stepped aside. I saw Dean first. He had already spotted me. I smiled at him and immediately recalled Sam entering me hours before. Guilt made my cheeks flame, and I moved to my right to avoid his stare.

Matthews was a daunting man, dressed again in full uniform. He took command of the room with his voice only, but seeing him up close sealed the deal. His presence would strike fear in anyone, even without knowing the events of yesterday. This unit was definitely in the higher-ups' pockets, but why? *For fuck's sake, this can't all be about lettuce.*

"We won't be screwing around, and I don't give a shit what anyone likes to eat. If it's fast and easy, we will grow it." A few heckles comparing vegetables to women came out from the crowd. Matthews stepped forward with two huge strides. He grabbed a man by the throat and yanked him nose to nose. A few of us stumbled away, slack-jawed.

"Is there something funny about starvation?" he spat. The man shook his head no as Matthews continued to squeeze his airway shut. "You'll be the last to eat. Every day. And if we run out, you can eat your words." He freed the man and turned on his heel to leave. Dean nodded to Matthews in understanding that the order was his to execute, and then Dean headed in my direction.

"Hi darling," he drawled, tucking a piece of hair behind my ear. He wanted to console me or butter me up. I assumed we would avoid talking about what had happened the day before, which was fine by me. I wanted more than anything to forget. "You're with me for the next few hours. Lucky me."

I gave him a weak smile in response. Part of me knew this was the beginning of whatever plan Dean had for himself and us, and part of me still felt a little terrible for fucking Sam earlier and loving it.

He led me by my elbow to a boarded room in the center of the unit. I noticed drones lined the roof as we waited for the security door to read his palm and eyes.

"This is the control room," he explained. "As leadership, we'll grant you access. After we finish here, I'll get someone to do your retina scans and handprints." He dropped a large binder in the center of a small table as I took my seat. The room was simple and well guarded, stocked with a few file cabinets and tables. Several screens covered one wall and displayed images of empty greenhouses. "And this is your AGP, Agriculture and Growth Plan. This keeps us all alive. We're starting with radishes, carrots, and squash."

Dean went on for over an hour about the overall projections and my responsibilities. I knew how to farm, so he skimmed most of everything. The vegetables chosen were fast growers. A child could be successful. "What about the chemistry piece?" I asked.

"Not today," he said and reached across the table for my hand. "This week we just need to get it all planted. Your team starts with your direction tomorrow. Some things will be ready in thirty days, God willing."

"What about science willing? Is chemistry a way to grow things faster?"

"Not today," Dean hissed. He gripped my hand so hard it almost hurt. I tensed my shoulders and scooted away from him. He yanked me back. "What's going on, Row?"

He was pulling me closer to him. The chair squeaked along the cement floor as it moved. His jaw tightened, and he cocked his head to the side. I knew struggling would only entice him, so I conceded and lifted myself to move closer.

"Nothing is going on. I want to do a good job is all. We can talk about chemistry tomorrow."

Dean narrowed his gaze and loosened his grip on my hand. His eyes moved down my body and back up to my lips. "Okay, Row, whatever you say. How's married life?"

It took everything in me not to roll my eyes. He would see that as disrespectful, and I knew when I was being baited for a fight. "It's cramped, so I appreciate getting his clean work clothes today."

"Hopefully, he'll be able to walk and shower soon. I'm sure it's been difficult for you."

"I'm grateful, Dean. You won't hear me complaining, but it's far from a honeymoon."

Dean seemed pleased with my response. He gave me a wide grin and reached for the radio on his belt. "Intake complete. Please bring in the appointment for Mrs. Lawson."

"So, I guess we're almost done here? Do I get scanned now?" I asked. He placed my palm on his thigh and leaned forward. He smelled like he always had of coffee and mint, even now. His fingers pushed up and between my legs, teasing me to notice.

"Do you remember the cruise we took all those years ago?" he responded. "Maybe it's the water or us together again, I just keep thinking about it."

"This ship is a little different. Fewer margaritas and more, you know, overall hopelessness."

"I can be happy with you here." His other hand lifted to my cheek, rubbing his thumb along my bottom lip. "Remember our first night on that trip? I made you very happy."

I hated to feel it, but the thoughts came rushing back, and the warmth in my core grew. There had been a time once when I craved Dean like a drug. He was arrogant, but he had a right to be. He never left me unsatisfied, and reminiscing about better times had me holding my breath. His hand on my jaw became stronger, and he drew my face to his.

"You did, it's true," I admitted. "But we agreed that part of our lives is over."

"I think life is different now," he pointed out. "You know why I need you here, Row? Why I really need you?"

His mouth was on mine, pushing his tongue between my lips. He gripped my throat, holding me in place, and he moved my hand to his cock. It twitched and pulsed from my touch.

He was aggressive, always was, and I'd probably leave the room with a few bruises. Dean had regularly blessed me with love marks when we were together. I loved the feel of them on my body. His force was never unwanted, and a bite mark or hand slap didn't bother me.

But today, when he gripped the back of my hair, yanking my mouth open further, I was... confused. I kissed him back in my shock and possibly my fear. I still needed Dean to keep me here, to keep *us* here.

What I felt for Sam was real, but his life, all our lives, were in Dean's hands. The same hands that moved over my body as if he owned me, and I yielded to his will, trapped by my circumstances.

The door opened, but Dean refused to stop. He was the boss of all things and he would finish when he wanted. Knowing someone was watching, I grew uncomfortable. I pulled back, making his grip on my hair tighter, and I mindlessly moaned in response.

Dean's smile was criminal as he yanked us apart to look at me. "You like that, baby," he boasted. Someone at the door gave an awkward cough, and he released me.

When I turned to see Sam, my heart stopped beating.

No tears fell. I looked at him with dead eyes, my heart sinking in my chest. I bore my gaze through him like he was nothing. *Dean will not win.*

Sam glared at the wall behind us as he gripped the sides of his wheelchair, a spoke breaking free with his bare hands.

Chapter Twelve

Cults

"Sam, it's so good you could join us. Rowan grabbed your clothes, so I sent for you to get your intake done." Dean rose from his seat, shoving his chair back with a kick.

Asshole.

The vein on the side of Sam's neck throbbed. He brought his hands to his lap and cracked his knuckles. "Thanks for leaving the chair on the deck, Dean. It helps a lot. Rowan was worried about how I would manage," Sam spit out. The sound of his strained voice pierced my heart.

"Well, we may need to get you a new one," Dean replied, tapping his boot on the side of the wheel. "There seems to be something wrong with the spokes." Dean opened the door and ushered in a few men. "These two will do your scans and finish up your paperwork." I kept my expression detached and fixated on Dean. He shouted back as he stepped out of the room, "Tomorrow at 0800, Rowan, and we will see you next week, Sam."

"I'm fine to start tomorrow," Sam gritted out before Dean shut the door. "I have this chair, which is in great shape. Put me to work."

Dean turned and moved his jaw back and forth, considering the offer. "Your call, Sam. If you feel up to it, 1300 hours." Dean left with a wink, and I smiled at the bastard. *Am I passing enough of your tests, Dean?*

The two men got right to work. They meticulously scanned every part of my face and hands and drew more blood. We received maps of the agriculture area and I made a note of the building that read, *Chemistry*, at the center.

They finished with me first, and I announced I would stay and wait for Sam. "No need," he snipped without looking in my direction. He avoided eye contact the entire time. The thick tension made our guests eager to finish and leave us.

I had no response to his attempt at brushing me off, but I didn't move my ass either. After fifteen minutes of agitated breathing and teeth grinding, we were ready to leave. Sam had the lead on me with wheels, but I would catch him at the stairs. I wanted to run after him, call his name, and make him stop to listen, but there was a fucking drone flying overhead.

I was highly agitated for a woman freshly fucked, but Sam had every right to act like a man scorned.

I tried to wrap my arm around him as he started towards the stairwell, but he pushed my hand away. "Drone," I hissed in his ear. His eyes moved upward, and he conceded until the stairs covered our heads. He then thrust my arm off him, sending me stumbling backward.

He hesitated in regret and mumbled, "I'm sorry." I rolled my shoulders back and walked behind him in silence.

We entered our cabin, which felt even more like a cell because of my outfit and current mood. He stretched out on the bed, defeated. We had a few hours until we picked up the boys.

"Should I leave and waste time in the mess hall with Lori?"

"Yes," came his sharp reply.

"You know, the only way marriage works is if you communicate." I was testing the waters with a joke. Avoiding each other failed before, so at some point, we had to talk. BeLew needed to come back to a happy home, or room rather. *No one would think this place could pass for a home.* The boys deserved better. The world had damaged them enough as it was.

He let out a harsh breath and covered his face with his hands.

"I didn't mean that," he mumbled through his hands. "I don't want you further away than you already are."

"I'm right here, next to you, ready to talk," I said, moving to my side of the bed.

"The truth is, I don't know how to feel. I'm torn between feeling like you cheated and questioning if I took advantage of you before. I'm fucked up from this." He rolled to his side, scooting over to let me lie next to him. I ran my fingers through his hair and met his eyes. I'd hurt him. I'd hurt us.

"I wanted to be with you. I still do. Dean set that up. You have to see that." My guilt washed over me. *I had kissed Dean back.*

He nodded, "I do, I'm not stupid. I also saw how you responded to him, which is what he wanted. You fell right into his arms and hours before..."

"Dean and I have a history. You know that." I wouldn't lie to Sam or make promises I couldn't keep. "But forget about any feelings for a minute and listen to me. If Dean wants to kiss me, I'm not in a position to say no. If he wants to fuck me, I can't say no to that either. Our survival depends on him. This is something I knew before you were a body we picked up on the side of the road. He holds the power. I won't choose my pride, or yours, over BeLew. I'll do anything for them."

Sam tensed, and his face became contorted in rage. "You would just give your body to him. It means that little to you."

"Yes, I would, because BeLew means everything to me. I would give myself freely if it meant they would be safe. And for you too, by the way."

"Oh, please don't do me any favors, Row," he spat. "I don't need you prostituting for me."

His comment enraged me. His feelings were hurt, yes, but he should have some empathy, too. I bet if he was being flung off the side of the ship in zip ties he would think, *"I wish Row had spread her legs a few times instead of preserving her honor."*

I grabbed a pillow and chucked it across the room. I got up and crawled over him, careful to avoid his leg because I still cared about the bastard. He opened his mouth to stop me, but I cut him off. "You know, when I was a little girl, I always thought maybe I'd show horses, or be a vet, or a mother. I also said to myself, Row, how about you be a whore? Maybe, oh my God, wouldn't this be great? Maybe you can be a mother, but it means you have to lose your sister and then you get to be a whore at the same time. All my fucking dreams coming true on this floating purgatory."

I paced inside our small space. Anger flooded out with every word and I knew they weren't all for Sam, but I couldn't stop myself. Dean had put me in this position. He'd entangled me in his net again, but I had pushed those feelings down. My rampage spewed out at Sam because I could never say these things to Dean.

"And you have the nerve to tell me what I shouldn't be doing. You don't even know what you need, Sam," I seethed. "Just sit back and let me rescue fucking everyone and then judge me for it."

I wasn't crying. My old self had taken hold, and I was becoming an expert at holding in my tears. My body shook with fury. Sam continued to stare at me, speechless. I kept on, "Don't you forget who dragged your bloody, lifeless ass across land and ocean so you could lie there and tell me what I shouldn't do for my family. Fuck you, Nico. Excuse me while I whore it up to keep us all alive. You just stay right there. I'll bring you back a snack, you asshole. Anything else you need? Would you like my body again, or is it too loose for you?"

I turned and started through the door as he called my name. *That ungrateful piece of shit.*

There weren't a lot of places I could go in my ferocity. The boat was huge, but BeLew had to be picked up in a few hours, so getting lost was not an option. The deck would have watchdogs, and I had already showered. Lori was my only choice. I would come offering helping hands. She could always use those.

Sure enough, I found her running around the kitchen barking orders. I stepped through the swinging doors. "Need any help? I need to keep my hands busy."

She ushered me to her side. "Is it alright?" I asked. "I don't know much about a kitchen."

"No health inspector is coming," Lori chuckled. "We are flying by the seat of our pants here." She was pouring flour and water into an industrial mixer. I grabbed the bags from the corner and started carrying them over to another mixer on her left. "Speaking of pants and busy hands, I would think you would want the time with your husband. I saw him getting around better this morning. And sorry, not sorry, I would climb that man like a tree. Shit, you are one lucky lady."

I slammed a bag of flour on the floor. "We got into a fight."

Lori raised her eyebrows. "I've been there. How long have you been married?"

"Oh, long enough for him to know better." I made a mental note that we had to get our love story in line as soon as I was ready to speak to him again. "I'm embarrassed to say I don't know, but are you married, Lori?"

She scribbled baking instructions on a whiteboard in front of us. There was a third mixer, so I gathered I would make dough for the duration. "I was," she muttered. "He joined the Assembly of the Eternal."

My agitation left me at that moment. No one had spoken about the Assembly of the Eternal since we boarded. I was all too familiar with that cult. Some liked to think it was a religion or a way to handle the unknown, but it was a damn cult. Most of them were long gone, at their own hands.

"I see," I mumbled.

"I won't change the subject right away, as you love to do," she chided.

I gnashed my teeth and poured the increments she had written out into the mixer. "Why, whatever do you mean?" I sneered. There was a thick layer of sarcasm letting her know I picked up her meaning.

Lori continued. "He took the tonic, but we were separated at the time. I left him to stay with my family, which was close to the coast. They went inland, and I came here with the boys. He was long dead by then. Fucking coward."

My stomach dropped. My outburst with Sam seemed stupid after Lori told me about her husband. Terrible men were everywhere, and in my heart, I knew Sam wasn't one of them.

"I'm sorry, Lori. Truly, you are a strong woman. You and the boys deserved better. We all do, and I'm not trying to be distant. I want to be a good friend to you. I'll do better."

"Did you know anyone in the AOE?" Lori asked. She stepped over to fiddle with some dials on my mixer.

"Didn't everyone before they took the plunge?"

"I suppose," she deadpanned. I'd disappointed her. I was too candid with Sam, but not honest enough for my only friend. I shook out my wrists and dragged another bag of flour to the third mixer. She shifted to the counter and started chopping something with the aggression and the precision only a chef could pull off.

I took a long exhale, steadying myself for the conversation. "The Assembly of the Eternal was the most despicable gathering of dumbasses I've ever seen. They preyed on weak and scared people. I heard leadership took everyone's money and built some crazy bunker in Idaho or some shit. I'm sorry your husband fell in with them. I know what it's like to lose someone you love to that special brand of crazy."

Lori sat her knife down and turned to face me. She crossed her arms and tilted her head. "Well, we all knew someone in it before they took the plunge, as you say."

I ripped open the flour, lifted it, and poured. "My brother-in-law joined the ranks early on. He loved feeling powerful. Anyway, it killed him and my sister in the end. Almost killed BeLew."

She lowered her eyes and took a step toward me. "Did they take the swim? Did they try to take your sons?"

"No, they didn't get the chance." I struggled with how to explain the next part. She took my silence as pain, which was partly true, but it was too soon to confide in her that BeLew were not mine. Not yet.

This topic made my skin prickle. It felt wrong to discuss things like this. The Assembly of the Eternal had become folklore or urban legend, and speaking about it somehow brought it back to life. I never said Bloody Mary in the bathroom mirror with my girlfriends. Fate was unkind enough without pushing her limits.

The cult started after a few tragic back-to-back weather events. They acted like a church at first, and millions live-streamed their so-called sermons. They would predict a catastrophic event, and like clockwork, it would happen. At that point, anyone could foresee the next hurricane or flood, but people were losing control. They wanted something to trust, and it wouldn't be the government. For millions, it was the Assembly of the Eternal.

The influence started slow. First, they all wore only blue, the color of the water, to pay homage to mother earth. The only jewelry they could wear was a pin of the AOE's symbol. When food went scarce, they gathered by the hundreds and took over entire warehouses to feed their collective. My sister left offerings for me hidden in the barn. She went along to get along, but she knew she was in over her head. Her husband rose in the ranks of the AOE, and it trapped her. This place helped me understand that feeling – being trapped by a man and scared for your life.

There were late night hushed talks about escaping with BeLew, but we didn't know what was coming. No one knew. We never imagined it would end in mass suicides across the globe. They called it "*The Swim*".

The dreams came back, and I'd ignored them. I'd convinced myself they weren't true.

It was time to confide in Lori. I wanted someone else to know, and she would understand without judgment. Or, if she judged me, she wouldn't be alone. Hate lingered in my heart, hate for myself. The things I did were unforgivable.

"My brother-in-law was going to take the family to the lake for "the swim". BeLew were living with them at the time. He didn't say what he was doing, but my sister found the tonic. She heard him talking to his counterparts about the date and location. She cut the battery lines to their cars. I went over to help them but he made them walk. He had completely lost his mind by then, convinced if they didn't take that fucking tonic and drown themselves, it would damn them for eternity. I had my gun and, well, he had his."

Lori stood next to me without speaking. The flour bag was empty, and I was staring at the bowl of powder. My chest hurt like a broken part of my heart had re-opened.

"We fought. I don't have to tell you what about." My shallow breaths made it hard to speak. Lori's eyes were wide as she stared at me, touching her fingertips to my arm. "BeLew ran back to the house at some point. Everyone was screaming at each other. It got really chaotic. He raised his gun to the boys, and my sister got in between. I shot him. He shot her. It happened really fast. It's not like in the movies. You hear bullets, but people don't bleed right away. They kind of fall to the ground and it takes a while for your brain to register what's happening. You can't understand that they are dead, that they are gone. Then there's the denial part, where you just stare at someone. You look at the body of a person you loved every day for your entire life, and you wonder if it truly happened. Then you wonder how you keep loving people."

Lori had a tight grip on my arm. "That's horrible, Row." We said nothing for a moment, and the mixer buzzed, an awful sound breaking my trance.

"There's nothing you could have done, Row. That group had them all mind fucked. He's responsible. Luckily, nothing happened to the boys. No - not luck. You saved the boys, Rowan. Do you understand that?"

"I'm just not so sure about that," I winced, my voice a few octaves too high. I saw the scene in my mind, as clear as it was that day. My sister lay crumpled in the dirt, her breaths muddled with blood. BeLew had stopped their run in the distance, their little legs frozen, not knowing which way to go. I remembered how heavy the gun had felt in my hands, but I kept hold of it, afraid to let it go. Then the fear washed over me, the fear that I had made a terrible mistake.

"The thing is Lori... I can't tell you. That is, I'm still not sure... who shot first."

CHAPTER THIRTEEN

FORGIVENESS

SAM HADN'T SPOKEN TO me in days. I understood, but hated it all the same. I gave him the time to process our fight. We had nothing but time in this place.

He started work as promised and, much to Dean's pleasure, avoided me at all costs. He caused himself visible pain by lifting out of his wheelchair and walking away from me more than once. This fight taught me nothing except that we were both stubborn as hell.

Even with his disdain for me, Sam loved BeLew. He helped them study and played games with them in the morning before school. When he would come in at night, I pretended to be asleep. He kissed the boy's heads before begrudgingly nestling his large body next to mine.

My feelings didn't matter. BeLew deserved safety and happiness, and Dean seemed to be pacified for the moment. I wanted things with Sam to be okay, but maybe that was asking for too much. I had developed feelings for that bastard. He needed time, and we had at least eleven more months of that.

I helped Lori in the kitchen when I felt restless or lonely in the evenings. The boys would play or do homework in the mess hall, and I stayed occupied with whatever task I could manage. I knew twelve-hour days were not ideal for the long haul, but the alternative was too much to endure. Alone with my thoughts was a dangerous place to be.

Lori and I were closer. My admission to her meant something to us both, and she took every opportunity to reinforce her opinion that I saved BeLew and did not kill my sister. I wanted to believe her, but my deep-rooted self-hatred remained.

"Still fighting with Sam?" she asked one evening. Her question was rhetorical. She saw we ate separate breakfasts and during an inventory meeting Lori attended, we stood on opposite sides of a ten-foot room.

"You know it. I'm nothing if not consistent," I clipped, taking ingredients to each mixer. I could bake with little direction by then, but the ingredient list lingered on Lori's whiteboard, just in case.

"You may not have noticed, but the man pool is slim pickings around here, Row, and I've been looking. I don't need your hot ass in the mix, so work it out."

"Thanks for the pep talk, Lori. It's really helpful."

"Remind me what the fight was about again?"

I shut down, and she knew I would. I'd told her I wanted to keep the details of our fight to myself. How would I explain the complexities of this argument? I could fill the entire ship with my secrets.

"He's not willing to make the sacrifices I am to stay here. Can I just leave it at that?"

"He almost sacrificed a leg!" Lori stopped what she was doing and was staring at me with her hands on her hips. "You are cranky as shit. I appreciate the help, but you are driving me crazy. You need some dick, and wouldn't you know, there is a fine specimen in your quarters."

I slammed the ingredients into the mixers. "I'm working on it. He's adjusting. We are all fucking adjusting. Please change the subject."

Lori fidgeted with her hands, a solid tell she had something to confess. She walked over and stood next to me. "Enough with the flour! Oh my God, it's like someone set off a fire extinguisher in here. I have something to talk to you about. It's about the chemistry assignment you seem so keen to get started."

That perked my interest.

"So, I should start by confessing I'm sneaking food to the two hundred," Lori continued.

Momentary confusion quickly turned to fear. "Wait, what? First, we've named the stowaways now? Second, you were there on pirate day, right, Lori? Did you push that into your subconscious? Breaking the laws here is punishable by a horrible death."

"Listen, they cannot work effectively on the rations they're given," she seethed. "I can make provisions stretch. I'm already under quota and trust me, it's working out. You aren't the only one with friends in this place."

I rolled my eyes, trying to wave the puffs of flour out of our faces.

"I've been talking to some of them, and well," she drifted off. "Um, it's just odd. They're growing in the chemistry building."

I stood there, waiting for Lori to give me more. I waved my hands in front of her. "Everyone is growing in the ag unit, Lori. It's the sole purpose of the whole place. Is there something else?"

"They're growing flowers," she explained. "That's odd, right?"

"What the fuck?" I blurted. "I don't know. Are you sure?"

Lori brought her hands to her hips and groaned. "I'm sure that's what they told me. I'm not sure what that means, but I've warned you, and now you know."

"Okay, well, thanks. I guess." I didn't know what that tidbit of information meant, or if it was even valid. I was sure that Lori was tired of my sulking.

"Listen," I said. "I know I'm not the best company right now. Thanks for putting up with me." I plastered a smile on my face and finished with the batter.

She squinted her eyes and crossed her arms. "You're welcome, but seriously, I think you should walk softly with your job. Something's not right. And get over this shit with your husband."

"Okay," I agreed. "I'll keep my eyes open, and I know Sam and I will work this out."

I mopped up the white powder that rested all over the floor. Lori told me it was pointless until the end of the day, but I still wanted to keep my hands busy. It helped push thoughts of Sam away, if only a little.

All I could do about Sam was wait for him to come around. The facts hadn't changed. Dean had been a perfect gentleman the past few days, borderline kind. He'd visited BeLew's classroom and had even brought them some plants for science class. I couldn't explain to Sam that Dean had backed off, because he refused to look at me, let alone talk to me.

Lori nudged my arm. "Hey, could you keep an eye on the boys for me? I'm running down to the lower decks." Lori had a large cloth sack hung over her shoulder like some sad, apocalyptic Santa.

"Oh, wow, so you're doing this on the regular I see. You're making this horrible decision, like now. You are insane. Seriously, are you a strong swimmer without the use of your hands?"

She pushed through the swinging doors, ignoring my commentary. She took a pause and turned back to me. "Why don't you come with me?"

"And leave four boys to run amuck without super-vision? That's another way to get thrown overboard zip-tied."

"Sam's out there with them." Lori gave a nod of her head towards a corner table. I walked up to see for myself, and there he sat. A fresh plate of food was placed in front of him while he rustled BeLew's hair. He had that big, stupid grin on his big, stupid face.

I miss him.

Maybe it was frustration or the desperate need to get away, but I snapped, "Fine, let's go. I can point out how crazy you are after seeing it for myself. Then you'll have to believe me. You tell Sam to watch the kids."

"Oh, for the love. This stupid fight," Lori hissed, putting her sack down and walking towards their table. They spoke for a moment while regret coursed through me. Going to see the two hundred was a terrible decision, but I wanted to help Lori and avoid Sam until he talked to me first. Sometimes when you win, you lose.

She sauntered back, and too stubborn to back out, I picked up the heavy bag, and we headed out.

The path down took over half an hour, and at some point, I groaned, realizing I would have to take all the stairwells back up. It got colder the deeper we went, and the sounds of the ship were ominous. Every creak or clang made me flinch, as if the floors above us would collapse. My nightmares of sinking deep into black water crept into my mind, and I shook my head to break them free.

When we entered a large room of flickering lights stuffed with people, I knew we had arrived. There were mattresses strewn on the floor, hanging bunks, nets draped from the ceiling, and a few tables scattered around. Overall, the conditions were deplorable.

I helped Lori unpack containers and bag up empty ones. There were maybe a dozen kids that watched us, waiting for the first turns at snacks.

"Are you all liking school?" I asked. I had a basket of rolls, still warm, that I passed out to them.

"They don't go to the school," a male voice came from behind me. Startled, I shot around, almost dropping the food. It took me a moment to register, but I knew him. It was Luke from the RHIB all those weeks ago. It seemed like a lifetime ago. He reached out and hugged me. "Did he make it?" Luke chuckled. "Your husband?"

"He did," I smiled. "He's doing well."

"She isn't talking to him," Lori chimed in. "But his leg healed up. You two know each other?"

"So, there's still a chance for me, then?" Luke beamed and turned to Lori. "We had a wild make-out session when I was sure her husband and all of us were going to die a grisly death." He took a few steps back from me and raised his hands. "Oh shit, am I going to make it? How healed up are we talking? Should I watch my back? I remember him being a large guy."

I gave a guttural laugh, and the tray of rolls almost slipped out of my hands. I couldn't remember the last time I truly giggled. The kids laughed because kids are like that, sponges that absorb the feelings of those around them. I needed to be happier around BeLew. They needed me to laugh and feel joy.

"Oh, wow. I wouldn't call it a make-out," I laughed. "You got a kiss as you saw us off. I can't say I'm sorry about it."

Luke beamed in my direction, and Lori grabbed my tray before I poured our hard work all over the floor.

"Well, aren't you just swimming in available men?" Her tone was jovial, but there was a nip to it. "Luke is part of the medical team. He comes down here to check on everyone when he's done with his shift. It's kind of him."

"It's nothing," he brushed Lori off. "What else am I going to do, pace around the boat for the hundredth time?"

I certainly understood that. "Why don't the kids go to school? I thought we had an oversupply of teachers?"

"Because they want more growers," Luke answered. "Not that we would ever be short on food the way Lori works her magic."

God, this man is a flirt. I love it. We need some shameless romance.

"So, the kids are working in agriculture? Are you serious?"

"They are reporting to chemistry," Lori interjected. "To grow... flowers."

"Who told you they were growing flowers?" Luke asked.

"I have my sources." Lori's eyes shot around the room. "Let's not talk about this anymore, okay." We nodded in unison, uncomfortable with the shift in conversation.

I enjoyed my time in the lower decks more than I thought I would. My plans to talk Lori out of going dissipated, especially after seeing how many children inhabited the space. Everyone was content that they could stay on the ship. They counted blessings, not burdens, and the kids, although working and not learning, seemed well fed and playful. Someone had given their mothers some chalk, and they lined the walls with lesson plans and games.

"Lori, I'll be back the day after tomorrow. What about you?" Luke asked.

She blushed, and I backed away from their conversation. I packed everything up and moved it into the hallway. When I finished, and Luke and Lori remained deep in discussion, I joined a young boy in a rousing game of Go Fish.

I decided I would come back before Lori told us it was time to go. It was a miracle my newfound family was still on board and not down here with everyone else. It was my responsibility to help in any way I could. Maybe it was my guilt again, but my heart needed to pay some kind of penance.

"So, what's the story with you and Luke?" I snickered as we headed up one of many stairwells. *My ass better look amazing after this year.*

"I think we are going for a walk together the next time we come down. Maybe he can find a place to fuck me where I won't get spotted by a drone."

Another guttural laugh left both of us this time. "I hope that works out for you."

"Me too. There's nothing to look forward to besides carbohydrates and sex around here. Mark my words. In about ten or eleven months, this place is going to be bustling with newborns. No one rubbers up when it's the end of the world."

Shit, that's true.

The days after lacked the excitement of the lower decks. Sam still hadn't spoken to me about anything that mattered. The boys enjoyed school and their friends. They slept deeply and peacefully. It was routine, and I couldn't complain.

My nights had been dreamless, but I still woke randomly. I sat up one night, not sure of the time. I knew I was off the next day and so was Sam. In fact, most of the department had the day off. It was well deserved. We had been breaking our backs to get everything planted.

Then it was nonstop soil moisture checks, fertilization, and temperature control. I already hated radishes, and my disdain for them grew by the day.

Out of habit that night, I placed my hand in front of Sam's mouth, checking for his breath. It was a routine now. I would awaken, ensure he was alive, then lie in bed and question the choices I made in life.

He was getting around better, but I might never stop worrying. The wheelchair was still necessary, but he could stand for almost an hour unassisted.

This night, however, Sam's eyes shot open and found mine. I pulled my hand back, startled that he caught me. "Checking to make sure I'm breathing again?" he whispered, nearly silent.

I nodded, inches from his face. I longed for him. He felt so close, but also miles away. *Are we still in this together?*

He brushed my face with his hand and let out a breath. Inching towards me, his lips met mine, and we clung to each other. He kissed me slowly, and I couldn't get close enough to his warmth. The barrier closed us off from BeLew, but I heard Sam whisper, "Quietly," as he pulled down my shorts, and I wiggled my legs free.

I clawed at his pants to remove them, panting while trying to be silent. The feeling of hot skin touching mine immersed me in calmness and relief. His cock twitched against my side, already leaking and sliding against my thigh. I'd missed this. *I'd missed him.*

"I'm..." he trailed off, staring at me in the darkness.

I pressed my finger to his lips. "You don't have to say it. Me too, Nico."

His hand moved down, pulling the sheet back. I felt his gaze cast over my body. "Sam," he said.

I cocked my head and inhaled, slow and deep. My chest rose and fell and his eyes flicked to my peaked nipples, apparent through my thin shirt.

He wrapped his fingers around my leg and drew it to the side, exposing my wet center to the cool air. "Sam," he repeated. "Say it." He inched lower, until he was on his knees at the edge of the bed, looking up at me spread before him. My body shook, and I tried to press my legs together, but he pushed his huge body between my them, moving his shoulders under my knees and locking me in place.

"Say it," he commanded. "Sam."

I nodded, but the words caught in my throat. His fingers squeezed, pushing into my skin and pinching, and he waited.

"S-Sam," I stuttered.

He lowered his face between my legs, rewarding my obedience with a languid lick. A thick tongue dove inside me, massaging my walls and drawing out, only to flick at my clit.

Oh, fuck yes.

I shuddered and moaned, and he repeated the action until my legs shook uncontrollably against his hold. Before long, I had to pull back, the pressure was too great. My orgasm threatened to burst from within me already. He didn't allow my retreat, yanking me back down against his face. I feared I might bruise from his grasp, keeping me flush with his mouth, refusing to let me go until my release.

That skilled tongue circled, and his lips sucked at my clit in an unrelenting motion. I lost all control. Sam could feel it coming. My body shook, and heavy breaths hissed out from my throat. He paused only to drag a pillow to my hands, which I placed over my open mouth in case I screamed. And when the wave of pleasure spread through my limbs, I pressed that pillow against my face and cried out. I didn't remove it until the pulsing ache left me. It fell to the floor, and my legs slipped from his grasp. Breath made its way back into my lungs, making my head spin.

Sam rose from the floor with a grunt and crawled over my limp and sated form. His firm body hovered over mine, and I gazed at every line and curve of muscle, the perfect V that mapped the way to his massive cock. It jutted out against my center, and I smiled, knowing what came next.

When he entered me, I cried out again, and his hand moved over my mouth, smothering my whimpers. He kept it there, pinning my head to the mattress as he thrust. The only sound was the chain of the bed gently clinking and Sam's ragged breaths as his pace quickened.

He held back, taking his time. Slow, even strokes filled me and brought me to the edge. A few times, he stopped to stare at me while I writhed underneath him, so close to another climax. He occasionally lifted his hand to kiss me, but placed it back, claiming me over and over, keeping my moans silent.

"Dean doesn't get this," he hissed into my ear. "Not anymore."

I had no response. I couldn't move my head to nod either way. He was stating it as fact. There was no point in refuting what he believed to be true.

I clawed into his back, drawing him closer against me, wanting to feel that warmth. I craved more of it, more of him. We were still in this together. He needed time, but he also needed me. I felt him swell inside me until he shuddered, filling me with his heat and growling into my ear, "Mine."

I'm yours.

Another surge of satisfaction washed over me, softer than the last, but still full of pleasure.

He released his palm from my mouth again, replacing it with his lips and tongue. Our kissing slowed as my heart rate calmed.

All was forgiven.

CHAPTER FOURTEEN

ON THE HORIZON

FIVE YEARS AGO, MY brother-in-law had branded my sister. She told me she had an accident with a controlled burn. "I got a little careless with the lighter fluid. It shot up and bit my arm. No big deal," she'd said as she brushed me off.

"Why were you adding lighter fluid when the burn had been going all day? It didn't rain," I questioned. She'd shoved her sleeve down as if that would erase its existence. I had noticed the bottom of the symbol, curved lines that resembled waves.

She motioned for me to move along with my chores. When she killed a conversation, there was no way to bring it back to life.

Dean had come over that evening, and I'd told him what I saw. He knew how to get people to answer questions – to confess. After a card game and some whiskey, they revealed everything. The Assembly of the Eternal had spread its roots in our little town. Tattoos must have been cliché, but stigmatizing a follower, that meant loyalty.

Later, Dean told me about their admission in confidence, confirming my suspicions. He told me that my sister was anxious about the branding and their conversation. "She will tell you during the weekend trip into town. She's a grown woman, and she's made her decision."

I'd lain in bed, angry and numb, after he told me the news I had already known in my heart. Her family had bound itself to the will of a cult, the Assembly of the Eternal. Her arm would forever bear their mark. The mark had waves that intersected with a circle and a twisting of flames throughout. I knew what it looked like. I had seen the full branding in my dreams as a child.

I saw it again that night on Sam's back.

A scarred circle around the edges of a faded design was all that remained of a failed attempt at removal. My fingers felt the rough skin when I traced the lines in disbelief. There was so much to each other's story left to tell.

He awakened at some point, feeling my fingertips along the lines. He drew in a deep breath and turned to face me. "I was hoping to tell you about that before you saw it."

"Who else has seen it?"

Sam paused in thought. "Oh, are you worried about Dean? At the clinic?"

"I don't know, really. Anyone seeing that... it's dangerous."

"I changed myself into scrubs after they finished with the torture, er, I mean, medical attention," he chuckled.

"I'm being serious. They hunted those left from the Assembly of the Eternal for sport. I can't say it would be much different here."

"Lots of things are different here. No one needs to worry about some long-dead cult."

"Not all dead," I whispered.

It was almost morning, and BeLew would be up soon. I didn't want them to hear a discussion about the AOE. Anytime it came on the news or radio, they stiffened with fear. Once, in a food bank line, we'd heard a couple of men talking about survivors. The suicides had swept the country, but not everyone had obeyed. They'd spoken about killing those that were left. I was used to that kind of talk. Political correctness had been long gone, along with social decency. We were simple people, and taking the law into your own hands had become commonplace.

When the line had moved and I'd turned to usher the boys forward, I saw Beau had wet himself. Lewis had stood in front of him, protecting his brother. The intensity of their fear was justified, and I couldn't do a thing to lessen their emotional scars. Their bodies weren't branded, but their minds still felt the burn.

"We can't talk about this now. The boys, my sister..." I trailed off, my voice giving out from the memory. "My sister was in the AOE. It killed her."

"Did she take *'the swim'*?" His forehead creased with worry. He reached for me, and I folded into his warmth.

"No. Her husband tried to take them. She died, and BeLew and I got out. Again, we can't talk about this around the boys. Not ever. Do you understand?"

"You know I do. Row, I'll just tell you this. I didn't join out of belief or faith. I did it... I did it to save people. Do you understand? I was trying to get inside the organization. Do you believe me?"

"Yes, now go shower. You smell like sex and sweat."

"Wow," he smiled. "Way to end a conversation and kick me out. Has anyone complimented your skill at changing the subject?"

"Well, speaking of that, are we going to discuss the fight? Do you want to talk about that, instead?"

Sam blinked a few times and shook his head no. "I had to process what you said. Let's agree to disagree, but I understand I can't control much of anything here, not even your decisions. I'll take what I can get with you... whatever that means."

"I care about you," I admitted. "More than I should... more than makes sense."

Sam kissed me and stroked my hair from my face. "I care about you, too. You and the boys. More than makes sense."

I turned over to face the wall, smiled to myself, and pressed my back against him to cuddle. "Actually, I take back the sex and sweat comment. You smell like fertilizer, Mr. Lawson."

"Okay, Mrs. Lawson." He kissed my cheek, squeezing me tight. I didn't remark on his Mrs. Lawson comment. I had already made enough marriage jokes, and his tone was endearing. It felt right to be called Mrs. Lawson.

BeLew rustled in their bunks moments later, and Sam got up and opened the divider. "You boys want to get cleaned up? And you can make sure I don't fall over, okay?"

"Do we have to use soap?" Beau asked.

"Yes," I rumbled in response, making Sam giggle. "What kind of question is that, honestly?"

"Well, Beau's question was a yes or no question. Your question is disjunctive," Lewis added.

Sam cracked up laughing, and he had to place a hand on the wall to stay upright.

"Well, I'm pleased you are learning new things in school. Now get," I giggled.

BeLew grinned from ear to ear at their smart-ass remarks. They all gathered some fresh clothes and headed out the door. They left me with the room to myself on my day off, and the boys had only a few hours of school. My body hummed, knowing what would fill those hours. I didn't want anyone but Sam to have me. That may not be true forever, but it would be for now.

Later that day, Lori and I took a trip to the deck. The sun shone down on us, and I loved the feel of heat beating down on my skin. We stretched out on our bunk blankets in sports bras and panties while the boys played in makeshift saltwater pools. No one had a bathing suit and once a few people had mentally said, *"Fuck it,"* and got down to their underwear, everyone else followed suit.

It was hot. The world was ending, and the kids were playing in plastic barrel drums that someone melted on the sides and bonded together. The entire scene was a mix of parental desperation and creativity.

So really, who gives a shit that we're in our panties?

There were close to fifty people at our impromptu pool party. We traveled as far away from the agriculture unit as Lori would walk. Drones were fast, but the distance gave the illusion of privacy.

Scanning faces, I saw a familiar boy and girl from the lower decks. "Look who it is," I said. I stood up to greet them, and Lori grabbed my hand and yanked me back down. I almost landed on my ass with the sheet sliding underneath me.

"You can't act as if you know them," she hissed. "Don't be stupid."

My face fell. She was right. "I'm not used to that kind of isolation," I admitted. "They're just kids, and it's like they're hidden in the basement."

Lori tilted her head to the side and looked up at the sun. "We're doing more than we should, honestly. You can't hug two hundred people in public. That doesn't make you or them isolated. What, you don't have enough friends on this boat with me and Dean?"

I rolled my eyes and laid back down.

"You care about Dean," Lori said. "But there's something between you both that isn't right."

"You could say that."

"I did just say that, Rowan. Throw me a bone. I'm shockingly bored on my day off. Speaking of, have you noticed everyone is off today? And I mean everyone. School even closed early. Doesn't that seem odd to you?"

"Lori, everything seems odd to me. I'm numb to the insanity that is my life right now."

She planted a playful smack on my ass and dropped the subject. The boys ran over to grab snacks with a few friends in tow. No doubt they knew that being nice to the sons of the cafeteria lady was a good move.

They cleaned us out and then went back to running and splashing. The boat felt almost bearable today. I closed my eyes and pretended I was on a beach.

My mind went back to the morning with Sam. We had exhausted each other. He used whatever energy he had left for my pleasure, and I adored every minute. He had a way of being strong and sweet at once. He moved in and out of me while pulling my hair. He slapped my ass while we cuddled. It all worked with him, and I couldn't get enough.

"What's that grin on your face?" Lori asked. "You look like you just did something naughty."

"I *did* do something naughty," I shot back. "Sam and I made up. And then he made up for having to make up in the first place. He's sleeping it off right now." I raised my arms over my head, stretching in satisfaction.

"Well, your mood is loads better. Are you spirited enough to help me in the kitchen tonight? I want to get some prep done and get ahead. Especially since I need to make another run downstairs this week."

"You know I will." I closed my eyes and continued to unwind in the sun.

She tapped on my forearm minutes later, bobbing her body in excitement. "What?" I stammered. "I just started to relax." But she didn't need to tell me what. I saw Luke headed our way out of the corner of my eye. He looked edible, and Lori was salivating.

"Well, what luck? I come up for a break and find... what exactly have I found? You're both undressed, and I'm into that. Damn, ladies." Luke rubbed his jaw with a playful glare, and he fixed his eyes on Lori. She ate it up, lifting onto her elbows and pushing her chest forward.

"This is more than you will see tonight," she boasted. "So, get it while you can."

Luke licked his lips and turned to me. "Did you know Lori is making me a Michelin quality meal tonight after we get some chores done?" He made air quotations with his hands when he said chores. I knew he meant help with the lower decks.

"Oh, well, should I bow out then? I was going to help with said chores," I replied.

Luke waved his hand at me. "No, please help. The faster we get done, the faster I can prove Lori wrong."

"Wrong about what?" we said in unison.

"That this view right now is the most I'll see from you." He leaned down and whispered something dirty in her ear. Her body flushed, and her cheeks turned a neon hue.

"Why are you working?" I interrupted. "It looks like everyone has today off. Lori and I were just talking about how odd it is. You're in uniform, with guns."

My eyes darted to his sides. He had two firearms holstered to his sides, something I was sure I had never seen before. Luke's back became rigid, and he stood back up. "I'm essential. They didn't grant my department the day off."

"The kitchen is fucking closed. We had people take food with them after dinner for today. The clinics just opened and people have done fine without them," Lori commented. "And why the guns, Rambo?"

Something didn't add up. Lori had the same line of thinking, and she shot me a sideways glance, but something else caught her eye. I followed her line of vision to see a pack of boys running our way with frantic expressions.

"Maybe it's to help you with that stampede," Luke joked.

BeLew skidded to either side of me, their hands on their knees as they gasped for breath. "Mama," Lewis heaved. "Look, it's coming."

I stood up, as did Lori. We began looking around, but all I could see was a ship deck and the ocean.

"What?" I demanded. Other kids jumped and pointed with confused looking parents. Their arms flew all different directions, desperate to make us see. I grabbed my clothes and started shoving them onto my body. "What's coming, BeLew?"

Lori raised her hands in exasperation. "What the hell?" she griped. Clearly, she had gotten nowhere like the rest of us.

"Up," Beau shrieked. "Look up." His little hand pointed behind me and towards the sky.

I watched the horizon for a solid minute. *Did these kids see a weird bird or something?*

"Oh, shit," Lori's voice came from behind me. She grabbed my face and pointed it more to the left. And there it was.

"Is that a...." I couldn't even get the word out.

"That's a helicopter," she finished my sentence. "That's four helicopters. Luke, what is this? What is going on? Luke!"

Luke had left, taking his opportunity to exit the line of questioning.

"Oh, that asshole," she whined. "We need to stay on deck, but I think we should take shelter. Can you get into the ag building?"

"Yes, I think so. Are you sure we shouldn't go below? These helicopters are landing on this deck, not in our bunks."

"I'm the one with the real military background, so trust me," Lori snapped, grabbing our things and starting towards the agriculture gates. My stomach dropped at her words.

Real military background.

She had little concern for my reaction. Her only focus was to get us moving. "Let's go!" she yelled back at me. Drones darted overhead. The boys made headway in front of us, now understanding the plan.

"I won't even get into what that's supposed to mean," I grumbled, chasing after her.

"It means I'm a friend you can trust with your secrets. It means whatever happens next, let me make the orders and do the talking."

I kept my mouth shut as directed. She knew something. She always had. That worried me, but not as much as the question that spun in my head as we approached the agriculture gates.

What happens next?

CHAPTER FIFTEEN

THALASSA

I HEAVED A SIGH of relief when the gates to the agriculture department opened. The sound of the helicopters blocked out everything else. My hair whipped
around, stinging my face. I had been too jittery for the
first scan, so it took another try to get through.

"We need a building with two exits and a roof," Lori
barked.

I jogged forward, and everyone followed. The greenhouses had roofs, but you could see through the foggy
plastic. We made our way to the center of the unit when
Lori stopped us and grabbed my arm.

"Not chemistry," she said.

I turned to her and cocked my head. "Why not, Lori?"

"Not now. Not chemistry."

I surveyed the area. There weren't a lot of choices that
didn't leave us out in the open. "There's a storage shed
next to chemistry. It's empty with a roof, but it doesn't
have two exits."

She gave it a moment's thought, then nodded. "Okay,
that will have to work."

Another scan to enter and we piled inside. The roar of the helicopters stopped as we closed the door.

The four boys crawled underneath a wooden work-bench. I unfolded a cloth tarp that lay on top, and Beau pulled it down over the sides.

"It's like a blanket fort, right, boys?" I said. I heard the shaking in my voice. Lewis gave me a thumbs up, and Lori's boys bobbed their heads. "Not a sound, okay." I adjusted the cloth around the table and faced Lori. "We should talk."

She looked at the floor and rubbed her temples. "I know you aren't military," she confessed. "I've known since the first day you came into the mess hall. Dean told me, and well, it's obvious. You don't have the gait. At first, I found it very odd that he would tell me something that put him in a compromising position. Then we became friends. He knew we would. You know how he is. He can read people and it's like he can predict the future."

I let out a sputtered laugh. Lori had no idea how ironic her statement was to present company.

"Anyway, it's become the veiled threat that we both have with each other. We both care about you and we kind of... let each other get away with things because of it. He has something on me and I have something on him. He knows I give food to the two-hundred."

"And?" I encouraged. "And you know what about him, or is it me, or is it Sam? Is it just that I'm not military?"

"Sam?" she questioned. "Is there something else with Sam?"

I paused for too long. She pushed her neck forward and widened her eyes.

"Sam's not my husband," I whispered. "We are together. I have strong feelings for him, but we aren't married."

"Oh, well, getting your boyfriend onboard makes sense. You wouldn't want to be alone, and you would need to be married to bring him if you were military. I get it."

I bit my lip and inhaled slowly.

"Rowan," Lori drawled. "What are you leaving out? How long have you been together?"

I twisted my fingers together. "Well, I've known him since, er, well, the day we boarded."

"Boarded what?" Lori asked.

I shrank back away from her. "The ship."

"The ship? This ship!"

"This very one."

Her eyes looked like they could bulge out of her sockets. She seemed desperate to pace, but the storage unit was too small.

"He got injured on the road," I continued. "We picked him up, and it just snowballed. I couldn't leave him hurt, and the boys somehow got attached to an unconscious stranger. I know it sounds insane."

Lori covered her face with her hands and dragged them downward, pulling at her cheeks. She smiled and shook her head. "I would have done the same thing. That's why we're friends, because we're both fucking nuts." She grabbed my hand and squeezed it. "Thank you for confiding in me."

Footsteps.

Lori and I ducked down and sat on the wood floor. I pulled the cloth back to see the boys all sitting calmly. BeLew held hands. I reached my finger to my lips and let the cloth fall back. The storage shed shook as the door to chemistry slammed open and shut. Lori and I inched towards its adjoining wall.

"What do you let him get away with?" I whispered. "What do you know about him?"

"Shhhh," Lori hissed. She pointed to a vent on the wall. It looked like a slotted furnace grate with screws on the sides. She put a fingernail on one side and turned the screw. I did the same on the other side. We gripped the ends once it was completely loose and pulled out the vent.

It gave us an unobstructed view of the chemistry building floor, and there were lots of shoes on that floor. Our eyes met in horror and excitement. I gulped, and we both maneuvered ourselves to our bellies to hear better. The storage room was pitch black compared to the chemistry building, so no one could see us. At least, that's what I hoped and prayed for.

The room fell quiet when someone spoke. "It's good to see all of you, but your visit wasn't scheduled for several hours. We didn't clear the decks or make the announcement." I was sure it was Captain Matthews's voice

Another man answered him. "Weather is coming in from the west faster than expected. It was now or never. Communications are shit and you know it. Make something up to the passengers or don't. What are they going to do about it, leave? You have control of this ship, don't you, Matthews?"

The Captain acknowledged his superior and the next twenty minutes of conversation almost put me to sleep. Not only was it in veiled acronyms I didn't understand, but it centered on supply needs, surveillance, and next steps. Nothing out of the ordinary or nefarious came up in their conversation.

The helicopters were from another ship that was partnered with ours and, due to weather, they changed the schedule. Communications continued to be an issue, but navigation was intact. It was more important to know where to go than to converse with other ships. The voices introduced themselves from different factions of government. All male, which made me give an eye roll in the dark.

Dean's voice boomed, causing me to jump. He was always glued to Matthews, but his presence in the chemistry building startled me. "What's he doing here?" he barked.

"Rivera?" another man questioned. "He came up in the facial recognition system a few weeks ago."

"Nico, it's good to see you, brother," another voice said. There were back slaps and handshakes.

My body trembled, and I lifted myself off the floor. "What the fuck?" I gasped. "What the actual fuck?" For a moment, I may have blacked out. My ears filled with a dull roar, and I saw spots in my vision.

Lori yanked me back down, begging me to be quiet. Blood rushed through my body, and I felt my heartbeat pounding in my skull. My hands trembled, and I stood up again, heading towards the door, trying to escape. Lori had wiggled in between me and the exit and pushed on my shins. "Stop," she hissed. "What are you doing? You'll get us all killed."

"Mama," I heard from below the wood bench. It stopped me in my tracks. My head spun and my pounding heart made me dizzy, but Lewis's voice brought me back down to earth. I crouched down to the floor and sat cross-legged. I reached for Lewis's hand and gave him a weak smile.

"Here," Lori said and shoved a plastic baggy in my face. "Are you hyperventilating?"

"Are you trying to get me to suffocate myself by putting a plastic bag over my head?" I answered.

"Well, you *did* seem suicidal just now." She crawled back to the vent, and I stayed put. My legs were like lead. Someone called him brother. Dean now knew his actual name. He's not who he says he is.

Who is he?

Lori's hand caught my eye, frantically waving me over. I willed myself to make the arduous crawl back to the vent, my body fighting me the entire way as if it were going into shock.

When I reached the vent, I heard Sam's voice. "I'm not leaving Thalassa."

"It's not your assignment," Captain Matthews answered. "And you're lucky you weren't thrown overboard. You were here under false pretenses. I want your file."

"He was to reach an island jumper, and he did," another voice snapped. "Remember your place in this, Matthews. You would also do well to heed that warning, Rivera. You don't make the orders here."

There was a silence, and I thought they would hear my heart thudding against the wood floor.

Sam cleared his throat. "I respectfully request a permanent placement on Thalassa."

"Are you still injured?" another voice asked.

"Yes, but for clarity, I have personal reasons for wanting to stay."

I saw Lori's face in the shadows dart back and forth from me to the vent. She recognized his voice. She knew it was Sam. I saw her mouth, "Oh my fucking god," and I covered my face with my hands, nodding yes.

I heard Dean's laughter in the room, a snide cackle directed at Sam. He had to be crawling out of his skin to pipe up, but there wasn't much he could divulge, given the situation. *How bad this would be for Dean if Sam was cleaning toilets?*

"We are growing here, too," Matthews barked. "If you care to be down a man that you didn't know survived in the first place, I'll take the able body. Well, as able as he will be when he's healed."

"Well, you can get Rivera up to speed then. Whatever your reasons are, son, I hope they're good. You're giving up a position on the Galene. Room with a view and all that comes with it," the man chuckled.

"I'm sure," Sam deadpanned.

"Dismissed," the Captain bellowed, and I heard a few handshakes and farewells as Sam left the room. Matthews gave only a curt dismissal. He sounded bitter about being put in his place. He was at the top of the food chain on this vessel, but not with our visitors.

The remaining men talked more about supplies, which led to a conversation about exchanges. Things were set to move between the two ships through the kitchen and the agriculture department. It made sense why the entire ship had a day off. They were moving things back and forth between vessels.

If passengers watched a helicopter land, then saw strangers go to the mess hall, take food, and leave, it would incite panic. The helicopters, even if they arrived when scheduled, would have caused enough confusion.

The crowd dispersed and left the chemistry building. My pulse was still sky high as Lori held my trembling hands.

"What do you let Dean get away with?" I uttered. "You look the other way on something, Lori. What is it?"

"He's storing Papaver Somniferum in the kitchen fridges. I noticed the bags and threatened a recruit that was bringing them in to tell me the source."

I gave an agitated huff. "In English please, for those of us not so kitchen inclined."

Lori gripped my hands so tightly I felt a few knuckles pop. "It's the poppy seed, Row. It's the flowers in chemistry. I think Dean wants drugs on this ship."

Before I could react, the door to the storage unit flew open.

Dean paused for only a moment before he took two huge steps forward, grabbed my arm, and dragged me out of the room.

CHAPTER SIXTEEN

SEVEN WEEKS

"WHERE ARE WE GOING? What about BeLew? Please, just stop," I begged. The boys were safe with Lori, but I was frantic. Dean weaved in and out of walkways, dodging view from anyone. He stopped in a dark corner with plywood walls and pushed me back against it, his arms encasing me.

We stood face to face without a word said between us for minutes. I felt his breath, tainted with anger and lust, hot against my skin. My eyes darted around him. We were close to the office.

"I didn't know about Sam," I admitted. He remained silent, baiting me to speak, and I failed to resist. "We are going to the office to destroy our files, aren't we?"

"I always admired your problem-solving skills." His sharp tone could cut glass. "I hope you didn't know about Sam, because that would put us all in immense danger. The only reason Matthews isn't in that office right now is because his senior is at his side until the Galene leaves. He'll be looking for them as soon as he can, and if he finds them..."

"I know," I answered. "We're all dead."

"BeLew too," he spit.

I shut my eyes, and hot tears fell. I had fucked up. I wished I could go back to that day on the trail and just keep walking. I hadn't seen this in any dream, or I would have known better.

"Let's go," I mouthed. "What are we waiting for?"

The office door next to us opened, and Dean wiggled his eyebrows. A few people walked out, and Dean slid his arm around the door, wedging his fingers inside the opening before it closed behind them. I shot around the cracked door and saw his face wincing in pain. "What are you doing?"

"They track the entries," he hissed. I opened the door fully and stepped through. "It's how I knew you were in the storage unit. I was in a meeting, which you obviously heard, and saw you where you were. Matthews can't know what we're doing." Once inside, Dean pulled me back against the wall. We stayed flush against it and he yanked a camera from the ceiling in one pull. He let me go and crossed the room, opening various cabinets and pulling out folders I assumed were our files. He flicked a lighter from his pocket and set the flame to a corner.

"You've been tracking me around the ship?"

"I see no point in being evasive anymore and especially in this conversation. Consider yourself lucky they haven't had time to enter all these electronically yet." His eyes were dancing in the fire he created. As each page burst into flames, he let it fall to the ground and put it out with his boot. "I'm reported to regularly about your movements - electronically and verbally. It seems my distrust was warranted. You know this means your marriage is over, right? To be more specific, Nico - Sam

- your husband, now lives alone. They have issued me larger quarters, and you will move in with me. I'll have someone get your things."

I had nothing to say in response. Sam asked to stay... for me, but now that Dean knew who he was, our time was up.

Why didn't he tell me? He put our family in danger.

The memory of the six falling over the edge entered my mind, and I stiffened with fear. I warned Sam about Dean, about me being here under falsehoods, yet he never said a word.

Still shocked by the new information, I took a page from our files and caught it with Dean's flame. I had no rebuttal and Dean knew it.

I had little to lose anymore, so I seized the opportunity to question Dean's actions. "Why do you care so much about what I do - about me? It takes a lot of time and energy to follow someone's every move. It's not love, Dean. What do you want?"

The fire burned close to his hand, but he never flinched from the heat. He moved his jaw back and forth and bore his eyes into mine, ignoring the sting. "It's dedication. That's more important than love, anyway. To dedicate yourself to someone and something. Idiots in love can't even do that most of the time."

Dean always got his way. He wanted me away from Sam, and now he had a good reason. I wanted the truth, but it was muddy now. I had given my body and our safety away to Sam, incapable of seeing clearly in his presence. He had chances to tell me, *didn't he?*

I watched the flame grow closer toward my hand and the words *Lawson Family unit* turned to black and crumpled on the page. All I had left were ashes of what our little family never was.

It had been four weeks since the visit from the Galene crew.

Four weeks since I saw our Lawson Family cabin.

Four weeks since Sam had been inside me.

We lived in Dean's room now. The boys slept on individual cots, which they pushed together in an adjoining room. It separated from ours with an actual door - a door I kept open at all times.

Dean held at me at night. His hands traced down my body, trying to rouse something to begin. I doubted he would wait for permission, yet he insisted on my consent. "It won't be any good if you don't want it," he told me. "I have other women on this vessel begging for it. I'll be faithful to you when you give yourself to me."

He meant what he said. I dodged shitty glances from random females more than once. He didn't fuck anyone from my work crew, thankfully, but my team loved to talk. They gossiped about Dean's latest conquest nonstop once they realized I couldn't care less. Sleeping your way to the top was the same in our new world as it was in the old. These women wanted status and protection.

All Dean wanted was to get off.

He never brought the women to our home, and he showered before he came back. He attempted to be respectful, but the effort was lost on me. Sometimes at night, I would awaken to him staring at me while I slept. He would ask if I was having another night terror and what I dreamed about. I must have cried out in my sleep, but I kept my dreams safe inside my head. I only had flashes now - blood on my foot, a fire, and trees.

Dean walked with us to BeLew's school and work. We ate together in the mess hall most days while his other women stared and I scanned the space for Sam. I never saw him.

I spent my days trying to ignore my pathetic messes of discarded relationships. I thought of Sam every moment. I pined for him like a sick schoolgirl. Dean didn't love me, but he wanted to own me. I loved him only because my heart had once. If I loved you before, I loved you forever. Despite that, I could not and would not give my body to Dean again. With a line of women ready to satisfy his needs, he could wait forever. I hated the idea that Sam may not wait.

With no choice but to carry on and survive, I focused on work. We had a full growth of radishes, which I proudly plopped into Lori's kitchen like I had cured cancer. They were sad little vegetables, but I had grown something in this hellhole that would nourish the bodies of others. That was something. I needed a win after all the mistakes I had made - mistakes that kept me in this place with men that tortured my heart.

I continued my nights helping her in the kitchen as the boys did school work and played. BeLew wanted to test out and be in the same class as Lori's kids. They were on a mission, and they spent every evening testing and quizzing each other. They needed consistency, and being together provided that. Being ripped from Sam was a step back.

They saw Sam regularly enough. I never took him off the guardian list for school and he visited daily. Dean allowed it, to my surprise. He accepted my explanation that BeLew loved Sam, and they had lost enough people in their short little lives.

Sam's paperwork had gone up in smoke, and the Captain assumed it was one of the men on the Galene who was responsible. I heard Sam worked in engineering and asked about me often.

He still went by Sam.

"He says it's his nickname," Lori told me one evening as we chopped radishes. We were trying to pickle as many as possible before they went bad. Decomposing radishes smelled like gasoline, and Lori didn't want any alarms in her kitchen.

"I used to eat these in tea sandwiches with my mom," I smiled at the memory. "We would play tea party and take the crust off the bread, stuffing them with odd combinations like radishes and mayonnaise. I hated them, but I thought they were refined or something."

"Do you still think of yourself as refined when you eat them? Give yourself a minute to mull it over, because we will eat them for months."

"I haven't thought of myself as refined since I was seven."

"How are you doing with... everything?"

I grabbed a knife and chopped. "Do you think the girls in the lower decks would like a tea party?"

"As I've said before, I love your ability to change the subject, Row. It's quite the skill. I hope you'll teach me one day."

"Maybe I should hold a seminar."

We chopped and piled the pieces high. Lori had machinery that did a lot of the work for us, but there was always more to do by hand. It seemed like most of the items that needed repair around the kitchen were fixed right away, and she implied Sam had a hand in that.

"What do you think of Sam's situation?" Lori pressed. "Row, what do you want to do? Tell me how to help you."

I ceased my chopping and stared at the knife I held, frozen in time. I set my hands on the counter, letting the knife clatter as it slipped from my grasp.

He still went by Sam. After knowing who he truly was, he still went by Sam.

Lori's chopping stopped, and she stepped over, hooking her arm in mine. "If you tell me to stop bringing it up, I will."

"No, you won't," I murmured. "Please... don't."

I wanted to hear about him, and I hated myself every time my heart fluttered at the mention of his name. He penetrated my soul and my every thought. I slept in a bed next to Dean, wishing I saw Sam's scarred yet beautiful body lying next to me. I had no information about who he was and why he was here. His ticket on an island jumper meant he was something to somebody, but I couldn't find a way to speak with him and find out what.

Dean kept guards on our floor, and they didn't permit Sam to even enter our stairwell. He had tried and failed many times. I wasn't blind to the random recruits that seemed to linger in front of the kitchen, either. A drone followed overhead when I walked the deck. Someone was always watching, always tracking.

Dean ripped Sam from me without my permission, but my distrust made me agreeable to our separation. He had hurt me, and he never had the chance to explain why. What if my heart couldn't take the explanation? I had seen us as a family - in this together.

"I miss him." I could barely exhale. "Every single day."

No tears left my body. I still hid those outward emotions when I could, even though the innermost part of me wanted to scream and cry and hurt him as much as he had hurt me.

Lori remained immobile, watching as I thumbed the blade of the knife that lay on the cutting board. I pushed too hard and watched the blood pool over the silver edge, hoping to feel something else, another form of hurt.

"It's been four weeks. I want to see him."

Lori pulled the knife from me and tossed it in the sink. "I can arrange a meeting."

My eyes stayed on the blood. Lori was angry with him for a few days after the incident in the storage unit, but something had changed in her after a conversation with him. Sam had gotten to her, and that changed Lori's perception of the whole mess.

The blood continued to drip from my finger. I was numb everywhere except for my love for BeLew, and my sick longing for Sam.

"We're bringing supplies to the two hundred tomorrow night. He can be there," she urged. Her eyebrows lifted as she wrapped my hand in a towel. "I'll call Luke and set it up."

I nodded as the rest of my body remained motionless.
Four weeks since we held each other in our bed.
Four weeks since I tasted his cum in my mouth.
Four weeks since I felt his lips on my body.
Seven weeks since I had a period.

CHAPTER SEVENTEEN

LIAR

THERE WAS NO SUCH thing as a weekend on a farm. Animals ate every day, and machinery broke down when it wanted. People complained about misplaced weekends more than anything else on Thalassa, and they loved nothing more than to gossip and grumble. In their lives before, they had looked forward to a Friday night. Now they worked ten days in a row with one or two off. Weekends weren't my reality for as long as I could remember, so it wasn't a loss for me.

The school remained open seven days a week. They either stayed on pace, repeated studies, or tested out. All four boys made it into the same class and planned to stick together. Lori and I kept them in six days a week, mostly because there was nothing for them to do outside those walls.

It was a mundane existence. Time meant nothing and days ran together, and that was how we carried on for several weeks. It wasn't until I had a reason that I started counting time.

Twenty-four hours until I see Sam.

How many weeks had I been on this boat? When was the first and last time I was with Sam? Where was my fucking period?

Time mattered again.

Dean hadn't returned to our cabin yet, and BeLew stayed with Lori and the boys to play on deck. I rocked back and forth on the edge of the mattress, contemplating what I would tell Dean. He had walked me home an hour ago and left again. He was with a woman, no doubt, not that it mattered. It might put him in a good mood. His mood grew worse each day, each time I rejected his advances.

He knew about Lori helping the two hundred, but we never spoke about me taking part. He might not care. Not once had I mentioned Sam's name, not in our four weeks together. He wouldn't suspect him to be there. *Or was that a lie I was telling myself to get through this conversation?*

When the door opened, I stilled my rocking, unsure of what would happen next. My dreams lately were pieces of an impossible puzzle - a fire with puffs of smoke reaching the sky, my foot soaked in blood, running through trees in the darkness. Sam wasn't there, and neither were BeLew. I shuddered at what that might mean. I wished I had concentrated on my visions over the past month, and willed them to show me something about this day or this plan. It might not have worked, but my nerves spun in overdrive, and I chastised myself for not trying.

I never spoke to Dean the first hour or two when he came home. He would be content from his encounter, but also frustrated. No need to poke the bear. Unfortunately, I had to get tonight over with, so I lacked the patience for our typical two-hour delay.

"How was your workday?" My question was simple enough, unassuming.

"Boring. Monotonous as always. As was the past hour after I got off work." He tilted his chin down towards me, begging me to inquire. His bait hung thick in the air between us.

"Come sit with me." I patted the mattress at my side, and he obliged. His hand moved under my shirt and up my back. I resisted the urge to wince or lean away. His other hand gripped mine and he moved it onto his leg, forcing an intimate seating arrangement. I gritted my teeth and crossed my legs in his direction.

"What's up, Rowan? You need something from me?" He moved to my ear, gently nipping. His nails ran down my back, and I did my best not to react. He knew me too well. What buttons to push.

"I want to go to the lower decks and help Lori. I have before, but I want to be honest with you about it."

He moved his head back, and I turned to face him.

"That's bold, Row. Your soft heart has gotten you into trouble before. What makes you think it won't again?"

"I've never thought of myself as soft-hearted, but I don't want to lose what's left of my empathy. Albeit there isn't much remaining." I grimaced, knowing that was pure honesty. It had been Dean's advice to stick to the truth as much as possible when I spewed lies. I had to see Sam, but I needed to help the stowaways before my heart turned to stone.

"Do you have any empathy for my situation?" Dean's nails scratched harder up and down my back.

"You know I love you," I admitted. "That can't and won't change."

"In what way, though? Love like a friend, or a man you want inside you? Somewhere in the middle, maybe?" His mouth moved back to my ear. "This broken heart of yours should have healed up by now. Sam is a liar. You think he's pining for you in that small bed he used to fuck you in? He's living it up a few doors down from Matthews. Now that he knows he's safe, he's getting more pussy than I am. And we both know I'm fucking everything I can to keep my mind off of your sweet cunt."

I flinched, and Dean moved his hand to the back of my head, pushing his fingers through my hair. "What part of that bothers you?"

"Both parts, if I'm being honest."

"Seems to be your motto lately, not that I mind." Dean's fingers curled around the base of my hair and tugged. My head dropped back, exposing my neck. He moved his mouth to it, gently licking and sucking. He moved my hand between his legs, and his cock twitched when my hand wrapped around his length.

Play the game, Rowan.

He gripped my hair harder, causing me to gasp. Lifting his face to mine, my breath turned uneven and ragged. I still had a visceral response to Dean. His force and confidence could make me wet, even when I feared him. I wasn't proud of it, but accepting your weaknesses gives you power over them. This encounter needed to stop, even if a fight took its place.

"You were just inside another woman," I hissed.

His grasp on my hair tightened, making my eyes water. "And whose fault is that? You lay next to me every night and feel my dick hard against your ass. You ignore it, pretend I'm not there, like you can't do a damn thing about it. When I'm not here, do you touch yourself thinking about Rivera? He's not thinking about you."

Tears stung my eyes from the pull at the nape of my neck. His hold hurt, but his words cut deeper. I felt Dean stiffen against me every night, and I wished it was Sam. I would close my eyes and pretend I was back in bed with Sam, running my fingers over his scarred back, feeling his ice-blue eyes watch me at night.

"Let me go, Dean. You're hurting me."

He released me and threw himself back on the bed. "I don't give a shit what you do with the two hundred, Row. I don't give a shit what you do at all."

"Thank you," I whispered, and made my way to BeLew's room. I made myself busy, making their beds and picking up their things, and hoping Dean wouldn't figure out my plan.

The stairwells I once thought took a lifetime to descend, now seemed to fly by at warp speed. Lori droned on and on about Luke and their time together. They were a couple, and she recited every detail of their relationship without hesitation. I was happy for her, but she never disclosed what I wanted to know. *What did Sam tell Lori that made her empathize with him?*

"It's not my news to tell," she would reply when I asked. "When you see him, he'll discuss it with you. If

I could, I would, Rowan. You know that. I don't keep things from you."

The sacks in my arms grew heavy, and I knew we were close. Dread coursed through my veins, but so did excitement.

"I hope you don't mind Luke teaching the boys first aid tonight in the clinic. He got called into work. But hell, they'll need it wherever we are going. Set the bags down there," Lori motioned.

"We aren't taking them in?" I lined the sacks against the wall of the common area.

"You aren't. The fourth door on the right. Sam's already there, has been for over an hour," Lori winked.

I nodded and headed down the hallway. I tapped nervously on my thighs with every step. My hand touched the door and turned the handle, keeping the door shut and flush with the wall while I drew on my courage.

Four weeks since I'd seen him.

The door pulled from the other side, causing me to stumble forward. I felt Sam's warmth wrap around my body in the darkened room. His familiar scent, the stubble on his cheeks, and the strength in his arms as they held me overwhelmed my senses. My knees felt weak beneath me as Sam lifted me, my legs wrapping around him as his mouth took mine.

The door shut behind us, and my eyes took a moment to adjust to the pitch-black room. That didn't stop our attack on each other bodies. He pushed me against a steel wall, and I clawed at his back, feeling him swell between my legs. His hands kneaded my ass, pulling me up to the right spot.

"Your leg," I stammered, breaking our kiss.

"Is better now," he interrupted, his lips back on mine as he lowered me to a hard surface. His hands opened my pants and pulled them down my thighs.

I yanked at his pants, moving them down. *Fuck, his body was perfection.*

"You lied to me," I reminded him as I dragged his shirt over his head. My vision had returned, and Sam hovered over me in his magnificent form. *Fuck, his body looked amazing.*

"I did, but I thought I could start over. It was a lie by omission."

I shoved his pants off and felt him spring free on my leg, then slapped his bare chest, pushing him away from me. "Still a fucking lie."

He grabbed my wrists and drew me to him. "I love you, Rowan."

"I know," was all I could manage as he pushed himself into me, his fingers digging into my skin as he plunged into my body. He was fucking me, not making love to me, and I preferred it this way. I wanted him to be ruthless and dominant. I wanted the fight, and I wanted the fuck.

One hand moved around my throat. I could breathe without trouble, but the message was clear. He craved my submission, my attention.

My response was to slap him again in the chest. "How could I love someone I don't know?" He barely nudged backward and kept a steady pace.

I hit him on the cheek the next time and immediately regretted the act. He stopped, still buried inside me, and moved his face to mine, nose to nose.

"I'm sorry," I breathed. "Sam, I'm sorry."

He exhaled and continued his movements, slower than before. "Hit me again if you want to, Row. Slap me." I shook my head no, and tears stung my eyes. "You want to hit me. You're angry. You have a right to be. Do it."

He pushed himself to the hilt, filling me completely, and held himself there for a moment before he pulled out again. He baited me to hit him – waited to see if I would. I pulsed with need, and he kept pausing. He entered me with such trepidation now I felt myself pulling him back with my heels.

"I hate that you lied to me," I choked out. "Don't stop. Please don't stop. I don't want to hit you. I'm sorry."

"I love you, Rowan." His control remained. He lingered inside me now as I rocked myself against him, desperate for release.

"I won't hit you again. Please don't stop," I begged. Not the place I thought I'd find myself — begging for him — but I couldn't go back now. He stopped, motionless except for his mouth and tongue, kissing my neck and chest. "I didn't let Dean have me, Sam. It's yours like you said. I didn't let him."

His back tensed, muscles rippling down his spine. He looked up at me and when his blue eyes met mine, a growl vibrated in his chest. Something had ignited inside him. His movements quickened, and his arms reached completely around my back, holding me against him and lifting me slightly off the table.

"You love me, Rowan." He was practically climbing onto the table, pumping and pinning me to the back wall.

I whimpered his name when I came, scratching my nails down his back, almost drawing blood. He swelled and filled me with heat, the pulse of his cock throbbing against my walls in an unbearable stretch. "You love me," he repeated.

I relaxed after my climax, and my body fell limp on the table. He was the perfect sight hovering above me. The man I wanted, despite everything, desperate for me to love him back. *What have I done?*

"I do, you asshole. I fucking love you."

Chapter Eighteen

Power and Control

W E DRESSED IN SILENCE, and Sam kept his eyes glued to my body. He licked his lips and sighed. I blushed under his gaze, even though he had seen every part of me.

"Where does Dean think you are?" he asked.

"Exactly where I am. In the lower decks."

"I've heard he's making his way through every woman on the ship. And you haven't been with him?" Sam stepped back and crossed his arms in front of his chest. "Is that true?"

I buttoned my pants and flipped him off. Immature, yes, but a fair representation of how I felt. "Who's the liar, Sam? Who, exactly, lied? This isn't a rhetorical question. I want you to answer me. I need you to admit it and then ask me again if I lied so you would keep fucking me like some desperate whore."

He dropped his arms and huffed out a breath. "I love your fire, Row. I lied to you. A lie by omission, but still a lie. A lie because I was desperate to start over with you... but... still a lie. Please forgive me."

His arms curved around my body and pulled me to his chest. "I've been dying of jealousy. It's been unbearable, imagining you in his bed every night. It killed me to accept it, and to hear it never happened... I'm just surprised after our last argument when you told me you would have to give into him."

Sam's scent intoxicated my senses. I folded into his embrace and breathed him in. I had learned that lingering on disagreements didn't do any good. We forgave each other every time, but he wasn't off the hook that easily.

"He hasn't... forced. He's made his intentions known, but he hasn't pushed it. He claims you are partaking in the same brothel he is. He acts like you moved on with every available woman too."

"Rowan," he seethed. "You cannot believe that." He stiffened, fury pouring out with every word. "That piece of shit would say anything to get his way."

"I didn't believe him."

Sam took a step back from me, growling under his breath. "Good, because it's not true."

"I know that. Lori said you were still only interested in, you know, us, I guess."

"Lori told you I was still in love with you and only you. Do you know how many times I tried to get to you? Do you know I have twenty stitches from fighting one of Dean's men to enter your floor? When I got there, you weren't even in the cabin."

I put my hand to his lips to stop him. "I know you wanted to see me, and I know Dean made it impossible, but I'm here now. Understand that I was hurting. I'm still hurting."

Sam's eyes pleaded with mine. His hands moved to my jaw, tracing his thumbs on my lips. "I died in that ditch. When I closed my eyes, I was ready to let go. But meeting you, being cared for by you, it woke me back up. I don't know how else to describe it. I never wanted life more. I want our life together. Our family and you, that's the only thing that keeps me going. I can't breathe without you."

His words were exactly what I needed to hear. It's how I had hoped he felt, like this place had given us another chance at more than just survival. It gave us life.

"It felt like a fucking heart attack every day without you, but I kept going out of some pathetic hope I'd have you again," he continued, each word more desperate than the last. "There is no one else. If you're gone, I'm done. Do you understand? You and BeLew are the reason I have the will to keep going on this piece of shit ship. I went about this all wrong. I should have trusted you more, but I wanted to forget, forget all of it before. Do you know what that's like?"

I kissed him, and every terrible memory disappeared for a moment. All my thoughts were of him and how stupid I had been. It was obvious he had a past he regretted, and I had been unfair because I was scared - terrified even. The more you cared about someone, the more you had to lose.

I hated the past as much as he did. The future that pushed itself into my dreams scared me just as much. I wanted right now, this moment, with him.

It was impossible to pull away from his lips, but the clock was ticking. Our time together was finite.

I touched his cheek, letting his face rest on my palm. "Dean knows where I am, but that doesn't mean I have all night. I need to know your story, all of it, and I'll tell you mine — everything."

Sam kissed the top of my forehead and stroked my hair. "You're so beautiful."

"You're stalling. Start with the branding on your back."

Sam's jaw tightened, and he sucked in a breath. Fighting the urge to smack him again, I stood motionless, waiting for him to concede.

"Okay, well, the boys aren't around, so now is good." He relaxed his grip around me and lowered us to the floor. We sat with our legs outstretched, backs against the cold metal wall. We held hands, staring into the dim empty room.

"You know I was married before. Her name was Cecilia. We sort of separated, and she died, or it happened the other way around." He ran his hand through his hair, pulling at the ends in frustration. "I can't really be sure. I'm not sure of anything anymore."

"I'm here, I'm listening," I whispered into his ear. I rubbed my thumb along the back of his hand and kissed his cheek.

"It all went to shit with the AOE. I mean, things were already going to shit, but with us, it was because of the AOE. Some of my wife's family entered the Assembly of the Eternal in its beginning. We thought they were insane, but when all their bullshit started, no one knew how outrageous they would get. Her parents joined and gave away their life savings, and unfortunately, ours as well."

I gasped and pulled my knees to my stomach, wrapping my free arm around my legs.

"Right, I know. She had some joint accounts with them, and they had access to some things. They wiped us out. I had to tell my employer when it happened."

"Your employer?" I interrupted. "And that is?"

"I was in the Navy for twelve years, got injured, and moved to a desk. I worked in engineering. As time went on, they assigned me to foreign threats. When most threats became domestic, I was on a team to investigate the Assembly of the Eternal. So, my bank accounts being drained by them didn't look great."

I nodded, enthralled by every word.

"When they found out, they had a proposition. My wife and I could join the AOE undercover. At first, I thought it was insane, but when I went to tell Cecilia, she wanted to do it. I think there was a mix of wanting to see her family because she missed and loved them, and a strong desire to claw their eyes out for betraying her."

I chuckled at his comment. Cecilia sounded like a strong woman who had been through some shit. I understood that. I went back and forth between hating and loving my family, so I related to how she must have felt.

"You would have liked her," Sam muttered, echoing my thoughts. "Anyway, we did it. We didn't have a lot to lose at that point. The government likes to make you think you have a choice in things, but we knew they would've made it an order eventually, at least for me. This way, we could be together. And it would guarantee our safety long term. Things had been going downhill fast on land and there were lots of underground bunkers and paths to safety at sea in process, more than just these ships. We needed a spot somewhere."

"There are people hiding on land?" I asked.

Sam squinted and looked up at the ceiling. He might have said too much, but I let him continue. "I can't be sure, but I think so. There were lots of schematics I had access to — places for survivors. I consulted on projects for several ideas. Some of them have to be out there, like Thalassa. Anyway, becoming a part of the AOE gave Cecilia and me protection somewhere. They would've given her a spot on the Galene."

"So, you were supposed to be on that ship from the beginning? What happened?"

"Besides being impaled on my way to find a vehicle," Sam grinned. He paused a moment, taking in a deep breath. "She was dead by then." He let out the air from his lungs.

"So that day, what happened that day I found you?"

"The storms came quicker than expected and upped the deploy date. I thought I had more time is all. I wasn't suicidal. I tried to get to the Galene."

I lifted my hand to his chin and brought it back down to my gaze. "Okay, so what happened when you were with the AOE?"

He gave me a chaste kiss and continued. "We received the brands early on to prove our loyalty, and they re-united Cecilia with her family. They never apologized for taking the money, and it was clear they never would. Their view was the AOE would save humanity. Our savings account didn't matter when it came to saving the world. They believed that with every fiber of their being and, with time... Cecilia believed it too."

I brought my hand to my mouth to prevent any words from escaping. She betrayed him. Whatever happened to her, she had killed herself. Alignment with the AOE ended in death, even when good people with good intentions joined. But I couldn't say that to him. I couldn't believe it myself with my sister's death, so I knew how he felt.

I reached for Sam and he gripped my hand, his fingers wound tightly around mine. I felt the cut on my thumb open. He trembled, but his voice kept steady.

"I was in denial at first. I believed she was in character and would snap out of it. But the truth was I lost her in there. We didn't train her to be inside an enemy camp. She couldn't compartmentalize the situation and, to add to the problem, her family was a powerful and comforting force, shifting her views. For the last few months, I was pretending to be in it with her. I still loved her, but I lost her. I didn't know what to do."

He shook his head, and I saw the pain in his face. "I'm deceitful. I betrayed you like I did Cecilia by pretending to be someone I'm not. She believed I was obedient until the day I left her."

"You left her? Then how did she..." I trailed off.

"The swim happened a week after I left the AOE. I had gathered the intel needed, and it was time to leave. The night I fled, I tried to get her to come with me. She sounded an alarm, and I had to knock her out. I almost took her unconscious body with me. I could have easily carried her, but I thought it was too late. I thought she was happier with her family in their ignorance. I didn't know they would all be dead in a few days." He slid his fingers out of mine. "You're bleeding."

"Oh, I cut my hand on a knife in the kitchen," I explained.

He attempted to stand, and I pulled him back down, keeping him on the floor with me. "You haven't lost me, Sam. I'm here, in love with you."

He pulled me into his lap. His fingers traced my jaw while his thumb pulled my bottom lip down.

"We are still in this together," he said. His face moved to mine, taking my mouth.

I separated my lips from him to answer, "Yes." Our foreheads touching, I left kisses on his cheeks and nose. "Is this what you told Lori? Is this why she has a soft spot for you?"

A coy smile crossed his lips.

"She doesn't know every piece of the story, but she knows enough. She knows I lost my wife to the AOE and my service. I told her I was miserable without you and in love with you. She knows that I stupidly thought I could put everything behind me and start over as your husband, not this broken man who lost everything and had to try again."

I ran my fingers through his hair and settled closer to him, trying to comfort him. I couldn't get close enough, knowing I almost lost him. "Thank you for telling me. Nothing between us anymore, okay?"

"Except Dean. Let's not forget that issue. So, what now? We sneak around like teenagers? How many times can you help the two hundred before he gets suspicious?"

Sam was right. Dean's passive-aggressive comment was a one-time deal. He went to extraordinary lengths to ensure that Sam and I stayed apart. Dean always got his way. That he hadn't won me over yet drove him further over the edge. If he knew Sam and I were together, there would be worse than toilets in Sam's future.

In fact, Sam's safety aboard this vessel surprised me. The Galene was not in a convoy with us. Accidents happened and Dean had friends on this ship. Sam could be zip-tied and chucked over the side in the dead of night, and who would do anything about it? "Has Dean tried to do anything to you? I mean, threaten you?"

"No, and I don't think he will."

"Don't be so sure."

"He would lose you forever, Rowan. If I disappeared or got hurt, you would never give in to him. He's smart. Probably the smartest fuck I've ever come across. It's too bad he focuses all that on serving himself."

"Dean is a special brand of horrible, but his entire focus isn't to hurt others. It sometimes comes out that way, I'll admit."

"No, he wants power at any cost," Sam shot back. "He wants to influence and control those around him. He gets off on it. You see that?"

"It is power, Sam. It has and always will be power. That doesn't explain his obsession with me."

"It's not love? You two have a history."

"No," I almost laughed. "He said it was dedication, in fact. I asked him. He said dedication counts more than love."

"Does he owe you something? Why is he dedicated to you? Is it because of the baby?"

"You're giving him too much credit. It's always what suits Dean, what gets him what he wants."

"And what could he get from you?"

Thoughts swam in my head about what Dean was after. He was involved in so many oddities with the agriculture unit, chemistry, and the two hundred growing poppy flowers.

His desire for me didn't make sense. It didn't fit.

My brain buzzed like fire and, for a moment, the mess we were in suddenly became clear. I stood and paced back and forth. I recalled his incessant questions about my night terrors. He drove me insane by constantly asking. How many times had I told him not to worry about them?

Sam studied my movements. "Rowan, are you okay?"

Dean knows. He knows about me.

"Sam, it's time I tell you about my past. And I need to start with my dreams."

Chapter Nineteen

The Seer

B EFORE THE THIRD STORM, I had dreamed about my sister. It had been so clear the facts were irrefutable, but I was an expert at denial. In the dream, I held the cold metal of the gun in my hand while my sister and her husband stood in front of me. Blood poured from their eyes, mouths, and stomachs. It trailed down her neck, dripped onto her shoulder, and encircled the flames that branded her arm. Beau and Lewis screamed in the distance, and then I awoke.

The first time I had the dream, I knew nothing of their ties to the Assembly of the Eternal. As months passed and the situation became desperate, the dreams increased in frequency. I was afraid of sleep and the nightmares it would bring.

When I stood in the field with them that day, I knew the outcome. When it was over, I remembered my sister's words from the week before. "If anything were to happen, Row, get Dean. He can help. He'll protect you. He knows he needs you. He knows how powerful you are."

I thought she meant to get Dean if she killed her husband or tried to run off with the boys, but that was denial. I knew the truth, even though I never told her this dream. The one dream I kept from her.

I replayed those words in my head repeatedly in the small room with Sam that night. "He knows he needs you. He knows how powerful you are."

He knew about my premonitions.

She told him.

She tried to protect me.

He'd known when he came to the field that day, undressed my sister and her husband, and burned their bodies. He'd spread their ashes in the lake, dropping pieces of their clothing on the shore's mud. AOE would assume they took the swim, that they'd obeyed. He'd searched for hours for the shells and cleaned the guns for half a day.

Only he'd known why he did that for us, the true reason. He had to keep me close and safe and in the dark about what he wanted from me. He got me onto this ship because he thought my sight would protect him. Dean desired more control and planned to use me and drugs along the way.

Sam knew my sister died because of the AOE, but I divulged all the details that night, starting with the dream. He listened intently, his face unchanged throughout, unsure if my admission made me crazy.

Sam held me and kissed my hair when he felt me quiver. "Sam, that day in the bunker, he said, *you're sweating and shaking. It seems more like night terrors again.* He said again. I never told him about my dreams, but my sister did. He wants me close, so I'm with him when I dream. He asks what I dreamed about constantly, orchestrating a way to get me closer, to trust him again. I can't believe I didn't see this before."

"Are you sure you aren't reaching?" Sam's tone was gentle. "Lots of people had dreams about losing loved ones when the world went insane. That doesn't mean you saw what would happen."

"Sam, my dreams show the future. I saw the stowaways sinking in the water with their hands tied behind their backs. I saw my baby die in my arms years before it happened. I won't bore you with the list of nightmares that have come to pass. You just have to trust me. This gift or curse, depending on your outlook, it's a force in this world. If the vision comes to me, it's fucking happening. And no one can stop it. What I see is inescapable."

Sam nodded, digesting the information, taking everything in. His pseudo-wife told him she was psychic. That was a big pill to swallow. "Dean wants drugs on the ship for control and status. And maybe... he needs you for protection?" Sam asked.

"Did Lori tell you what we think he's doing in chemistry?"

Sam nodded. "She let it slip. It's dangerous for you — for you both."

"Yes," I agreed. I shook my head erasing the worry. "But the dreams... they don't work like Dean thinks. I'm not a movie reel of what's coming. I didn't dream for years until the storms started. My whole life, I've gotten the visions wrong. When what I dreamed of comes to life, I recognize the signs, but it's always too late. It's like watching a car accident. There isn't enough time to do anything but scream."

"And you have tried since the dreams came back?"

"Well," I paused. "I haven't tried since having the pre-monitions as an adult. The last time was when I was a girl. The visions I'm having now, though, I can't figure out what they mean. There is a huge fire and smoke is covering the sky. I'm getting slapped by leaves running through trees. My foot is covered in bright red blood. A fire on the ship is bad, Sam — very bad."

"True, but as you said, it will happen. Are you sure this happens on the ship? Maybe this happens when we land."

Bang. Bang. Bang.

Someone knocked on the door, and our conversation came to an abrupt halt.

"It's just me. Time to go," Lori hollered. I opened the door, fully dressed, to Lori's apparent surprise. She tsked at me and looked us over. "You two fuck and make up?"

Sam wrapped his arm around my waist from behind and kissed my neck, answering her question. "Thank you, Lori," he said. "For helping me get the woman I love back."

"Why sir, I do declare." She blushed and gave herself a fan with her hand. "I'll meet you at the stairs in five minutes, Rowan. Sam, you need to be thirty behind us at least." Lori gave a wink, then left.

"In two days, you're coming back to help the two hundred," Sam said. "In the meantime, think about what the visions mean. And Row, Dean will bring you in with the drugs soon."

"W-what?" I stammered. "He won't. He doesn't think I know."

"Yes, he does. Why do you think Lori knows? He's smart, Row. Don't underestimate him. She's the bait to butter you up to the idea. He may think you already dreamed about people strung out on heroin. Who knows? But he told her because he wants you to know. Be ready."

Heroin. The word left unspoken until now. The drug had destroyed countless lives before the water and the wind had a chance. It had spread through our town and the world, ripping apart families. Every night the news would have the count of how many had died in our state from overdoses. There had to be recovering addicts on this ship - easy prey to help start a dictatorship. *And I was to be his seer?*

A part of my heart ripped out when I left Sam. Forty-eight hours until I saw him again. Maybe then I would have the courage to tell him about the seven weeks, but I had confessed enough today. Just like my visions, nothing changed what was already in motion.

I made it two flights of stairs before Lori started pumping me for information. It relieved her I knew about Sam's wife, but she was most interested in hearing dirty details about the sex. Some things I would never divulge, but I confessed to her I told Sam I loved him. She teared up a few times, acknowledging how she felt Sam was sincere in his feelings for me. He'd begged her to help him, and she was a sucker for second chances.

"I wish Luke looked at me the way Sam does you," she confided. "He looks at me like I'm a meal or something to be had. Don't get me wrong, I'm into it, but I think it may be lust, not love."

"Luke's good with the boys, and he seems infatuated with you," I assured her. "Sam and I had this traumatic horrible event, you know. We thought he was dead more than once, and I think it fast-tracked his way of doing things. Normal, healthy adults don't move this fast."

"Normal people don't look like him either, Row. That man is sex on a stick."

We put everything away in her kitchen, and I lingered. Leaving meant I had to face Dean and our bed together. All the while, my heart stayed next to Sam, wherever he was on this ship. Lori acted eager to get back to Luke, who was waiting for her, so my stalling was short-lived. I took the slowest walk down my hallway, stopped in the bathroom to give myself a hard look in the mirror, and then crept into the room to find Dean sitting up in bed reading a book.

Shit.

"Hey," I mumbled. I checked on BeLew who were sleeping soundly, strangling their stuffed ducks under their arms. I kissed them on the head and went to the sink to brush my teeth and avoid eye contact with Dean.

Dean kept his head down on the pages, but his eyes followed me. "Aren't you going to ask what I'm reading?"

"I can see what you are reading, and you have read it a hundred times." Dean read *The Kite Runner*, which I always found an odd choice for him.

"I like stories of retribution. What can I say?"

The story was more about forgiveness, but people see things through their own personal lens.

He slammed the book closed and chucked it under the bed, walking over to me. I felt his warmth press behind me and his hands on my shoulders. "How were the lower decks?"

I spit in the sink and looked back up to meet his eyes in the mirror. "Fine. Nothing too exciting." My skin buzzed from the lie.

He moved his hands down my back and kissed my neck while I stood there with toothpaste lips. "Dean, did you want to keep reading because I'm exhausted?" I wiped my lips with my sleeve and edged out from between the sink and his grasp.

"Sure Row, let's go to bed." He followed me under the covers, spooning me from behind, pushing himself against me. It was apparent enough what he was after without his dick stabbing me in the back. I tried not to move.

"No again?" he questioned, running his fingers down the side of my arm. "I didn't mean what I said earlier about not caring what you do. I care very much. I love you, Rowan."

He knew I was still awake, but saying it back was a betrayal to Sam. I loved Dean, but that love was out of obligation. "I know," was all I could manage.

What felt like an hour later, I assumed he was asleep. I turned onto my back. He reached around my middle, startling me, and spoke again. "I've made a lot of mistakes. I know that. But what I do, it's for you and the boys." I nodded in the dark, wishing I could just sleep and dream of Sam. I welcomed a premonition at this point if it meant this conversation and this night could be over.

His arm tightened around me, pulling us closer together. "I'll keep waiting," he murmured. His exhaustion set in, making his arm fall heavy and his breathing slowed. "And Row, tomorrow we work in chemistry. Just remember, I do it all for you and the boys. Because I love you."

He stilled, drifting into a peaceful sleep. But I was not as fortunate. That night I dreamed of Sam, but not in the way I wanted. It began with a blinding light, and I could barely see past the fire that burned my retinas. I wandered around the deck of the ship, feeling heat pinch my skin.

When I found Sam, he was too far away, and I couldn't get to him. He ran into the flames as smoke billowed up to the sky above us and I chased after him. I screamed his name, watching him disappear into the burning wall of fire.

CHAPTER TWENTY

FAMILIAR FACES

THE NEXT MORNING, REELING from my nightmare, I dressed in a fog. I asked BeLew to repeat themselves several times, unfocused on our conversation. Dean was no better, consumed with the day ahead. The boys knew something was wrong, but they were making volcanos at school that day, and that consumed their minds. Motherhood still perplexed me, but one thing I knew for certain was that young boys loved blowing shit up.

"Are you sure baking soda and vinegar make a volcano?" Beau asked.

"It is sodium hydrogen carbonate and if the teacher said it will, it will," Lewis asserted.

Their eyes gazed up at me for confirmation, and I stood slack-jawed, my mind one thousand miles away. "Um, yes, it will work."

"Why?" they asked in unison.

"How long will it take? Do we have to wait all day?" Beau continued.

"Something about molecules and hydrogen. It doesn't take long. Here, take my watch today and you can time it.

Don't lose it. Anyway, in about ten minutes when we get to school, you can ask all the questions you want. That's where you learn things."

"Right, because we're not learning much of anything here," Beau giggled. Lewis agreed with a nod. I groaned, and we shuffled out the door.

Dean held my elbow back as we turned a corner in the hallway toward the Classis rooms. "I'll meet you at work. I need to get there early and add you to the security board," he said.

"Right, okay t-thanks," I stuttered. I had almost forgotten that today he would take me to the chemistry building. Before I continued back down the hallway, he pulled me into a kiss. It was short but firm. When his lips left mine, his eyes looked past me and he smirked at the space behind us. When I heard BeLew squeal Sam's name, my eyes rolled. *Still an asshole.*

"You should come with me now," Dean ordered.

"Dean, please," I begged. "I don't want to miss the kid's volcano. I promised. There are parents everywhere. Don't worry about Sam."

He cocked his head, every vein in his neck protruding. I hugged the bastard, running my hands up and down his back, trying to get him to agree.

"I'll see you right after," he snipped. Dean pulled back, turned, and left.

Thanks for the hour hall pass.

I stomped down the hallway. The boys had their arms wrapped around Sam and his eyes met mine, burning with fire. He gave them a pat on their backs and steered them into the room.

We came at each other so fast we almost collided. His hands gripped my arms and held me against him. "You're pushing your luck already," I said into his chest. "Were you waiting for me?"

"You're just a pleasant surprise," he teased. "They asked me to co-host the explosion at school today. Volcanos and fire and all, they want someone from engineering to oversee the chaos."

"You volunteered."

"Yes. Yes, I did."

We stepped to the side, letting kids shuffle into the room.

"You know, that kiss, Dean, just..." I trailed off.

"I'm not worried about Dean," Sam scoffed. "I'm happy to see you. Even if I had to grit through that scene first. I want to kiss you more than anything right now, but I don't know how many spies Dean has in this place."

I moved closer, brushing my nipples against Sam's chest. "I want to do more than kiss."

"Down woman. Last Dean heard, you aren't talking to me. I'm surprised you're allowed near me."

"What time is the explosion?"

Sam gave a wide smile. "I'm sorry, what?"

I smacked him on the chest. "The volcano explosion. When is it? You're here before attendance."

"Oh, maybe an hour from now. What time do you have to be at work?"

"I have maybe thirty minutes, an hour. I can make up something."

I felt Sam grow against my stomach. The draw to him was worse than whatever drug Dean cooked up in chemistry. It withstood all reason, all common sense.

I thought I'd loved Dean once, but this obsession, this need I had for Sam, this love, made me irrational. It made me do senseless things.

Sam licked his lips and moved his mouth to my ear. "The hallway along the mess hall, when you get to the dead-end and turn right..."

"Those are the engineering cabins?" I interrupted.

Sam trailed his nails down my arm. "Bunk three seventy-two. Count to fifty and then start walking."

When he turned to leave me, the fire in my dream flashed in my memory and I pushed it away. Whatever our future held was all the more reason to make the present worthwhile.

I craved Sam, and why should I wait? What if there was no tomorrow? What if all I had left were thirty minutes with him worshiping every part of my body? It was worth it. The storms, the fear, the excitement - it was a fleeting point in time that could crash at any moment.

My plans for the future crashed and burned one hundred times over in my life. I accepted my lack of control in this world. My dreams told me that. No matter what I did, destiny had its own plans.

I waved to the boys in the window as I flew down the hall minutes later. Sam and I were in this together, and we would be together... in every way.

His new cabin was twice as big as our first one, further confirming the politics of this ship overshadowed practicality. A single person in all that space was a waste, and we both knew it. The sooner we could be together, the better for our family.

We only had twenty minutes, and I hit my knees as soon as the door shut behind me. Undressing while I had his dick in my mouth was a new timesaving skill.

He had bent me over a desk, merciless with his force. I basked in the pain and pleasure as my hips slammed into the cold metal.

He panted, "I love you," as he came inside me, and it reminded me of the seven weeks that had passed.

Sam had been rough, and I would have the bruises to show for it later.

To keep my story straight, I joined the class for the initial test and, thankfully, BeLew went first. If asked, they could corroborate my alibi. My satisfaction from our morning overpowered my small twinge of guilt.

Flushed and sated, I stepped into the chemistry building alongside Dean. He held my wrist as we stepped inside like he was walking a pet. He was short-tempered about my tardiness, but when I explained the boys had to show me the volcanic explosion in all its glory, he calmed down.

"Where's your watch?" Dean spat. He held my wrist up as we stood in the empty white room. Only chairs and tables filled the space.

It took a moment to register his question. "Um... you were there. I gave it to the boys to time the volcano. They won't lose it. Sometimes I think they're more responsible than me."

"Well, be sure they are."

I shot Dean a look of annoyance. He was protective of his things, and that included me. "This looks like a meeting room. What is this?"

He tugged my arm and brought me to the corner of the room. Releasing me, he opened a drawer at a nearby table and pulled out a crowbar. Placing the flat edge in a slot of the tiled floor, he pulled the bar towards him and a piece of the ground lifted to reveal a stairwell underneath. It resembled a hidden basement, and I would never have guessed it was there.

"Pull it over," Dean commanded, and I did as I was told. He placed the tool back into the desk and we descended, closing the entryway behind us. The room above us looked as if nothing was out of place.

I kept my questions to myself. I led the way but didn't know where we were going. I walked slowly, looking back at Dean every so often. The dim lighting flickered like a bad horror movie. Determined to hide my nerves and fear, I directed Dean to lead as we entered a grey hallway. I kept my shoulders back and my chin up, but butterflies filled my stomach. There was one door at the end of the hall, making the destination clear, but I wanted him to go in first.

I had nowhere to go but through, nowhere to escape without Dean. We were in a dark hole in the center of the ship. Would the hatch to the stairwell even open for me without a key or code?

"You may see some familiar faces in here," Dean explained. "It's best you absorb it all without asking too many questions."

"Okay," was my response. The tremor in my voice gave away my fear.

"Don't worry, Row. I'll take care of you. This is all for you and the boys, remember."

Dean did the handprint and retina scan and announced our presence on a monitor. I repeated the process, and we stepped inside a growing room. Lines of plants with workers monitoring and watering. I recognized them as the two hundred. Shielded by Dean walking in front, I shook my head at a few of them to signal they shouldn't react to my presence.

Where the lines of plants ended, crisp white lab rooms began. Six separate spaces with what looked like eighth-grade science class equipment lit up a back wall. Bunson burners and test tubes filled the tables. This was way beyond my expertise, but I knew what I was looking at.

They made drugs here.

Now I made drugs here.

"I know this seems bad to you, Row, maybe even criminal," Dean began.

Maybe criminal? Jesus, he was out of his mind.

"But this is for everyone's safety. As soon as we make landfall, someone will look for and make drugs. A quarter of the population uses it and needs it. I'm not making anything horrible, just opium. It will help people get through life on this boat and the future hardships we are about to face. We have limited morphine and pain relievers. How are you going to handle a tooth extraction without something to get rid of the pain? What if BeLew gets hurt? We need something to help with physical pain."

I understood his explanation, but his methods were self-serving. He said it himself, someone would do this.

He had to be the first. He had to have control. All I could do was nod in response.

"You will report here from now on. I need your help with the logging and inventory of what's coming. The poppy plants will be ready in one to two weeks. You don't have to take part in making anything, just the administrative side of things. This is the right thing, Row. We can't let anyone else have an operation like this. In the wrong hands, it could be dangerous for everyone — for the boys especially, if someone wants to recruit the next generation."

There was his manipulation — the last nail in my coffin to push me to his side of things. He threatened the boys' lives to remind me we needed his protection.

He held my wrist again. "This way," he said, and we entered a space next to the labs with a desk and file cabinets. "I've made a short list of what we need to categorize. Today, I need you to focus on our inventory. I need you to list how many plants we have and what that could produce. Talk to the workers. They will help you with the logs. This binder has everything we have written so far, but it's clunky and disorganized. I know you can put your touch on it. The last hour of the day we will check on your regular team to keep up appearances."

Our inventory... how many plants we have. He already spoke as if this was a family operation.

I moved behind the desk and gave him a weak smile. Observing and reporting were all I could do today, and I planned to memorize every inch of this space to tell Sam later. Dean wanted obedience in the bedroom and I refused him, but I could submit here to please him.

Hours later, desperate for a bathroom break, I asked one of the two hundred to lead the way. Her name was Mary, and we had spoken several times. We walked in silence, aware of all the eyes on us.

"You can go," I said to her, opening the bathroom door. "I can make my way back."

She turned to leave, and I heard her say a loud and familiar hello before the bathroom door came to a complete close. I opened it back up, peering in the direction she walked. The man beside her looked familiar to me, but I could only see the back of him.

My mind played tricks on me sometimes, but I swore I knew him. I didn't recognize him as one of the two hundred, but I watched them leave, waiting for a spark of memory.

He moved through the growing room without turning back. When he stepped out of the only door, I silently cursed to myself.

Still baffled but compelled to work it out, I looked back to Mary.

When I saw her face, I froze. She pleaded with her wide eyes, telling me I should recognize him. I tilted my head and questioned the person who came to mind. Could it be him?

I gave a terse wave. She tilted her chin up, and we both turned away.

The confident stride of his walk, the broad shoulders, and the gun holstered at his sides all pointed to one person.

It was Luke.

CHAPTER TWENTY-ONE

A DUO OF DREAMS

I DIDN'T HAVE WORK the next day, and the boys were bundles of energy after all the volcanic activity. I wanted to see Lori, and if the timing was right, talk to her about what I saw.

She already suspected what Dean was growing. She had the seeds in her walk-in and knew he had nefarious intentions with them. She may even agree with Dean to an extent. Lori was practical in that way. This dangerous world always had and would always have drugs.

I made her jump when I rushed into the kitchen and announced I planned to stay. She had just picked up her boys and the pack of them rushed off somewhere to see what else they could blow up.

"I could use the help," she admitted. "I got behind today with some things, but I still plan to visit the lower decks tomorrow. Three kids are having birthdays down there this month, and I want to see if I can get away with a cake. You're coming tomorrow, right?"

"I told Sam I would," I blushed.

Lori fluttered her hand against her chest and made a swoon sound. "You two lovebirds picked up where you left off."

I gave her a grin and nodded. "Is it just us tomorrow? Is Luke coming?"

"Not sure yet. He may join us in the fun later. The man loves sweets, but he's been so busy lately."

"I bet," I mumbled under my breath. "Did you tell him about Sam and me? About yesterday? Does he know I'm seeing Sam again?"

Lori raised her hands to her hips and gave me a sideways look. "How many ways can you ask the same question, Row? And no, I made a point not to tell him. It's your business. But he wants what's best for you, just like I do."

I raised my eyebrows. "You kept it from him? That's good and please don't tell anyone, but why? Is there something going on there?"

Lori shrugged and stepped over to the dry goods. "Come help me with rolls. I love you, but it's all you've got." She took a step stool to a high stack of flour and lifted bags from the top, dropping them to the floor. "Luke is great at a lot of things. Being a medic, being sexy, making me come until I pass out, but there is something weird with him. Maybe he's not that into me. I don't know."

I dragged the flour over to the mixers, remaining quiet. Lori lowered from the ladder with a solemn expression. "It's not like I'm the woman of his dreams, and I get that. It's not love, it's lack of options, but he's always a million miles away. Sometimes I feel like he's ticking a box with me. Like, go to work, eat, fuck Lori. We don't talk about anything real."

"What do you talk about?" She felt something was off with Luke. That meant she would believe me.

"Bullshit lately. Nothing of substance. What I plan on cooking or what the boys are doing in school. It's a lot about me which I was into at first, but he never opens up about anything. He gave me this watch, like yours. That was sweet."

I took her wrist and ran my thumb over the face of the watch, an identical copy of mine. "That was nice and thoughtful."

"Yes and no," Lori chuckled. "I'm a chef. It's not comfortable to wear a watch all day when my hands are getting dirty and drenched. He didn't think that part through. When he came by earlier today and I didn't have it on, he got all shitty about it."

"Right, when I gave mine to BeLew Dean was..." I trailed off.

"He was what?" Lori asked.

My mind ticked through the sequence of events. Anytime I walked around the deck, a drone found us. For the past month, Dean knew my every move. It upset him when the boys had the watch when I went to the lower decks.

He's tracking me through the watch. Now he has one on Lori.

"Lori, I need to tell you some things. You won't like it."

"Worse than the apocalyptic nightmare we are currently in? Or on par with it?"

"Depends on your opinion on the loss of orgasms. Where would that be on a scale of, things are fine and another apocalypse?"

Lori chucked the last bag of flour by the mixer and sucked in her cheeks. "Well, shit."

As we talked, Lori came to realize how much Luke pumped her for information. He veiled every conversation with intel about me. He asked her if I was having nightmares and what I dreamed about. Dean had trusted Luke to tell him that much. Or, Luke was such a lackey that he didn't know why he was asking the questions.

What were the chances I would see Luke again on this ship? How insane were the odds that the man that was at gate forty-six the day we arrived onboard would connect with Lori to help the two-hundred? Lori — the only friend I made on the boat. He weaseled his way inside our lives.

Was he in medical the day they fixed up Sam? How did he find us on deck the day the helicopters arrived? The day no one else was working, and he waltzed up to us to question our day. Did he see us run into the agriculture department?

I felt like a complete idiot.

Too many coincidences.

Luke was in Dean's pocket.

"Why all the questions about nightmares and your sleep?" Lori snipped. She agreed her boyfriend misled her, but that didn't mean she had to act happy about it. She paced the kitchen with sharp movements, her anger rising with each revelation.

"He thinks I can predict the future. He may want to exploit that. Well, he definitely wants to exploit that. I'm sure of it now."

Lori stopped dead in her tracks and pivoted her body to face mine. She had tears on her cheeks and my heart panged with guilt. "Dean's not an idiot."

"No," I confirmed. "He's slightly misled, but far from an idiot."

She took a few cautious steps toward me, pointing her finger in my direction. "Slightly, Rowan? You cannot be slightly psychic. That's like being slightly pregnant. You are or you aren't. Which is it?"

I stilled myself and looked to the floor, remembering I was inching closer to eight weeks. I couldn't face her. I trusted Lori, but I struggled to say the words out loud. I hated the thought of hurting her more by keeping this secret.

"Funny you should say that," I replied. There was no point in keeping it to myself any longer. I was furious about Sam's lie by omission, but I played the same game with her. I needed her support.

"Funny?" Lori raised her hands in the air and slapped them back down on her sides. I opened my mouth to speak, but she raised her hand to silence me. "Just give me a moment." She moved her head from side to side, then marched over to a thin cabinet in the corner. She lowered herself to the ground, reaching her arm inside, shoulder deep. She yanked out a thin bottle of Kentucky bourbon and rose to her feet.

"I only have a few of these if that tells you anything about the severity of my panic attack right now." Two glasses clinked on the table as she opened the bottle.

"None for me," I said, and pushed the glass to the side.

"Beggars can't be choosers. This is good stuff and we could use it." Lori gave herself two fingers of bourbon in the remaining glass.

"I love bourbon, but I haven't had a period in two months. Sam and I haven't been careful. I don't need to add fetal alcohol syndrome to this ever-rising pile of shit."

Lori's mouth went slack. "Oh my God, Row." She shot the drink back in one pull and poured another. She poured a small amount into the second glass and slid it over. "It won't do shit. I had a pitcher of margaritas with each kid and didn't even know it. You need it." She sipped on her second glass.

"Also, I am a little psychic," I added.

"Just a little?" she murmured into the glass.

"Like maybe mediocre at best. The kind of psychic where you dream about the future but the premonitions don't make any sense until it's happening, and you're already fucked."

"Right, so did you dream that the man I'm fucking is a complete waste of a human and a total piece of lying shit?"

"No, that one escaped me."

We both took a pull. "I'm so sorry about that, Lori. I know you care for Luke."

"Be more sorry you are only a mediocre psychic. You could have seen this coming if you were expert-level. You could tell me if we'll survive this mess." She twirled the glass in her hands, staring at the brown liquid.

"You believe me? You don't think I'm crazy?" I asked her.

"I thought Dean's obsession with you was crazy. He always cared about rising in the ranks more than anything else, so the thought of him being in love with someone and sacrificing for them was crazy. This makes more sense. Fits with his narcissistic persona."

"Right," I nodded. "And because I know you want to ask, my dreams right now aren't clear. There's a fire that I've seen a few times. I dreamed last night Sam was running into it and I'm scared, Lori. They always come true. I can't lose him again."

She poured her third drink and walked the bottle back to the cabinet. I swirled a small amount of the burning liquid in my mouth and swallowed. Guilt followed, but a taste wouldn't hurt.

Lori made her way back and held her last drink to her chest. "What about the boys?"

"They don't know. I'm doing a shit job of protecting them, but I've kept this from most everyone."

Lori waved her glass in front of me. "No, that's not what I meant. What about their dreams?"

"Oh, they don't have the premonitions."

Lori set her glass down and placed her hands on my shoulders. "Rowan, the boys have been talking about BeLew's dreams for weeks. They have been dreaming about fire too. You didn't know? They keep having the same nightmare. Black smoke everywhere and a fire on the deck of the ship."

I dropped my glass, and it shattered onto the floor between us. Lori's grip on my shoulders tightened. She gave me a small shake.

"Did they tell you about the shore with the broken wood? Did you dream that too?"

CHAPTER

TWENTY-TWO

INTENTIONS

KNOWING THE WATCHES TRACKED our every movement changed our perception, but not much else. We still had jobs to do, school for the boys, and time on our hands.

I skipped the visit to the lower decks with Lori. We had no plan for what to do next. Dean had to approve of my comings and goings. And what if, in the time they gave Lori the watch, they gave Sam a tracking device of his own? Lori told Sam what we had discovered. She told me he appeared detached, mumbling something about missing the signs. She left him like that, not knowing what to say.

Dean's desperation showed itself in his every action. He asked about my dreams multiple times a day and became more forceful at night. He gave subtle threats about our future when I refused him. I had to wrap myself in the sheets like a burrito to avoid direct contact.

I created inventory logs over the past week for the drugs we grew. Dean labeled it as pain management and held morning meetings, thanking everyone for their help in our necessary endeavor to relieve the passengers from undue duress. That was how he described this venture. He acted as if we were nurses or war heroes out in the fields of battle with wounded soldiers.

No one wanted to feel the pain of a tooth pull, but there was no way they remembered to pack toothpaste but forgot the lidocaine and general anesthesia. A few days before, they had set boxes of condoms out in the mess hall. Two months too late, but nevertheless, those things had made it onto the ship.

Some workers bought into the hype, or they knew enough to get along to survive. Mary, my tipoff woman, gave a subtle eye roll each morning, and I would exchange a lopsided grin with her. I hadn't seen Luke since my first day there. Every time the door opened, my head shot up to take a record of the person. They may have been there against their will, but Dean had spies everywhere. If I ever had the chance to see Sam again, I needed to be sure of who I passed in hallways or stood next to me at the bathroom sink.

Yes, I was paranoid. I had every right to be.

That night, Dean had planned an evening with friends. I heard his version of events along with everyone else's. He said they set up a large card game in the mess hall and wagered some personal effects. Others explained gambling was part of it, but so were some resident whores who were performing for the group.

Luke had opted out, citing he was faithful to Lori. She had kept up their relationship as if nothing had changed.

He had to remain in the dark until we had a plan. She encouraged him to have a night off for the card game, but he told her it would be a brothel and he wanted to spend the time with her. When he bowed out, it threw her into a spiral of confusion.

Neither of us knew his genuine reasons for skipping the event. My opinion was her company was better than the high chance of contracting herpes. She agreed and then resigned herself that she may have sex with him out of obligation. She was being a martyr, but part of her still wanted him.

I would never judge. I was partially to blame.

Time continued to tick forward without my period. Nothing else felt out of sync, so I choose full-blown denial. Maybe along with the missing lidocaine, we were sans pregnancy tests, so I would have to wait it out. How would I even get one? The only person I knew in the medical department was Luke.

My file cabinets burst at the seams. The labs were not in use yet and had loads of storage space. I waddled into one room carrying a stack of binders that almost blocked my vision and dropped them on an empty desk. Most of the workers had left for the evening and I was ready to call it a day myself.

With Dean gone for the night, I had the chance to talk to BeLew about any new dreams. I would need to take them out of our cabin in case Dean had it bugged. The thought of Dean knowing the boys had premonitions sent a shiver down my spine.

I pulled open a few cabinets that held random papers. Not willing to clean anything out, I kept looking for a clear drawer. On my third pull, a symbol caught my eye.

It was two jacket pins hooked onto a blue folder - rose gold metal with waves that intersected with a circle and twisting flames. They were pins from the Assembly of the Eternal.

"Not the shit I need today," I mumbled to myself.

"And what would that be?" Dean's voice answered from behind me.

I slammed the cabinet shut with my pinkie finger still on the opening. "Shit," I wailed, yanking it out. I shook my hand up and down and swallowed the pain. "I'm just out of storage and I would like to get going. I'm tired and the boys have been picked up late from school every day."

"Well, let me file those for you."

"No," I yelped. "I've been... I've just... been working so hard on this system and the organization. I'll take care of it. I'm almost done. Are we walking to the school together or are you about to start your evening? I thought you had left."

"I would much rather be spending the night with you."

I dropped the paperwork into the cabinets, covering the pins with my stacks. "You're hosting, don't be silly. I'll just take the boys on a walk. It's a pleasant night outside."

"Well, I was thinking the boys could spend some time with Luke, Lori, and her sons. I banned her from the kitchen tonight, and I have it all to myself until people arrive. I could cook something for you, for us."

I searched for a key to the cabinet with no luck. "It's been a long week, Dean. I appreciate the offer, but you have a big night ahead of you, and I'm looking forward to spending time with BeLew. I'll see you later on. Have a nice evening."

I attempted to squeeze through the doorway, and he gripped the gaping waistband of my pants, yanking me back. "You know, I think I will have some fun tonight. Maybe I'll bring that fun back to our cabin," he hissed in my ear. "I've been such a gentleman until now. How could you blame me since you've been such a cold fish?"

I swallowed hard and counted three breaths before I responded. He would take my excitement as anger, and that was exactly what I wanted. Dean's pride would be his undoing. He believed every woman would eventually fall under his spell, his manipulation. He gave me an out, and I gave him my fake jealousy.

"You won't find me in our bed when you do. Condoms are still in the mess hall. Have a blast."

I jerked his hand off me and stormed out of the lab. Dean just gave me a ticket to roam. I could go anywhere under the excuse that I was avoiding his whores. It took everything I had to keep the smile from my lips as I left the growing room, looking for Sam.

My first stop was Lori's cabin. I had only been there once. The way our shifts aligned, I always met her in the kitchen. I knocked on the door and waited, pacing the hall. It may have been ten seconds or a few minutes, but my patience waned. I banged my open palms on the door and called her name.

I heard noises from inside. First, I planned to talk to the boys somewhere quiet on deck about their dreams. Then, if Lori was willing, I could leave them with her and locate Sam. By that point, Dean would be drunk with his dick down some girl's throat.

More shuffling and my anxiety levels reached an all-time high. "Jesus, Lori, what are you doing?" I screamed at the door. Her door swung open and Luke stood with nothing but a hand towel over his junk. I despised him, but the sight of him flushed heat through my entire body. He was rock solid and had a sheen of sweat on his chiseled chest. The towel didn't cover all of him, and I failed to avert my eyes. My jaw fell open.

"Sorry to keep you waiting, Rowan. We can't seem to locate my pants," he grinned.

My attempt to sound annoyed came out like a pathetic stutter instead."Oh, y-yeah, I s-see that." I pointed at his groin, which furthered my mortification. "Not that I s-see anything." *Fuck.* "Just get Lori, please."

"Found them," she bellowed from behind Luke. He turned to shut the door, displaying his perfect ass.

A moment later he exited, wearing pants. I entered Lori's cabin with a neon flush on my cheeks.

"Before you say anything," Lori chided, holding her hand up. "I think we may have jumped to conclusions with his involvement."

"What?" I threw my hands up. "Are you orgasm drunk? Listen, I don't care if you still want to fuck Luke. God, I just about creamed my pants when he opened the door. But hormones lie, Lori. They tell us things like, 'Men change', or 'I'm the only one he feels this way about', or 'Luke isn't a lying asshole'. The pieces fit. He's part of Dean's plan."

"I'm aware he's part of Dean's plan."

"Okay, so what are you talking about, then?"

"Luke has a lot of outstanding qualities, but he's a glorified boy scout. He's been in the military since he was seventeen. He's kind and loyal, to a fault."

I made a drumroll on my legs. "And, Lori? What's your point?"

She scrunched her shoulders to her ears and inhaled. "He's as dumb as a box of rocks. I'm talking common sense dumb. The man is a genius with memorization and facts in the medical field, but he's not a problem solver, more like an order follower. But he can find my clit, and that, my friend, is genius."

I laughed, my shoulders shaking as my eyes watered. I wrapped my arm around Lori. "I know you care for him, but I saw him in the growing room. He's part of the drugs."

"I could say that about you, too. You are in the growing room. He's following orders, Rowan."

She had me there. From the outside looking in, I was as guilty as sin and with Dean until the end.

"This isn't about my feelings," Lori interrupted my thoughts. "He's oblivious, and maybe a bit by choice. You've never been in the military, so let me enlighten you on some things. When your superiors say to do something, you don't ask why. It's not a discussion, ever. After so many years, you don't even care why. He's following orders."

"He's still in on Dean's plan!" I shouted.

"But he doesn't know it," she shot back. "All I'm saying is, he has no idea why he's doing the things he's doing. Dean has used him like a pawn in chess. You could say the same about me, you know. Dean introduced us, got the boys together. How can you be so sure I'm not into ship domination with a side of drugs and premonitions?"

"Because I know you," I insisted.

"And I know Luke, with or without hormones. He follows orders. He doesn't question. He does it in bed too, and that shit is amazing."

I wrapped my arm tighter around Lori. "It doesn't change much. If and when it all comes out, Dean will just give him an order and as you said, he'll follow."

"It changes everything, Rowan. Because in my heart, if that happens, he'll choose me. He will choose us. He doesn't know Dean's intentions, but he's man enough to follow his own when the time comes. I don't have to be psychic to know that."

Her eyes pleaded with me to understand, to agree. Doubt filled my head, but there was still a glimmer of hope in my heart. "Okay. If you trust him, I can too. Just ditch the watch."

CHAPTER

TWENTY-THREE

ESCAPE

I WALKED THE DECK with BeLew, my head filled with questions and desperate for answers. Their new watches, too big for them, hung on their little wrists. It was the best plan we had. I had told Dean I would take the kids on deck, and if he tracked us, he would assume Lori was in attendance. I doubted he would look for her in engineering, where she would find Sam and arrange a meeting.

The Assembly of the Eternal pins combined with BeLew's dreams had me in a tailspin. Not too long ago, you saw people wearing them everywhere as a sign of loyalty. After the swim, they were nowhere to be found. I never found my sister's after her death. *Why are they here?*

I asked the kids about school and their friends. Volcanos were still a popular topic, and I regretted not knowing more about magma and explosions. My sister would have made a paper-mâché replica and videoed the entire experience.

"BeLew, I need to ask you some serious questions," I said.

"It was Lewis who said shit," Beau confessed.

"You said damn in class," Lewis countered.

"What? No, I don't care about that." I waved my hands at them. "I mean, shit, I do care. Don't say shit!" I stopped walking and put my hand to my forehead, feeling the pulsing headache start in my temples. "Please stop cursing, okay?"

They nodded in unison, looking devilish but adorable, blonde hair whipping in their faces as we began walking again.

"I want to talk to you about dreams. Your dreams and my dreams." They remained silent, and I continued. "Sometimes, Aunt Rowan has dreams that feel very real. And a lot of times, they repeat - the same dream over and over. It feels like it's happening to me while I'm asleep, and it may not make sense."

They only shrugged, and I realized I needed to give them an example so they could understand.

"You remember the old camera that your mama had? She would flip through all the pictures she took, one image after the other, but they might be pictures at different times and on different days. Sometimes those pictures could tell a story, but other times, they didn't go together at all. My dreams are like that, the same as pictures from an old camera. What about you?"

The boys held hands, glancing at each other in the way twins do, speaking a silent language that had no words.

I knew they had something to tell me, but they were deciding if I was worthy of the information.

Lewis reached for my hand. My brave boy cleared his throat. "We have the same dreams a lot, too. Sometimes they're scary."

Beau looked out at the water, and Lewis continued. "It feels like being at the beach. We've never been, but we've seen it on TV. But it's not like a vacation. No one is in a bathing suit, which is so weird. And you're there, in your clothes, but your feet are bleeding. And there's lots of wood like someone broke a fence. Mamma would say it's just a dream. I just wish it would stop. I don't want you to hurt your feet."

I tried to calm my reaction to the news, giving a soft smile and running my fingers through Lewis's hair.

"It is just a dream, boys. No matter what happens, I'll be okay. I'm tough. What about you, Beau? Do you have any dreams?"

Beau nodded and continued looking out at the ocean.

"Could you tell me about them?"

Beau turned to me, bewildered. "We did, Aunt Row."

"No baby, tell me about what you dream. And boys, let's keep this between us. It needs to be our secret. Do you understand?"

They nodded, and Beau turned back to the water.

"Beau," I urged. "Please, baby. What are you dreaming about?"

"We just told you. The beach and the broken wood. Your feet are bleeding."

I shook my head, pinching the bridge of my nose in frustration, and then it hit me. "Boys, do you have the same dream? You each are having the same dream on your own?"

"That's what I just said," Beau responded, with a hint of frustration. "We always dream the same. We used to dream about the ditch. Sam was scarier in our dreams, though. He looked like a zombie. He was nicer when we got to meet him."

They had the premonitions.

They could see what was coming, more than I ever could - clearer than I ever could.

They saw Sam.

I hid my shock as best I could, and we talked about volcanoes for the rest of the time. All the while, I wondered how long they knew Sam would be in our lives, and how we needed to be together again.

Later that night, I waited for Sam on the lower decks, my heart still lodged in my throat as I paced. I felt like a terrible mother. My sister would have noticed that her sons were having the dreams. Maybe she had known all along, and there was no time to tell me.

I heard his footsteps down the hallway, and my pacing quickened. I hadn't seen Sam for over a week and there was so much to tell him. When the door swung open, I jumped into his arms. His presence made me weak. He kicked the door closed behind him, running his hands up the back of my shirt.

"Wait," I breathed. "A lot has happened this week."

"Lori filled me in," he said, bringing his lips to mine. I moaned in response as I undressed, our mouths locked together. I had a moment of clarity as my shirt hit the ground and pushed Sam away with my palms on his chest.

"Filled you in on what? Do you know about the watches and Luke?"

He nodded while undoing his belt. "Lori's a fool. Luke is Dean's pet." His pants hit the floor, and I saw how ready he was for me. His hand moved to my pants, unbuttoning and pushing them over my hips.

"And the pins? My dreams? And the boy's dreams?"

"We had a very detailed discussion. Yes, all of it. Take off your panties before I rip them off."

I obeyed but continued my inquisition. "What does all of this add up to? What is Dean's plan?"

Sam stood, completely naked and stroking himself. He took a step toward me and I stepped back. A growl came from his throat.

With both hands, he lifted me and pinned my back against the wall. I yelped and then fell silent as he knocked the wind from my lungs in a single thrust. I wrapped my legs around his waist and my arms clung to him while we found our rhythm.

When he was inside me, it felt like everything was as it should be. I was meant to be with him. I was safe. I had forgotten about my ex-fiance's desire for domination in those moments. I forgot that the boys and I were in danger because of our gifts.

Sam's mouth moved with mine, and each pump into my body made me desperate for release. He pulled himself from me and placed my feet on the floor. "What's wrong?" I gasped, clawing him back.

"Nothing," he said, digging through his pants pocket. He grabbed a condom and opened it with his teeth, walking back over. "These are around now, and I know you are concerned about being safe."

My face fell. In all the chaos, and after being reunited with Sam, I let the possible pregnancy evade my thoughts. That was too much time - that meant something. That something might have a heartbeat.

"I don't think that will help," I stammered. My high from just a second ago crashed, and I picked up a piece of clothing off the floor and held it against my skin, covering myself.

Baffled, he brought his hand to my chin, lifting it upward. "Help with what?"

My mouth opened, but no words escaped. It went dry and my throat closed.

My true fear, aside from losing Sam or the boys, was that this news would be Sam's death sentence. Pregnant and alone, I would have to give in to Dean. So far, Dean was a necessary evil. If there was a baby and if Sam were gone, I would have to succumb to keep us all safe.

Sam threw the condom to the ground. "What's going on? Please, talk to me."

Tears pricked the corners of my eyes. Sam's worry grew upon his face.

"What is it?" he asked. "Did I do something wrong? I just want you so badly. I can't stop when I see you."

I moved my forehead to his chest, painfully aware of the tears that threatened to escape. Each pull of oxygen burned my lungs. My fingernails dug into his skin as he wrapped his arms around my back.

"I-I'm not sure but, it's possible," I stuttered and paused.

Breathe in, breathe out.
Breathe in, breathe out.

"I may be pregnant."

Sam stilled for a moment and then I felt his chest move, filling with air.

"I haven't had a period on this ship. I was never with anyone else. I haven't been for... a long time. My body could be acting crazy, but I'm normally on schedule. I'm really sorry."

Sam eased back and placed a soft kiss on my lips. "Sorry for what? Don't be stupid. Don't be ridiculous. I love you and BeLew. I'm surprised, yes, but I'm happy."

"How could you be happy, you crazy man? If Dean finds out, you're dead. And pregnancy is hard to hide. Harder when you're in bed with the person you're trying to hide it from."

Sam brought his mouth to mine again, and I felt the passion pass through his lips to my soul. We kissed for minutes and I lost focus on the problem. When my body relaxed, he wrapped my legs around his middle and entered me, slower this time. Even and unhurried, he filled me completely.

Moving his mouth to my ear, he whispered, "We need to escape. We'll leave the ship. Not in nine months. We leave now, Row."

I nuzzled my face into his neck and made myself believe he had a plan. With every stroke of him inside me, I told myself we would figure it out, together.

Before we left each other, I no longer needed convincing. We would leave this ship, together and safe... tonight.

• • • ● ● ● • ● ● • •

Lori paced her cabin and whisper screamed at me. "Well, I was always team Sam, but he's fucking insane." It was the middle of the night and all the boys were asleep. I stayed with Lori overnight, and Dean could take all the whores that he wanted back to our room. I had my hall pass to be away from him.

I held my finger to my lips, urging her to chastise me in a lower tone. "He's lost his goddamn mind," she hissed. "We don't know what's going on out there. The reason we're on a ship is to avoid certain death — death that is coming at us from all directions. There hasn't been one day this ship hasn't been moving, and it's moving away from something, you know?"

I raised my hands to her shoulders, urging her to sit on the bed with me. "Yes, I know."

She pulled away and continued to pace. "It's moving away from death. Did I mention the death?"

I sat on the bed and crossed my arms. "What the fuck do you think this ship is? Because it's no safe haven. So far, we have had people zip-tied and thrown overboard and slave laborers fed half rations and forced to work in a drug den — a den that has symbols from the Assembly of the Eternal. If Dean knows about my premonitions, and your sons know about BeLew's, how long before people outside our tight circle know?"

Lori lowered her shoulders and hung her head. She knew I had a point.

"This place is a ticking time bomb for my family. Not to mention if I'm pregnant, I'm completely fucked. The only reason Sam is still alive is because Dean thinks he's slowly winning me over. If he finds out I'm pregnant, I will have no choice but to depend on him fully. Sam will be as good as dead. It's not safe here, Lori. This ship is my death sentence."

"What symbols from the AOE?" Lori snapped.

In the chaos of revealing all my life's secrets and the latest happenings to Lori, I had missed that one. "Before you freak out, I simply forgot to mention it. I wasn't keeping anything from you."

"I'm not fucking freaking out!"

I paused and took a deep inhale, lifting my chin before I spoke. "I found the old fire and waves clothing pins in a cabinet. I'm not sure if Dean knows I saw it. He walked in as I found them. He seemed more occupied with telling me about all the screwing he was doing tonight, so who knows. Also, I think you *are* freaking out a little. Just a little."

"And you're a little pregnant."

I pursed my lips and crossed my arms. "Point made, but calm down before you wake up the boys."

Lori whined and sat down next to me on the bed. She put her face in her hands and lay down, resting her head in my lap. "I think they already have drugs here," she sniffled.

I played with a strand of her hair. "The poppy isn't ready."

"Dean brought something into the kitchen today. I think the party tonight is to introduce the product, get people hooked."

"Well, he got me and the boys on board, so I'm sure a gallon of white powder wasn't too hard to smuggle as well. It proves my point. Things are getting worse, not better. It is for me, at least. I hate that I've dragged you into it."

"Not your fault. Dean had a plan before I stepped into that kitchen. I'm panicking because you know this means the boys and I have to go, too. I can't survive here without you. We go together, or you don't go at all."

I stroked her hair, and my heart raced. I'd known Lori for such a short time, but I understood her. There was no changing her mind, and I felt selfish for not wanting to. I needed her with me. She grounded me in a way only good girlfriends can. They supported your crazy while nudging you in the right direction. I was good at survival, but Lori helped me live.

So much like my sister. My sister whom I let die because of a man.

"I suppose you'll want Luke to come," I gulped.

Her shoulders moved on my legs with each deep breath. She crept her hand up to mine and intertwined our fingers. "He'll make the right choice when the time comes. When do we leave?"

I bit my lip to stop myself from snapping at her. Lori had decided about Luke. I told her I trusted her. The topic was dead.

"We leave tomorrow."

CHAPTER
TWENTY-FOUR

LET GO

THANK GOD SAM DIDN'T end up cleaning toilets. Despite the unfortunate four weeks I was without him, the visit from the Galene was a blessing. His job in engineering gave him admittance to anything with an engine, navigation, and global positioning systems. Mobile navigation and GPS systems were under strict security measures, but because of his position, he had the key. He could take anything and everything we would need with most of the men at Dean's party.

He planned to load a tender boat with food, water, clothing, necessary electronics, and medical equipment by dawn. If a storm was coming, we would board the boat and leave its path until it passed. I insisted we should slow down and think through the plan, but we only had a small window to leave.

The Thalassa was a four-hour ride away from a chain of islands that could provide food and shelter. With every passing moment, we drifted further away. Thalassa crew had scouted the islands and found them barren. They checked most of the boxes for relocation, but they were too small for the ship's population. We were leaving and not coming back.

Sam also felt that with so many in quadrant C going to the event tonight, there would be a lot of hungover, sluggish workers on duty tomorrow. Circumstances offered the perfect time to make our move, and we wouldn't likely get another.

I had already visited my cabin and packed a bag for BeLew and me, leaving a note that I was staying at Lori's for a few days because I was mad after our fight.

I had an alibi and a plan. I also had the urge to vomit all the time, which could be nerves or could be a fetus.

Lori slept for only an hour, and when I awoke, she was packing bags for herself and the boys. I kept quiet, watching her from the bed. Fear and excitement coursed through my body.

What was Sam doing at this moment? Would he sleep tonight?

I didn't know how to drive a boat. He still had a slight limp, and I worried about all the physical energy needed to get us to safety.

I curled into a ball and thought about my dreams. Why was I bleeding on the sand? Would it happen tomorrow or years from now? And the blazing fire from my dreams happened on this ship. If everything went according to plan, we would leave the ship in a few hours. I trembled at what that could mean. Lori's face was solemn as she chose things for herself and the boys. She placed each item into her bag as if it held special meaning.

I rolled over and drifted to sleep, almost praying for another dream to come, one that would have more clarity or something helpful. Once my eyes felt heavy, I heard a click, and the walls vibrated.

My eyes shot back open.

The room went pitch black.

A loud buzzing echoed throughout and a red light blinked from beyond Lori's door.

"Was this part of the plan?" Lori's voice quivered as she asked.

"No," I said. "Grab your bag. We have to go."

The boys stood on wobbly legs, half asleep, as we put bags on their backs.

I dropped to my knees in front of BeLew. "Boys, do you remember the farm a few months ago, when we were going to the jeep?" They groaned, tired of this routine. "We had rules. Do you remember them? Stay where I can reach you. Run if you can. Do exactly what I say when I say it."

"What's happening, Mama?" Lewis's calling me mama made my lip tremble. I caught an empathetic look from Lori in the blinking red light.

"I need you... to trust me. I love you both so much. More than anything in this whole universe. Do everything I say when I say it."

They were waking up a bit more and their eyes grew wide as they nodded again. I took a hand from each of them and we left.

The dark hallway concealed our bags. We had no choice but to walk with the masses that headed upward towards the deck. I needed to get to one of the engineering tunnels. I had seen it a million times and there was an entry point five minutes down from where we lined up at the last red out. It was still night, and I prayed they didn't have time to set up a stage for whatever shitshow Matthews had planned.

The captain's voice boomed through the hall's intercom. "Please move in an orderly fashion towards the decks. There is no need to panic, but we require that all passengers are present at the top of the hour."

Many of us were already jogging down the halls, and this only quickened our pace. We took the stairs two at a time, and I wedged in front of our group to lead the way. If there was an opportunity to get to the planned meeting spot, I would take it.

My hopes were crushed when we got to the decks and witnessed the crowd of people blocking us from walking forward. A few drones flew overhead, sealing our fate.

"Fuck," I snarled. The boys looked at each other with open mouths. "Shit," I continued, as my inner voice had no filter tonight. "Don't say fuck... or shit." Beau broke the silence with a giggle, and Lewis punched him in the arm.

"What's the plan?" Lori whispered in my ear. We stood at the end of a lineup and people filed in behind us. My eyes adjusted to the darkness. It was night, and the only light came from the blinking red lights. The banister of the ship was on our right. I looked over and, unlike the other side, it wasn't a straight fall to the ocean below.

Mounted on the side of the ship, maybe eight feet down, appeared to be an old apartment style fire escape. It had open steel gratings for a walkway and a handrail on the side. It reminded me of tracks that run alongside roller coasters. Still terrifying as hell, but it wasn't a

plummet to your death as long as you didn't misstep.
If we stayed flush to the hull of the ship, we would be
concealed from view. The drones kept their primary
focus on the decks, not the sides of the boat or water
outward.

The slotted pathway looked like it ran down the entire
side of the ship. It was a gamble, but I would bet it
traveled far enough to reach the engineering entry point.
We had to get around, and this was the only way out of
the chaos.

I met eyes with Lori. "Crawl over. I'll pass you the
boys."

She took a hesitant peek over the side. Her knuckles
turned white on the metal that was as high as her chest,
there to prevent the very thing we intended to do.

She turned back towards me, still gripping the edge
with both hands. The wind whipped her hair in all directions, hiding her expression. "Fuck it," she heaved.
Turning back, she hoisted her body upwards, stomach
to the bar like a gymnast. Her right leg lifted over and
then her left, so quick no one shuffling around in the
dark took the time to notice. It was chaotic, and the
crowd remained focused on where the stage was last
time. Time was running out. I heard the clang of metal
as she landed. Her boys had their chests pressed to the
sides and their heads peeked over.

"Now boys," I barked. I helped them lift over, one at a
time, and saw them land with a thud next to their mother. Lewis had already lifted himself as best he could.
When his body made it over the side, I kept hold of his
arms, reaching over as far as I could before letting him
go. He fell onto Lori, taking her down, but they both

were safe. Beau had a steady shake to him, and I knew he would panic if I threw him over like his brother. I moved my bag to my front and had him climb onto my back. His arms wrapped so tightly around my neck, that I struggled for air.

Both of my legs were over the side when the red blinking stopped and the outdoor lights flickered on. At that moment, the sudden change captured everyone's attention. I extended my arms, hanging on the ship's side with only my hands visible to those on deck.

I released one and gazed downward. Lori stood with open arms, but Beau's grip was tighter than ever. I had no choice but to drop and hope we both made it onto the thin rail. I could twist my body so Beau was closer to the hull of the ship. If anyone fell over the side, it would be me. Make your decision and move was still the mantra that day.

I let go.

Chapter Twenty-five

In Flames

W HEN I WAS TWELVE, I had the same dream every night for a month. A broken cuckoo clock went off every ten minutes. Snow fell so deep it came up over my knee. Our neighbor dropped a boiling teapot on her foot.

No one slept that month, especially my sister. She resigned herself to sleeping not only in my room, but in my bed. I would stir and she would sit up, rub my back, and wait for me to wake up. She was a nurturer from a young age - born to be a mother. Every time I was startled awake, she spoke to me in a calm voice and told me everything was alright.

By the end of the month, her patience waned, and who could blame her? She was barely a teenager with her own emotions and problems and a crazy baby sister that kept her up all night.

She had paced the room one night when I shot awake from the nightmare. I sat in the bed for what felt like a long time to a twelve-year-old watching her sister wear out the carpet.

Back and forth and back and forth, her arms wrapped snugly across her chest. The white nightgown she wore flowed behind her as she walked and spun around.

She stopped and turned to face me. "Why do you fight the premonitions?" She raised her arms in thought like a schoolteacher in mid-lecture. "Have you ever tried to concentrate on the images or meditate on what you see? Do you know what meditate means?"

I shook my head no, scooting closer to the edge of the bed.

"Meditation is when you sit in silence and you let your thoughts go. You relax your mind. Sometimes people repeat a word or phrase when they do it. You could... repeat the images. See if your mind opens more. Try to make yourself see more. What if you could control this? Could you try?"

"Okay," was all I could say. The idea terrified me. I would never do what she asked, but she was so tired and worn out. I didn't want to disappoint her.

She smiled, and the worry left her face. "Yes, I think this could work." She brought her hands together in a clap. "I know you're worried about it, but something is calling to you, Rowan. You put forth no effort, and yet you see all these things." She stepped closer to me and rested her forehead on mine. She was smiling now, her burden temporarily replaced with hope. "What if you tried? What if you focused on this as a gift that could help others? Oh, wow, what will you see?"

"Okay," I repeated. "I'll try."

I fidgeted when our eyes met. I wanted her happy and freed from this turmoil we now shared, but I would never do what she asked.

That was the first time I lied to my sister. It was the first time of many.

I'd prayed that night my dreams would stop forever. They were something I wanted to get rid of, not learn more about, or control.

We had recently discovered my dreams were premonitions. Traumatic events circled these visions, not events I wanted to think about more. I never saw kittens or couples walking on the beach. I saw blood, pain, and fear. That my sister wanted me to experience more visions showed me how desperate she had become for either sleep or relief.

I saw my sister's face when I landed on the walkway below. I had blacked out for just a moment, and she was there, wearing that white nightgown, telling me it would be alright.

I had injured my hip, crashing into the handrail of the shaky steel grate. Beau had tumbled into the center of the walkway. He would have a few bruises but was alright.

Unfortunately, I had landed directly on my pelvis, folding over the side as hands from behind me grabbed my shoulders and arms, throwing me back to safety.

It had knocked the wind out of me. My sister had been a flash of a forgotten memory, and I opened my eyes to frantic faces.

Eventually moving to my knees and then standing, I started our walk and everyone followed behind me like ducklings. The wind kicked up, but it was manageable. I heard Captain Matthews' voice over the dull roar that filled my ears.

"We need to address another issue that will not be tolerated on this vessel. I hate to even say the words and bring attention to this, but we must be vigilant and swift with our no-tolerance policy. There are those among us with wishes to reestablish the Assembly of the Eternal."

An audible gasp came from the crowd above. We continued our path down the side of the ship. When he mentioned the AOE, my step faltered for a moment, but I continued. I had a general sense of where we were and how far we needed to go, and I used Matthews' voice as a guide.

The speech grew louder at the halfway mark. We had to be right next to where he was standing. "This kind of insubordination will kill us all. It was brought to my attention that a senior member of our staff has become involved. I do not show favoritism. We went to discuss the matter with the individual and found AOE paraphernalia. When we located him on the ship, he was stealing supplies."

I stopped, overpowered by the words, unable to move forward. Lori's boys stumbled behind me. When I turned, Lori's face flashed with the panicked expression I felt in my gut.

Crack. Crack. Crack.

The sound of bullets rang out, and I felt my legs falter beneath me. Lori was too far away and the walkway was too narrow to reach me, so I fell to my knees in shock. "Up," Lori barked. "We don't even know... We have to keep going."

I gripped the side rail and brought my numb body back to standing, turned, and kept going. Those were gunshots. I knew it, and no one could convince me otherwise. It had to be Sam. He had the symbol branded on his body, and Dean must have seen it at some point. Those pins had been Dean's. He planned this all along.

The crowd cried out in uproar, silencing Matthews' words.

We kept walking.

People screamed nonsense above our heads.

We kept walking.

The rustling of feet and bodies on the deck slowed.

We kept walking.

"Please calm down. We have the suspect, but as you can imagine after hearing gunfire, I can say with certainty, he is guilty."

What the fuck? The Captain just made himself judge, jury, and executioner?

We had reached the point where the engineering tunnel, by my estimation, was just over the side. The journey felt pointless now, but we still had to get off the side of the boat.

Rage filled my body. Thoughts about murdering Dean took over my mind. I would end him and be alone with the boys and my baby. This was my child and no one else's because no one on this miserable forsaken planet would do except for Sam. No father at all was better than what Dean offered.

I killed a worthless man before, and the world was better for it. The last thing this world needed was more pathetic, manipulating, insignificant men. I could do it again.

Lori insisted I go first because I had hurt myself in the fall. I hated to admit it, but she was right. Without someone else pushing, I was unsure if I could pull myself over.

When I made it to the side of the boat, no drones were in sight, and the agriculture building blocked any view of Captain Matthews. Most of the passengers had stilled, waiting for something. They twisted their faces in confusion and disgust. I trembled with the thought of who they saw and in what state that person was in.

Had he been shot or killed?

I made it over the edge, numb to the pain that radiated throughout my body. Lori's boys followed, and I pulled them by the back of their shirts until they fell to my feet. Beau and Lewis were in deep conversation, and when it was their turn, Beau, to my surprise, stepped forward. He used the flat palms of his hands to balance as Lori pushed him upwards with his legs and then the bottoms of his feet. I gripped his wrists and grimaced as the metal pushed into my hip.

"Like spiderman," Beau said, wrapping his arms around me.

I placed him on the ground. "Forever my superhero, baby."

Lewis was at his side less than a minute later, and Lori made it up after only a few tries, and I ignored the searing pain that shot up my side. It throbbed and burned like nothing I had ever experienced, but we were all safely within twenty feet of the entryway.

"Who is it?" Lori breathed. Sweat beaded on her forehead and her eyes were wild.

"I can't tell. I can't see." I surveyed what I could from our vantage point. "I think this may be our opportunity to go, but I can't. I have to know if it's him."

"You heard the gunfire. If it is, he could be dead."

My mind spun, weighing every option. I had children to care for, but there was also the child inside me. That baby deserved the chance to have a father, and that man might have a gun to his head right now. I could speak up for him and plead with Dean. Then I could sort out killing that fucking bastard later.

"It's Sam," Lori whispered. She rocked my shoulder, but I kept staring off into space.

"We don't know that," I argued, but my voice was uneven. The quiver in my jaw came through every word.

Lori slapped her hand on my thigh. "No, it's Sam."

I spun my head to face her. "We don't know that. Just let me think."

"Dammit, Rowan! Over there, it's fucking Sam. He's right fucking there."

My heart leaped from my chest and I sprung to my feet, but the sharp pain in my hip brought me back to the ground. Before I landed on my ass, I was in Sam's arms. His panicked eyes met mine. When he wrapped his arms around me, I yelped from the pain.

He pulled away with a start. "Are you hurt?"

"Not too bad. I landed on my hip. What the fuck is going on? I thought you were..." I trailed off.

Sam brought his lips to my ear. "When the red out happened, I waited by the entrance thinking you would be here..." The screaming of the crowd stopped his sentence short. Everyone quieted as the Captain urged them to calm down through the speakers all around us.

Sam reached past me and grabbed Lori's arm. "We need to go. Is she okay? Are the boys."

Lori nodded her head. "We can manage. I was hoping I could find Luke. I - I just..."

Sam's eyes widened like saucers, so big I could see myself in them. But it wasn't my face that looked back at me. It was bright orange streaks that flickered in the blue and black. And then I felt the heat. It came in waves that hit my back and stung my exposed skin.

Lori screamed for the boys to get up. I felt them move around me and heard Sam's muffled voice somewhere in my brain, but I remained still. "Boys!" he yelled. "Take the entrance... twenty-seven floors down... go without us... Rowan, are you listening?" Lori pulled at my arm. I smelled the smoke that fogged the outdoor lamps and filled my lungs. My brain clicked back and forth between reality and my dreams.

The billows of smoke escaped into the sky.
The fire on the deck.
Sam ran towards it.

This was the time to take control, to change my fate, to change everything. Next, Sam would run to the flames, and I couldn't lose him. I could never do this for my sister, but I could find the strength for him, for us, for our baby.

My eyes closed, and I thought back to my visions. I pictured myself in my dream. The sensations were the same, but the intensity felt stronger. Reality mixed in with my premonitions and I searched my mind, making the pictures flash in sequence over and over. The smells and feelings were familiar but brighter and stronger.

Fire and smoke cover the sky.
Sam is running towards it, and I'm left on the deck.
I'm bleeding on the sand.

I'm slapped by leaves running through trees.

The same pictures in the same sequence again and again.

Fire and smoke cover the sky.

Sam is running towards it, and I'm left on the deck.

I'm bleeding on the sand.

I'm slapped by leaves running through trees.

What happens next, Rowan?

Fire and smoke cover the sky.

Sam is running towards it, and I'm left on the deck.

Luke sits handcuffed to something on the deck. He's calling out to Sam.

Sam shook my shoulders, and I pushed him away. "Stop," I yelled. "I'm seeing it. Stop!"

Fire and smoke cover the sky.

Sam is running towards it, and I'm left on the deck.

Luke sits handcuffed to something on the deck. He's calling out to Sam.

He's screaming as wild flames engulf his body.

My eyes shot open. "It's Luke," I screamed. "We have to save Luke."

CHAPTER TWENTY-SIX

BROKEN THINGS

"LORI, TAKE THE BOYS to the boat." When I turned to give her the orders, I saw the flames. They were smaller than my dream, which I took as a good sign. Maybe we had time.

Lori gave a weak nod, still processing what I had said. Sam threw the bags back on the boys and led them to the entrance. People scattered, and the microphone barked with orders in acronyms that meant nothing to me.

I strapped my bag to the front of Lori. "Twenty-seven flights down. Count as you go. Do you hear me?"

"Twenty-seven," she gave a weak reply.

"This isn't like my dream. I'm seeing it. I'm stopping it." I dragged her to the entrance while Sam led each boy by his back into the doorway. The sprinkler system sputtered on, and it soaked us before I got Lori to the door. It had little effect on the fire that continued to grow.

Lightbulbs popped and shattered around the flames, and the stream of commands grew louder in the speakers.

"BeLew, I love you," I shouted down the hallway after Lori stepped inside. "Lori, do you know where you are going?" We had talked about it in her cabin, and I relayed the instructions that Sam had given me. But Lori was in a state of shock, and she had never been to the tenders.

"I'll get the boys there," she said. Her voice was small and tears spilled from her eyes. I believed her. I trusted her strength. She met my gaze with everything she had left. "I can do this. Will you... can you?"

I hugged her and gave her a small shove inside the entrance. "I'll get him. Luke will be fine."

I took Sam's hand and sprinted towards the fire. My lungs burned from the smoke and exertion. Sam never questioned and followed me step by step.

I took control of this premonition. I had accepted it and given into the vision, and I could use the power of that. I would give into my ability, hoping we could change the outcome. All my life, I had fought the dreams and what they told me. I should have let them in, seen the picture, so I understood it. Now that I surrendered to it, I could do something about it.

Sam saw Luke first and darted ahead of me. He tried to release my hand, but I clutched it harder and ran faster to keep up. I still feared the image in my head.

The flames were far enough away from Luke to approach him safely. He banged his handcuffs against a pipe and pulled one arm with the other, trying to break free even if it meant breaking a bone. We called out to him and his face calmed for a moment. Dozens of people scurried around the flames with extinguishers and hoses, but no one seemed concerned about the man handcuffed ten feet from their blaze.

"They think I'm in the AOE!" he yelled. "I was coming to tell you. They found me by the boats."

"Later, man," Sam stopped him. "We need to take care of this first."

"Have you been shot?" I asked, surveying Luke. The only blood was a ring around his wrist where he pulled at the handcuffs. The fire was growing hotter, and I felt it sear my skin.

"No," Luke shook his head. "I ran up through the growing room. I thought they would stop there... but they didn't stop. They fired at me. They started this fucking fire trying to kill me, and I haven't done anything."

Luke yanked at his wrist while Sam examined the cuffs and the pipe where they had attached him. His panic returned even though we were here to help. "What are you going to do?" he pleaded.

Sam held Luke's wrist up with one hand. He pushed his shoulders back and gave me a solemn look. I closed my eyes, knowing, without even seeing, what we had to do. Sam had no tools to break the pipe, but with my help, he could free Luke.

I opened my eyes and lowered myself to the floor next to him. "Let me hold you, Luke." He hesitated for a moment, but then he understood, and wrapped his free arm around me, laying his head on my shoulder. I moved to his lap and wrapped my legs around his waist, prepared to keep him as still as possible. When I gave Sam a nod, he lifted Luke's arm and smashed it down on the pipe.

Luke's scream stopped a few of the men fighting the flames. He thrashed in my limbs while I kept my arms and legs wrapped around his body with all the strength I had. My hip throbbed, but it was nothing compared to having your bone broken and then maneuvered through a metal circle.

"Once more," Sam yelled. Luke kept his cuffed arm limp while he pulled so hard against my middle, that I felt my spine strain. I nodded up at Sam, and he crashed his wrist into the pipe, breaking the bone completely.

Luke's tears felt cool on my shoulder, reminding me this fire was hotter and closer. Sam wiggled Luke's floppy wrist free from the handcuff while his good hand dug bruises into my side. Now free, I released my grip and stood to help him up. He was sweating, but that could be the fire or his now broken wrist.

I held his face up to mine. "We have to run. Can you run?"

He kept silent but began a slow jog after Sam. One by one, we stepped into the stairwell I had shoved Lori and the boys through only moments ago. Sam went first to lead the way, and Luke followed, cradling his arm. I went last, my body tingling from the adrenaline.

I had done it.

Luke didn't burn to death.

Sam never ran into flames to save him.

I had conquered the premonition.

I shut the door behind me, hopeful. Twenty-seven floors were all that stood between us and freedom.

Twenty-seven floors and Dean.

Dean, whose stare I caught across the deck as I shut the door behind me.

"Fuck!" I yelled down the stairwell after the men.

"I know," Sam hollered. "I saw him as we ran back. There's nothing we can do about it. Luke, how are you holding up. Are you going to be sick?" Luke's face was a mix of disgust and horror.

"Maybe, but I'll keep going."

We kept a steady pace down the steps. I lost count after the first few flights, but Sam knew where he was going. I tried to picture my feet bleeding in the sand. The constant movement made it difficult, and I realized I may trip and fall trying to do both at the same time. I had to wait until we boarded the tender and try again.

"Luke, is it a bad time to ask you what the fuck happened?" I asked.

He chuckled and cleared his throat. "Is it a bad time to ask where the fuck we're going?"

"We are leaving this ship on another smaller, less on fire vessel. Care to join?"

"Well, yes, thank you for the invitation. And what the fuck happened is Dean was having me plant Assembly of the Eternal pins in Sam's bunk. That piece of shit gave me a key and told me to leave him a package on the desk. Well, I forgot the key and tried to slide it under the door. It seemed thin enough, and I was being lazy. Well, it ripped, and I saw the pins. I know he doesn't like you, Sam, but that's some next-level bullshit. So, I went looking for you."

That fucking asshole. I would never forgive Dean if he killed Sam, so his next step was to turn me against him. *We have to get off this boat.*

"Dean wasn't answering his radio, and I'd be damned if I walked into his party with AOE shit. I went to engineering and someone said you signed out to do some inventory. When I got down there, some of Dean's goons asked what I was doing. I don't even know how they got down there. We fought. They said I was stealing stuff, which I wasn't. I had just gotten there. I ran off through the growing rooms to grab one of Dean's guns. I never fired a shot, though. When I got up through the ag unit, they started shooting at me around all the pesticides we were storing for the islands. Complete dumbasses. They lit the place up."

"That's good, though," Sam muttered.

"What is good about any of that, Sam?" I huffed back. Even going downstairs, I was exhausted, and my hip was killing me. Each step shot pain through my leg and each breath felt like fire in my lungs. I must have inhaled more smoke than I realized. "And how much further?"

"The good thing is the fire started in ag. Those chemicals will burn loud and hot, but they should be able to keep it contained. More people won't die, which is good. And Luke, sorry, but I was the one stealing. I have a boat stocked and ready to go. Five more flights, Row. Are you okay?"

He looked up the stairs to me, and I gave a frail smile. We were so close and my hip would not stop us. "Just fine," I lied.

Sam continued a light jog down the stairs. "What you saw back there, Row, the stuff with Luke and who knows what else. Do you think you can do it again?"

"What?" Luke mouthed back at me.

"I'll try when we aren't in the middle of an Iron Man, but yes, I think I can do it again. Jesus, Luke, I'll just have to catch you up later."

"Yeah, you know, I think I'm done with mind-blowing news for the day. Thanks," he shot back.

Sam got to a doorway in what felt like the hundredth stairwell and paused. I knew his hesitation because I felt it, too. *Was Dean on the other side? Had he beaten us down here?*

"Wait," I snipped. "Luke, you said some of Dean's guys grabbed you by the inventory and you didn't know how they found you. Did Dean ever give you anything? Anything that could track your movements? Could that anything be on you right fucking now?"

Luke's eyes tracked back and forth in thought. He held his limp arm close to his chest and shifted his weight. He lowered the bum arm and gave it a hard look. "My watch is gone. He gave me a watch. The same one I gave Lori. He said he would be pissed if we lost them."

"I ripped that off to break your wrist," Sam added. "I think we're good."

Luke gave a lopsided smile. "Thanks, I guess."

We all nodded and opened the door. The hallway was dark except for some flickering overhead fluorescents. It smelled like mildew, but I saw a light at the end of the hall. Sam pointed toward it as he picked up the pace and we all ran after him.

Lori's head popped through the shadows, and it gave me the extra adrenaline I needed.

"They made it," Sam cheered. The boys were then at her side, and I sprinted down the rest of the hall until we all collided. I could smell saltwater in the air as I pulled them close.

"We have to go," Sam insisted. He tried to raise me by the elbow, and I whimpered at the slight pull. "I knew you were hurt." His tone was angry, but also full of concern.

"I think we're all dealing with a few injuries here," Luke added. "Let's fucking go."

Several boats hung on thick black lines. We followed Sam and piled into the one he had loaded. I could hear the rushing of water all around us. The ocean was right below the thin metal grating that lined the floor under the tender. Sam scurried around the machinery, hitting buttons and codes. Underneath us, the floor moved and screeching metal revealed rushing water in its place.

"Just the release now," he yelled. "You are going to drop, but I'm coming." He pulled a yellow crank downward, and the boat jolted. We all steadied ourselves from the sudden drop. Then the boat lowered at a slow pace as Sam made his way back to us.

"You ungrateful fucking bastards," someone yelled from the hallway. I knew the voice and the man behind it.

"Sam, that's Dean. Run!" I screamed, but Dean had already sprinted into the room with his gun drawn.

"You piece of shit. I should have killed you when I had the chance in the medical bay, but Luke was too much of a pussy. Well, it looks like you aren't such a pansy-ass now, doesn't it?" Dean barked. He pointed the gun towards the boat that continued to lower at an excruciatingly slow pace. I covered BeLew with my body. I wanted to send them down below, but I had no idea where that entrance was or if the movement would make Dean shoot.

"Dean, if you are pissed at me, then deal with me. Leave them all out of it," Luke shot back.

"You know I'm pissed at all of you." He waved his gun around like a maniac. His eyes were wild and the veins in his neck throbbed. He ripped open the top buttons of his shirt and rubbed his free hand across his neck and throat. I had seen Dean angry, but never like this. It was his mannerisms and stance that were different. He came across as jittery but focused.

He was high as fuck.

"I'm the only reason you are all alive - and what do you do? You steal from me. You take my woman. You try to fucking leave. And go where, you idiots?"

"Dean, let them go," Sam interjected. "You want me dead, fine, but let them leave."

"And, you. I mean, where the fuck did you come from? Who invited you to the party, you asshole? God, I should have killed you so long ago. Why the fuck did I wait so long?"

The scream that left my throat was foreign to everyone, even myself. "Dean, no," I screeched. My body shook and my voice was hysterical. "I know how much you have done for us and me, but you know it was for yourself, too. I can't stay here. If you ever loved me, if you still love me, please, I have to leave this place."

Dean paused with his gun pointed at Sam. He cocked his head to the side, still eye to eye with him. The boat made a thud as it hit the water and rocked back and forth, begging for release.

Seconds felt like an eternity while Dean kept the barrel of his gun pointed at Sam's face. I heard Lori whimper, and Luke moved beside me.

"You know what true love is?" Dean croaked. "It's dedication."

The shot exploded in my ears, and a dull ringing took its place.

I closed my eyes, and I was back in the field. I saw my sister fall to the ground and the boys running away. Her dead body lay motionless in front of me. I refused to open my eyes and see Sam the same way.

"Rowan," I heard from behind me. The voice sounded like an echo. "Rowan," louder this time. I shook my head and covered my face with my hands.

Lori shook me. "Rowan," I heard Luke calling my name. "Rowan, open your eyes. I'm sorry that was by your head. It was my only clear shot."

I curved toward his voice but kept my head low, terrified of what I would see. "I still had the gun," Luke explained. "Those pricks never knew I had it in the first place."

I met his gaze in shock. He had what my sister would have called a shit-eating grin on his face. I twisted myself back around to see Sam mid-jump from the dock.

"Is he dead?" Luke asked.

"I'm not staying to find out," Sam answered. "And excellent shot, by the way." He grabbed me and crashed his mouth on mine in a quick kiss. "I'd like to finish that when we are safely away from this shithole."

"You know," Luke pointed out. "Rowan seems to have this kissing habit when being whisked away on a boat."

"Not funny yet, Luke," Lori scolded. He wrapped his good arm around her and they kissed, breaking only when the boat shot forward, leaving the Thalassa. I ushered the boys below as we made it into open water. After settling the children, I walked back out to be by Sam and leaned into his side while he steered. I searched the dock for any sign of Dean. I thought for a moment I saw movement, but I was out of his reach. After all these years, maybe I could live without being bound to Dean Riggs.

We rode to the islands in silence. With little to say, we huddled together, looking outward until the shoreline came into view.

"Is that our new home?" Beau asked.

"For a bit," Sam answered. "We may be nomadic for a time. Do you know what nomads are?"

"Like a tribe," Lewis said. "Tribes that go from town to town."

Sam lifted Lewis to his shoulder for a better view. "Something like that. For the time being, this is our home." Beau reached his arms for a turn and by the time they both had their fill, we were reaching waters too shallow to continue.

This boat was large enough for everyone, but we had to forage for what was available on the island and try to make a home on land. There was a lot of work ahead of us, but I would do it with Sam, and that made it all worth it. There was a smaller inflatable that we paddled to the shore after anchoring the boat. We could swim the distance, but everyone was half broken. Later we would search for a harbor or cover, but our getaway boat could bob out at sea for now.

Sam's muscles bulged through his shirt as he paddled. Over the past few hours, I realized Sam and I were now free to be alone again as a couple. Luke was pushing along with his good arm, and Lori admired the view. BeLew reached their arms over the sides, skimming the water with their fingertips. When we made it to shore, we all pulled the boat onto the sand, careful to keep it out of the current.

Once settled, I saw the devastation this island had taken. Broken houses laid everywhere a few steps inland. Pieces of wood lay scattered across the grass and flattened trees. This used to be someone's home. People got married here, raised their children here, and loved each other here. Splintered lumber and garbage were all that remained.

And broken wood.

My voice raised in a question as the memory returned. "BeLew is this what you saw? Is this the shore of broken wood?"

No answer as I scanned the devastation. "BeLew," I repeated, but they were staring at the sand, at the shore. I looked down and saw the blood. It made spiderwebs of red on my still wet feet. It was coming from inside me, running down my leg.

The tears came easily this time. After holding them back for months, and the freedom I felt only a moment ago, they flowed down my cheeks at the horror of what I was seeing.

"Sam," I whimpered, and he lifted me and carried me to a spot of grass. Lori found a blanket in the dingy and laid it out across the ground.

"It's okay," Sam whispered, moving me to the blanket.

"No, it isn't okay. This is bad. I saw this, but it wasn't like this. I never thought it would be this."

"Shhh, baby."

Luke cleared his throat and tapped Sam on the shoulder. They spoke for a minute and Sam returned.

"Luke has medical training. He delivered a few babies on Thalassa. Could you let him check you out?"

I nodded and swallowed the lump in my throat. Then I prayed this baby would survive. I prayed I could hold it and raise it with Sam and BeLew. I prayed for all the things I never allowed myself to want. Lori pulled the excess of the blanket over me and told the boys to sit by my head. Her sons stood far back, and she let them explore where we could see them.

Luke was gentle, but the pain still carried through my body. I didn't know if it was from my hip or losing this baby, but my entire middle felt like someone had hit me with a baseball bat. More silence and he examined me, and when he was done, he told me to rest on my left side and try to relax. "It's very possible this is bleeding from exertion. Lori said you crashed on a railing. The placenta could have shifted. I don't think it's placenta previa. The bleeding seems to have stopped. All we can do now is have you rest and wait."

Luke took Lori by the hand, and they walked to the water to give us a moment. He may be common sense dumb, but he was a skilled nurse. I said another prayer.

"We should name her," I said. "It's good luck. My baby Samuel came back to me. His love, I think, is in you. It's different, but the same, you know. That sounds crazy, right?"

"No, not crazy. And yes, I think we should name the baby. Are you so sure it's a girl?"

"No," I admitted. "But the name I want, it won't matter."

"Whatever you want." His eyes were tearing. It scared him, the possibility that this could be it. We could lose her today, and that almost felt like our journey was for nothing. We loved her, and the thought of one more death, especially this one, might be too much for me.

"The name I give her, she will make it. We are having a healthy, beautiful baby. A perfect baby girl, I think."

He chuckled and wiped his eyes. "You seem so set on a girl. What's the name?"

I touched my hand to my stomach and smiled. BeLew brought their little hands to the side of my belly and did the same. I met their gaze and spoke to them so they knew everything would be okay.

"I'm naming her after my sister. I want to name her Morgan, boys. Do you know what the name Morgan means?"

The boys gave excited nods, rocking my belly slightly.

"Will you tell Sam?"

Beau cleared his throat, and Lewis looked at his brother with pride. Beau had grown braver and more confident each day. "It means 'from the sea.'"

Sam clapped his hand on Beau's shoulder. "The perfect name for her. It's the most perfect gift your mother gave us. Her name and her spirit. Although, it still could be a boy. Either way, it's perfect."

"Oh, no," Lewis interjected. "It's a girl. We saw her. And yeah, she's perfect. She has our mom's eyes. I know you are upset about the blood, mamma, but everything will be fine. She cries a lot, but we are pretty excited. You cry a lot too when she's born."

Beau interrupted his brother, "But why are you in the way back of the island when she comes? Your legs get all cut up by the trees when you take the shortcut back home to have her."

The thud as Sam fell over was enough to break the boy's attention and giggle in his direction. My focus stayed on them. They were beyond perfect.

There was something about how clear their visions were. It was more than I could comprehend. I was leagues behind their capabilities. A flash came into my mind. It was the first time that happened when I was awake.

The image was of the boys holding Morgan wrapped in a blanket. They sat on a plywood floor with grins stretched across their faces. Their cheeks held less baby fat and just as much joy. She was curled up in their arms with heavy eyes.

She was blonde, sleepy, safe, and ours.

Chapter

Twenty-seven

In This Together

"**L**ORI TELLS ME YOU see visions of the future. Did you see my busted arm or the torture she is putting me through right now?" We spread Luke out on our kitchen table. His good hand gripped the side and sweat covered his brow. Lori wrapped his arm in another splint.

"Nah, I saw you burn alive. This sucks, but it's better."

"At this exact moment, Row, I'm not so sure." Luke let out a howl like a wolf, making the boys laugh. He tried anything to distract himself and refused to take the painkillers we had found. His arm took too long to heal, and I was worried, but Luke stayed in good spirits. He doped himself up when we first set the bone, but every splint change after he roughed through with screams and sweat. We had a limited supply, and he was afraid the kids might need them at some point.

Luke was a good man.

"Are you okay here, Lori?" I bellowed over Luke's animal noises.

"Yes, are you going to check the nets?"

"You know it. Wish me luck."

It had been five months since we arrived on this island. Every day we checked the weather, worked on our home, gathered food, taught the boys, and loved each other. We were not alone on the island either. There were a few survivors. We kept our distance, and things were cordial enough. The broken homes left plentiful supplies and there was land to farm and fish to catch. With less than two dozen of us, we rarely saw each other. We gave them a navigation device and so far, the storms seemed to stay away from this area. Weather had hit this place hard, and I hoped for the last time.

My stomach stretched outside my top now. This child wanted some sun shining through, anyway. The walk to the nets was peaceful. Sam would finish his current project soon. He had rebuilt homes in months, so everything else seemed like he was tinkering. It felt a bit like Little House on the Prairie, but who needs electricity and hot water? Whatever we went without, I spent my nights wrapped in his arms and that was worth all we gave up.

A rocky pathway stretched out into the water. Our nets swept farther past the coast where more fish could be found. I waded into the shallow beach, bending as best I could to bring in the net. The weight meant the catch was good that day. The ocean thrived without all the people polluting its waters.

I caught sight of Lori waving from the corner of my eye. I raised my free hand back to her. I heaved the net to my feet. A dozen fish flopped inside, blinding me with their silver skin reflecting in the sun. I pulled the rope over my shoulder and started my walk back.

I moved a wet hand to my stomach and spread the water over the growing bump. "Hey, baby. How about a fish dinner? Fish breakfast too, you say? Well, why the hell not?"

Lori still waved in the distance, adding a jump to her greeting. I dropped the rope and raised both hands overhead. Her motions continued and goosebumps covered my body. I rushed out of the water with the rope in hand, pulling the bag behind me. It was too shallow for a shark. Was a storm coming? Did we miss one?

She pointed with both hands in a violent back and forth to the horizon behind me. I turned, frustrated with this game that I was in no position to win.

My blood ran cold at the shadow in the distance. It could have been mistaken for a storm. It was large and foreboding, drifting across the water.

I had seen it before. My dreams for months had their return, but I was selfish. I dreamed of my child and longed to see her. Every meditation pulled me to her smile and giggle. She brought me joy, and I longed for images of her. Despite her overshadowing my premonitions, I knew what this vessel meant.

I had hoped we had years.

When I reached Lori, she had both hands on her head, staring out into the water. "Did you see this?" she uttered.

I nodded. "Some of it. Enough to know we should stay."

"Stay?" Lori questioned. "What if Dean is alive? We always knew we may have to leave. We need to be smart."

"Dean may be alive. I don't know for sure. I haven't seen that."

"So, you see my point."

"What I see, Lori, is The Galene."

She chuckled and dropped her hands to her sides. "I'm not going to ask how you know that." She grabbed the bag of fish and we walked back to the houses.

"Then don't ask why we need to stay, either."

"Would you tell me if I did?"

I thought about that as we walked in silence for a few minutes. I never gave my sister a warning of her death, and until recently, I held no regrets about that decision. Now that I knew I could change the outcome of things, I would have done it differently.

"I would tell you if you asked. It sets nothing in stone, but yes, I would tell you."

More minutes passed as we continued down the path we had worn into the brush and sand. It was hot, and I felt the sweat trickle down my back. Patches of wet covered the back of Lori's shirt.

Sam stood at the end of the trail. He reached out to take the fish from Lori and knew by her face something was wrong.

He put an arm around her and steadied her back to the house.

I saw her wipe her face with her hands and then stop for me to catch up. I stood by her side and tilted my head to her, ready for her question.

"I don't want to know," she said. "Just tell me what we need to do."

"Okay," I said as I hugged her, and she walked back to Luke alone.

"So, it happens now?" Sam asked once Luke had Lori in his arms.

"Yes, they're here."

Sam clenched his jaw and reached for my hand. I placed it in his as he pulled me into a kiss, our mouths moving in a familiar rhythm. The baby kicked, and we smiled through our lips, both halted by her movement. He took my face in his hands and pulled my gaze upward so we were eye to eye. "We are in this together."

I placed my hands over his and kissed the inside of his palm. "In this together. Forever."

THE FINAL STORM

B ELOW IS CHAPTER 1 from the next book in this series, The Final Storm.

The Final Storm is available for pre-order https://books2read.com/u/mY6eko

Check out my website for important release dates, https://lizhambletonbooks.com/

Slingshot

Silence fills the kitchen. It makes my skin prickle with discomfort. Before they arrived, there was only silence when the food hit the table. Even then, the boys would continue conversations with their mouths full. Four boys, all under the age of ten, and each one a bottomless pit. I'm the pregnant one, and they double what I eat at every meal. They laugh through bites and spit crumbs as they heckle each other. I miss their banter tonight.

The only sound tonight is pans and plates clinking as they hit the table. It's been a difficult day. A difficult four days since the Galene anchored just off the island. Its vast shadow looms in the distance and occupies our minds tonight, like every night since it arrived. No one has come ashore, and I know it will be on a day when it rains. I check the clouds morning and night to prepare myself. The anxiety of knowing too much keeps me in a constant state of fear.

Sam and I have no secrets, but Lori is in the dark... at her request. She doubts her decision now, asking open-ended questions I have no way of answering. The concern written on my face is my only and perpetual reply. The burden of it weighs on my heart when I lie down at night, waiting to dream. I have no date on the calendar for when people will arrive, but something inside me knows it's soon.

I meditate to see the visions of things to come, but at night, that's when true magic happens. All the pictures in my sleeping mind come to life, and I awaken with a movie reel in my head of future events. I'm blessed with pictures of my daughter, Morgan, my angel that will be here in a few short months.

I have the gift of seeing her blonde hair and sweet face. In my sleep, I feel the pull on my breasts from her nursing, and more than once I awaken to sheets wet with milk. Beau and Lewis have the gift, and they see her too. They feel her in their arms and see her take her first steps. It worries them that the steps are on a ship, not on this island. It worries Sam as well, but these visions don't have to come to pass.

We can change things, but should we?

Sam remains stoic and tight-lipped as we sit for dinner. He's always been strong physically and mentally, but the past few days have taken a toll. The way he looks at our friends, knowing things are not well beneath the surface, troubles me. He could fake it before we saw the ship on our shores. Its presence thrusts us into reality, and day by day, its shadow chips away at his happiness.

The Galene looms over our every move. It has an ever-present seat at this kitchen table where we eat, thinking about nothing but its outline miles out to sea. I want a family dinner where we enjoy each other and pretend that the damned ship won't ruin everything we've created these past few months.

I made the rule we would not discuss its presence at the dinner table. So now we sit in silence.

The Galene will bring what is necessary, and I know it, even if Lori doesn't. Luke will be sick soon, and the Galene is the only way to help him. Then again, it could save him and kill us all at the same time, but I never see the latter.

Luke's sunken cheeks and grey skin, misted with sweat, fill my nightmares. He has a relentless cough in my visions where blood leaves his lips and sprays the room, covering my body from head to toe. When I wake up, my hands run down my front to wipe it away. I shiver at the memory, and I shake my head to free it from my brain.

"BeLew, please eat some vegetables." The boys lower their shoulders and grimace. My nickname for them comes out in a sharp tone, cutting through the silence. Beau and Lewis look up from their food with only their eyes. My ears ring with the metal sounds of forks hitting plates. Beau pierces a carrot and looks over at his brother. They are seven now and have aged a lifetime in under a year. Each day I see more of my sister in my nephews, but as time passes, they feel more like mine. My children who become more capable of living in this harsh world every day. They can hunt, fish, start a fire, and cook outdoors. They would be littered with boy scout badges in our old life.

Lewis gazes at Beau and begrudgingly stabs the carrot on his plate. In a silent countdown, they both bring the vegetables to their lips and chew as if they are gnawing on acid.

Lori's boys follow suit when she glares at them. Luke is coughing a bit tonight, and every time the sound brings my shoulders up to my ears. Sam rubs his hand up my back and gives a gentle squeeze to release my fears. I'm hiding them from the others, but my mannerisms give me away. Luke continues his coughing spell, breaking our silence, and Lori pats him on the back a few times. "Did you swallow something wrong?" He shakes his head no, still coughing. I still myself, staring at him, knowing time is running out.

"You have to eat your vegetables too, Mama," Lewis drawls. "Morgan needs to eat healthy. Carrots are a healthy choice."

I crack a slight smile in their direction and start piling carrots on my fork. Sam rubs my thigh with his free hand, and I pretend not to hear Luke struggle to catch a breath. There is nothing I can do for him, nothing until they arrive. "What did you boys do today? All four of you were out of the house from sunup to sundown."

Lori's boys, Tanner and Hank, give each other a devilish grin. They are eight and nine, and BeLew's shadows. During our time on the island, long days in the sun had browned their skin and lightened their hair. When all four boys stood on the shoreline, I couldn't tell them apart from afar. I started calling them Tank, with Lori's permission. My sister was never fond of nicknames, but things were always easier with Lori, more relaxed.

Lori rolls her eyes and exhales. "They made a five-foot-tall slingshot. They finished their chores first. I'll give them that, but still. I can't decide if I'm annoyed or impressed."

"Boys will be boys," Luke wheezes. He gains control of the cough and reaches for a glass of water.

Lori pushes it towards him and continues. "They think they can make it big enough and shoot something far enough to, you know, er, hit the ship."

My eyes grow wide, and I can't hold back my grin. "Oh, wow. BeLew are you a part of this?"

"This is breaking the rule," Lewis said. "We don't talk about the ship at dinner."

More silence falls upon the table. The clatter of silverware and Luke's labored breathing fill my ears once again. My goal for stress-free dinners has failed. It would be better to discuss the ship than this, and I concede. "I want to hear about the slingshot. Forget about the rule."

Sam gives my thigh another squeeze. "Beau and I are more the idea guys," Lewis responds. "We draw up the plans, and Tank's on construction."

"And how's construction going?" I ask. "Are we ready to fire?"

"Oh, it's ready to fire," Hank pipes up. "But mom called us in for dinner before we could get it loaded."

Luke laughs, which is a pleasant replacement for his cough. "The fun police strikes again," he bellows. Lori glares at him and refills his water glass from the pitcher. "How about we make an after-dinner trip to this thing? Let Sam and I test it out with our brute strength. If anyone can hit that ship, it's the big boys. Am I right, Sam?"

Sam chuckles and nods. "It will be fun either way. I'm up for it, but only if the boys are." All four nod, bright smiles on their faces.

"Then it's settled," Luke says. "But we have to clean our plates fast. Rains coming in from the west. I saw it on the scanner."

My smile falls, and I drop my fork. Lori sees my expression and her back shoots ramrod straight. "Shit," I stammer, trying to reach for my fork with my stomach in the way. Sam pats my arm and brings it back up to the table. I meet Lori's eyes and bite my lip. She will ask me again after dinner. She needs to know, and maybe I need to tell her.

"But then again, a little rain never hurt anyone," Luke murmurs as he brings his glass to his lips. Another slight cough comes from the back of his throat, and he chokes it down with water. "The boys can just make a trip of it if you all want. You ladies can hang behind." Luke lowers his cup to the table.

A tinge of blood swirls through the glass as the raindrops start on the roof overhead.

Acknowledgments

I would be nowhere without a team of people support-
ing me every step of the way.
Thank you to my ARC team, a wonderful group of read-
ers that cheer me on with every release.
Thank you to my author friends, who keep me going
every day. Your support changed my life.
Thank you to my friends and family that remind me that
with love, anything is possible.
And thank you to every person who has picked up one
of my books and given my words the most precious thing
on this earth, your time. I love you all.

ABOUT THE AUTHOR

Liz Hambleton writes imperfectly beautiful romance. Her heroines are always strong-willed, and her heroes are resilient. Her characters live in alternate worlds and futuristic times, and putting yourself in their stories lets you escape reality while still feeling the power of true love.

If she's not reading, she's writing, and her deep adoration for the written word shines in everything she creates. Liz is married with two children, two large dogs, and a fish that refuses to die.

Connect with Liz for other works and important updates:

Sign up for my newsletter on my website for Affluence's extended epilogue, extended scenes, giveaways, and more: https://lizhambletonbooks.com/

Home - Liz Hambleton Books
Other works on Amazon are under my author page: https://www.amazon.com/~/e/B08N9XXBK8

Visit Amazon's Liz Hambleton Page

Like Liz's Facebook Page: https://www.facebook.com
/LizHambletonBooks/

Liz Hambleton Books (facebook.com)
TikTok: @lizhambletonauthor
Instagram: https://www.instagram.com/lizhambleto
nauthor/

@lizhambletonauthor • Instagram photos and videos